THE OTHER BROTHER

JAX CALDER

Chapter 1

I spot him as soon as I arrive at the party.

At first I think it's only someone who looks like Cody, because seeing him at Jamie Anderson's birthday is like spotting a vegan at a steakhouse.

The Cody lookalike is sitting on the couch. I watch him out of the corner of my eye as I circle the room, doing the usual amount of backslapping and fist bumping with my friends.

The party is already in its middle stages. Most people greet me with boozy grins and beer breath.

"Ryan, my man." Oz gives me the shoulder nudge and high five combo we perfected in year eight. A random girl standing nearby stares at us. I'm not sure if it's because she's admiring our awesomeness, or it's due to the fact that with the same blond hair, brown eyes and swimmer's build, Oz could pretty much pass for my twin after a few beers. "Why are you so late?" he asks.

"I was surfing. Lost track of time."

"Catch any good waves?"

"Yeah, some."

Harvey ambles over, clutching a beer. "You know what they say about surfing?"

"What?"

"You should always take out insurance in case the waves start breaking."

Oz and I groan in unison. Harvey is always good for a bad pun.

I flick another glance at the couch.

The guy who has Cody's dark curls and lean build is facing away from me, his T-shirt riding up to show off a sliver of tan back. He turns to reach for the cup on the coffee table, giving me a glimpse of his narrow face and large eyes.

Crap. It is Cody.

A mixture of feelings bubbles up inside me. Competitiveness, rivalry, comradeship, familiarity, nostalgia, and lots of other stuff all rolled into one tight ball that lodges in my throat.

I need beer to wash it down. I head to the kitchen, weaving through the next round of people saying hello, and help myself to the haven of magnificence that is the keg.

When I come back into the living room, I can't help glancing back at the couch. It's not like we're friends or anything, but I'm curious about what Cody's doing here.

But he's not there anymore. My eyes dart around the room, searching. I finally locate him standing up against the wall by the stairs. Actually, standing is a far too active term for what he's doing—he's letting the wall prop him up.

Holy shit. He's drunk. I can tell by the looseness of his limbs and the way his gaze isn't fixed on anything. Despite the wall at his back, he's swaying slightly, like he's moving to some song inside his head.

I can't help staring. I've never seen Cody out of control before. He's usually one of those people who makes Hermione Granger look badly behaved. I grab my phone and tap out a message to Mel.

Cody's drunk. Party at 87 Sylvian Street. He needs to go home.

A small part of me—okay, okay, it's actually quite large —is happy as I press send. Because Mel's had to bail me out more than once, but I'm willing to bet this is the first time she's had to deal with a drunken Cody.

Yep, it appears pettiness is my mojo for the evening.

After that, I try to get into the swing of the party, shooting the shit with Harvey and Oz, but I keep tabs on Cody the whole time. Cody, who's still drinking. Or trying to. Only about half of what he attempts to get in his mouth actually makes it there. The rest slops down his front.

On the plus side, it's taking him longer to get more drunk than if his aim was perfect. Unfortunately, he's getting enough in to slide from being pretty drunk to really drunk.

I check my phone every few minutes, but Mel doesn't message back.

Eventually, I give up and call her. It goes straight to voicemail.

Shit.

In the meantime, Cody has staggered to the bottom of the stairs and slumped over, his head between his knees.

Damn. I'd been looking forward to cutting loose with my friends before summer vacation sends us sprawling in different directions. Now it looks like my night has encountered roadwork and is heading for a major detour.

I'm not his keeper. I'm about as far from Cody's keeper as I can be. But I can't leave him here like this.

I stride over to the stairs.

"Cody." I shake his shoulder.

He stirs and lifts his head, opening one eye then the other. His gaze settles on me, and his eyes widen. Cody's eyes could trigger the least inspired person in the world to write poetry. They're bluey gray with dark flecks in them and a darker navy outline around the iris. Add dark curls, a straight strong nose, and the chiseled planes of his face, and he's an incredibly good-looking guy.

A flash of attraction shoots through me. It leaves a weird aftertaste in my mouth.

I'm an out and proud equal opportunities player when it comes to who I hook up with, so the moment isn't weird because he's a guy. It's weird because of who he is.

"Ryan?" he slurs.

When we run into each other accidentally, we usually pretend we don't know each other. I'm sure I started it five years ago when we were twelve and saw each other at the movies. I remember his eyes lighting up, and he opened his mouth, but I turned away, ghosting him. It gave me a thrill at the time but ended up just adding another complicated layer between us.

"Yep, it's me. The one and only." Going for minimum contact, I tug his arm, trying to maneuver him into a sitting position.

"Why are you here?" he asks as I prop him up. He's not actively resisting me, but he's not doing anything to help.

"I should be the one asking you that. How do you know Jamie?"

Cody appears to think for a while. "Music camp," he finally says. The words come out sluggish, like his tongue is set on slow motion.

His answer makes a little bit of sense, although Jamie is

in a heavy metal band, which is definitely not the sort of music I associate with Cody.

"It's time to go home," I tell him.

"Why?"

"Because you're a mess."

"Everything's a mess," he mumbles, his words coated in despair.

Shit. I definitely didn't sign up for the role of counselor tonight. That's taking it a step too far. A giant moon step too far.

"Come on."

As I try to lift him, I catch a whiff of his aftershave underneath the beer fumes. Cody lets me help him stand and does his best to get his feet to behave as if they've previously been acquainted and can work together. I support him with one arm as we cross the living room, ordering an Uber with my free hand.

I leave Cody propped up against the front door as I grab my jacket from the pile on the floor by the coatrack.

"Who's that guy?" Harvey saunters over, eyeing Cody curiously.

"Just someone I know."

I'm not about to explain who Cody is right now as it requires sitting down with pen and paper and sketching out some complex family trees. Once upon a time, before Cody and I were born, Cody's dad and my mum were married and produced my half-sisters Mel and Kate. But this is one story that definitely didn't end with a happily ever after. Instead, they had a bitter divorce before marrying other people. Cody's dad married his mum and they had him, while Mum met my dad and produced me. So Cody and I are connected by our half-sisters, along with the mutual hatred between our parents.

Harvey lifts an eyebrow suggestively, but I ignore it.

"You know what they say about alcohol?"

"What?"

"It might not solve all your problems, but it's worth a shot."

"Oh God, Harvey, that's bad. Even for you."

Harvey walks off grinning.

My phone informs me that Mitchell, my Uber driver, will pick me up in two minutes in a Toyota Prius.

Right, time to get outside.

The night is icy with a sharp wind. I shrug into my jacket.

Cody's standing there in a T-shirt with beer down the front. He begins to shiver. Shit. He probably brought a jacket with him, but there's no way I'm hunting it down now.

He sloshes up against me as we stand on the curb. I'm not sure if it's for balance or warmth. I've never been this close to Cody before. His body is firm against mine, the hard planes of muscles causing me to swallow. Cody is an athlete, a New Zealand age-group tennis representative, among his many other talents. His muscles are well earned.

But appreciating them is a worse idea than a Brussels sprout sandwich. Of all the people on the planet, Cody's reasonably high on the list of people I shouldn't be lusting after.

Our ride pulls up, and I'm relieved to put distance between us. Cody gets in first and fumbles with his seat belt. I lean across and snap him in.

"He okay?" Mitchell turns and eyes us suspiciously.

"He's fine."

"He throws up, you're paying for it," Mitchell says.

"He won't throw up," I promise.

I lean across to Cody. "Don't throw up," I instruct under my breath.

He obeys me until we pull up outside his house and climb out of the Uber, but two steps later he's puking in the gutter.

"Good timing."

"Shit." He wipes the back of his mouth with his hand and sinks down onto the edge of the sidewalk.

I tug on his arm. "Come on. We've got to get you inside."

I eye the porch of his house with trepidation. I've heard way too many stories about how strict his parents are. Sneaking him inside will be a fun mission.

We make it up the stairs to the porch without incident.

"Where are your keys?" I whisper.

"They're in…" He attempts to pat down his pockets, but he's got none. I take a wild leap of logic and guess his keys are in his jacket. Back at Jamie's house.

"I'm just taking a break…" He leans his head against the porch railing and closes his eyes.

Awesome. My night just gets better and better.

In desperation, I dial Kate. She's down in Wellington, the other end of the North Island, but at least she'll give me advice on the best way to handle this.

"Hey, Rhino, what's up?"

I loathe Kate's nickname for me, but I know that if I protest, she'll just double down on it. Although Mel and Kate are my half-sisters, they've never been halfhearted in their hassling of me. And despite them now technically being adults, with Kate twenty-three and Mel twenty-one, we haven't moved on from our habit of mocking each other ruthlessly at any opportunity.

"Yeah, I've got a bit of a situation here," I tell her. "I was at a party, and Cody was there, and he's totally out of it, and I thought I should get him home, but now I'm at his house and—"

"Cody's drunk?" she interrupts.

"Um… yeah."

"I thought he didn't drink."

Her words cause irritation to pound through my veins. It's part of the theme song that continuously plays in the background of my life. Cody the saint. Cody, the brilliant musician. Cody, the amazing brother.

I'm pretty sure I was permanently disqualified from the favorite brother race at age four when I gave military-spec crew cuts to Mel and Kate's Barbies, but even so, the knowledge that my sisters prefer their other half-brother always sits like undercooked meat in my stomach.

"If you like, I can send you strong photographic evidence that Cody does actually drink," I say.

"Okay, okay. Where are you now?"

"I'm by his front door. But he's lost his keys."

"There's a spare one hidden under the blue flowerpot."

Because my night color identification superpower is on the blink, I fumble around, lifting random pots before my fingers close over metal.

"Got it."

"His room is the second door down the hallway on the left. Be quiet, Dad and Heather's room is at the end."

"Okay. Thanks."

"Look after him, okay?"

"What do you think I'm doing?"

I hang up on Kate, and channeling my inner stealth skills, gently unlock the door.

But trying to be quiet when you're escorting a drunk through a house you're not familiar with is like trying to waltz with an uncoordinated giraffe.

At 6'1", I've got a few inches on Cody, and I'm bigger too, so I half drag, half carry him down to his room.

I've never been in Cody's room before. I leave the lights

off, but there's enough light coming in the window from a streetlamp that I can navigate my way around. It's tidy, which helps. Of course he keeps his room tidy. I wouldn't expect anything less. We stumble toward his bed, and I manage to haul him onto the mattress.

Cody immediately nestles into the pillows, his eyes closed.

I stand over him, looking down. I don't want to undress him, because that's taking this whole Ryan-rescue thing way too far. But I probably should at least take off his shoes.

I grab one of his Converse sneakers and tug. It sticks. I loosen the laces and try again.

It comes off just as light floods the room.

Blinking, I turn around, his shoe in my hand.

His mum stands in the doorway. My stomach hollows. She's the lesser of the two evils, but not by much. I've heard a lot about Heather from Mel and Kate, who in their teenage years had a Cinderella complex toward their stepmother. She doesn't look much like an evil stepmother now, though; she looks like a middle-aged woman who's been woken unexpectedly. She's got curly hair like Cody, only her curls are gray and currently sticking out in all directions.

The light causes Cody to stir, and he opens his eyes and turns his head towards the door.

"Hey, Mum," he mumbles.

"Cody." It's impossible to imagine more disapproval could be squeezed into one word. She stalks over to the bed and stands over him.

"Have you been drinking?"

"Just a… little." Cody's not helping his cause by trying to sit up against the headboard and failing.

She swings her gaze to me. "How did he get so drunk?"

Shit. She hasn't recognized me. It shows exactly how messed up things are between our families. Cody's mum has seen me lots at Mel and Kate's stuff over the years. Granted, I've probably spoken about twenty words to her in that time. And, the last time I saw her, my hair was still shoulder length, not short and spiky and bleached like now.

"I don't know. He was wasted before I got to the party. I'm not even a friend of his." I hold up my arms in a gesture of innocence, one hand still clutching Cody's shoe.

She fixes me with a suspicious glare. "If you're not one of his friends, then who are you?"

It's the million-dollar question. Who exactly am I in relation to Cody?

I take a deep breath before I answer her the simplest way I know how.

"Uh… I'm Ryan. Mel and Kate's other brother."

Chapter 2

I watch as the knowledge of who I am sinks in and recognition takes over Heather's face. I'm guessing she wasn't expecting to see the child of her husband's ex-wife tonight.

"I saw him at the party. I tried calling Mel, but she didn't answer. And I couldn't just leave him there…"

"Thank you." Her voice, now drained of anger, sounds tired. I get that tiredness. Families are complicated, especially broken ones like ours.

"He probably needs some water." I try to fill the awkward space. "He threw up before, he'll need to be rehydrated."

"Okay. Thanks."

She looks down at Cody then glances at me.

"How are you getting home?"

That's my dismissal. It feels abrupt. I don't know what I expected. It's not like I wanted to sit by Cody's bedside for the night making sure he's okay.

"I'll grab an Uber," I reply.

"Don't be silly. Frank will drive you."

"Seriously, it's no problem."

"Frank will drive you." Her words have a parental finality about them which I know not to fight. She heads for the door. I place Cody's shoe carefully on the floor before following her, sending one last glance back at Cody as I leave the room.

A few minutes later, I'm stuck in the world's most awkward car ride. Seriously, a dinner party with the ghosts of Hugh Hefner and Mother Teresa would be less awkward than this.

What do you say to someone who used to be married to your mum and had two kids with her before they split up? Who has then been engaged in bitter warfare with her for twenty years over the way to parent your two half-sisters?

If his relationship with Mum hadn't soured, she wouldn't have met my dad, and then I wouldn't have been born. So, I guess I owe Frank for being a first-class jerk.

I glance at his profile as he drives. I've only ever witnessed Frank looking immaculate, so it's mildly amusing to see his rumpled midnight look. He's pulled a sweater over his pajama top, but I notice the flannel bunched at the neckline, and his blond hair looks like it has been roughly finger-combed to hide his bald patch.

Frank's forehead is furrowed. I'm guessing he's trying hard to find something to say to break the silence.

"How's soccer going?" he finally asks.

"Good. We're in the semifinals."

"That's good."

"Yeah."

He switches on the indicator to turn right. We're leaving behind the sprawling lawns and shiny, large houses and venturing into my neighborhood, where the houses are stacked closer together and have a stale look about them.

My life has always been a slightly crumpled version of Cody's.

"Do your parents know you were at a party tonight?" Frank asks before the next silence can settle.

Ah. That's the Frank I was expecting.

"Yeah, they know." I can't help twisting the knife a little. "They trust me to be responsible."

Frank's face sours. He and Heather were way stricter about stuff like parties for Mel and Kate than my mum and dad. It was a major source of arguments when they were teenagers.

But given I've just delivered his baby boy home almost comatose while I'm sitting here relatively sober, I'm guessing there's not much wind propping up his sails right now.

He pulls up in front of our house.

"Thanks for the ride." I unclip my seat belt.

"Say hi to your parents."

It's hilarious how they do this. Act like things are normal and civilized between them all. Like we've never witnessed the hissed conversations that happen when they're together, the yelling on the phone, Mel and Kate's tears when they've been caught in the middle of whatever the current battleground is.

"Sure thing." I get out of the car.

He winds down the window to call after me. "Ryan?"

I thrust my hands into my jacket as I turn back to face him.

"Thanks for looking after Cody tonight," he says. His expression is so like Kate's when she's forced to do something she doesn't want to do that it almost makes me laugh.

"It was no problem," I reply.

THE NEXT MORNING, I'm lying on my bed ignoring the English assignment sitting on my desk that's due Monday when my phone beeps.

hey, Mel gave me your number. thanks for getting me home last night. Cody.

I stare at the message for a second. Then pick up my phone to type my reply.

no problem how much shit you in today

My phone beeps immediately with his reply.

shit is rating high on the shit-o-meter.

I bite down a grin. Suppressing my smile is overkill given no one is watching me, but I never want to give Cody the satisfaction of laughing at his jokes. He's got this dry sense of humor that comes out when you least expect it. But being the funny one is one of the few things I've ever had over him, and I refuse to relinquish ground on that front.

tried to smuggle you in but your mum caught me

no worries appreciate you tried

I stretch back on my pillow and think about Cody. About all the random stuff I know about him. He was obsessed with dinosaurs, LEGO, and Star Wars when he was a kid. He loves cornflakes with sugar sprinkled on top. He's great at Battleship but hates Monopoly. He always picks raisins out of anything. I've seen him remove every single raisin out of a slice of fruitcake. For the record, there's not much left behind from fruitcake once you've taken those nuggets of grapey goodness out.

He's not my friend, has never been my friend, yet thanks to my sisters and the time I've spent with him over the years, I know more random stuff about him than I know about all my friends combined.

I grab my phone and stare at his unfamiliar number. Then I save it under my contacts. Just in case.

TWO WEEKS LATER, I see Cody again at Mel's flute showcase.

This is when we normally see each other. Birthdays. Graduations. Concerts. Our sisters are overachievers like him, so our parents dragged us to lots of celebrations over the years.

He sits with Frank and Heather two rows in front of me, so all I can see of him are his dark curly hair and tan neck. He seems intent on listening to the music, while I'm having to pinch my thigh to stay awake. Flutes must be the most boring instruments on the planet. There's a reason all those Indian snake charmers use them to put serpents to sleep.

After what felt like hours but was only 20 minutes, the torture ended and I beelined for the after-concert supper.

The food is always fussy and pretentious at these things, but they serve alcohol. I toss up whether the bar staff will ID me but realize even if I get past that particular hurdle, I'll still have to dodge my parents and Mel. Not worth it. So, I order a Coke instead.

As I'm sipping on it, Cody walks up to the other end of the bar. He's dressed in a light blue button-down shirt with tidy black pants and polished dress shoes.

I think back to the party and the momentary sizzle of attraction I had for him.

He does have incredible eyes. And based on the experience of having him pressed against me, he also has an incredible body.

But I can't lust after him. He's my nemesis. Okay, maybe not quite nemesis, because that would imply we're an equal matchup.

Cody and I were born two months apart. So, I guess

it's natural we've always been compared to each other. Natural that our parents, who despise each other, would look to one-up the other when it comes to their nonshared offspring.

Unfortunately for my parents, Cody has always blown me out of the ballpark. He was reading by age four. Identified as a musical prodigy at age six. Not content to be simply intelligent and a brilliant musician, he also turned out to be exceptional at tennis.

Why can't you be more like Cody? Although my parents have never uttered those words, Mel and Kate have, plenty of times. Every time I pulled a normal little brother stunt like putting food coloring on their toothbrushes or balancing plastic cups filled with water over doors. Because apparently, Cody wasn't that kind of little brother. Apparently, Cody was the type of brother who volunteered to take their turn loading the dishwasher if they had assignments they needed to finish. Me? Not so much.

I sidle over to the perfect brother now. "So, not getting into the beer then?"

He scowls, grabbing his glass of orange juice from the bartender. "Are you going to give me grief about that?"

"Dude, I had to wash splashes of your vomit off my jeans. I think I deserve some mileage out of it."

The scowl fades from his face, and he shifts onto the other foot. "Yeah, sorry about that."

"No problem. We've all got to let loose now and again." I lean against the bar. "So, were you grounded?"

"Oh, yeah. A month."

"That's shit," I sympathize.

"It's okay." His voice is soft, his gaze on the ground. "There are worse things than being grounded."

Here's the thing. I've always been envious of Cody's focus. Not just for his talents, but for the fact he's so focused, so sure of his path in life. He plans to study at the New Zealand School of Music and become a professional pianist.

Meanwhile, my parents give me crap about being directionless. I'm about to go into my last year of high school and I still have no idea what I want to do with my life. Bumming around surfing every day isn't a legitimate career option according to both my parents and my career counsellor.

But as Cody looks at the floor, his eyebrows draw together and his mouth pinches, and I realize maybe being Cody isn't as easy as it looks from the outside.

"Hey…" I begin, hesitant.

"What?" Those otherworldly blue eyes lift and skewer me. My heart speeds up.

"You were pretty cut up at Jamie's party. And both Mel and Kate said you don't normally drink. Everything okay?"

He swallows, looking away. "Just some shit I'm dealing with."

"Well, everyone's always telling me how smart you are, so I'm sure you've figured out drinking isn't the best solution for dealing with shit."

"Yeah, consider that lesson well learned."

We share a wry smile, and for some reason I don't want to move away. We stand in silence for a few minutes. Cody's watching the crowd, an expression sliding onto his face that is both cynical and sad.

I follow his gaze and discover the reason. There's drama unfolding. Awesome. Our family always picks the best time to have their little histrionics.

Mum is having an intense discussion with Mel, who then has an intense discussion with Frank and Heather. Annoyed faces are sprouting like poisonous toadstools.

I know from experience that it's best to steer well clear

of these types of conversations, so I stay put. Cody meets my eyes, and I know I have an identical look of resignation on my face. Should I say something to acknowledge how fucked up it is that our parents continue to haul their past into the present?

But before I have a chance to conjure the right words, one of the other flutists comes up and starts talking to Cody. She must be Mel's age, but that doesn't stop her gushing over him with all the accompanying hair twirling and eyelash batting. He laughs softly at one of her jokes.

A quick scan of the crowd reveals all the parental expressions are back into the normal zone now. Standing here listening to the girl flirt with Cody isn't really filling me with happiness, so I head over to Mel.

"What was that about?" I ask.

Mel tucks a strand of her blonde hair that's straggled from her bun behind her ear. "Just the usual. Both parents wanting something from me that clashes with what the other wants. But I think we've found a compromise."

I idly pick up some weird pastry thing from a platter. "What's the issue?"

"I'd agreed to stay at the beach house so it can be painted while Dad and Heather are in Europe. But Mum wants me to stay at your house when her and Max go to Aunt Ethel's."

I narrow my eyes as my suspicion swells. "Why does Mum want you to stay at our house?"

"So I can babysit my itty-bitty brother." Mel tousles my hair, her eyes shining with suppressed laughter.

"Like hell," I mutter.

I stalk over to my mother, Mel close on my heels. She'll never miss out on a chance to see me humiliated.

"I don't need Mel to babysit me," is my leading line.

Mum gives me a look. "We don't want a repeat of what happened when we went to the Melbourne."

"You've got a memory like an elephant," I say grumpily.

"It would take a lot to erase the memory of your friends' butts as you all skinny-dipped in the pool," Mum replies.

"If YouTube hadn't been invented, you'd have never known about it," I declare. "I blame the inventors of YouTube for my current predicament."

"Perhaps instead you should blame your propensity to disobey the rules and get naked at any opportunity."

"If God gives you a thing of beauty, it's your job to share it with the world."

"It's all organized now, Ryan. I don't want to argue with you too." Mum's voice is weary, her forehead creased. She's playing the I've-just-had-to-deal-with-my-bastard-ex-husband card. It's a powerful one.

"How has it been organized?" Suspicion coats my words.

"Frank and Heather have agreed you can stay with Mel out at the beach."

Okay, I did not see that coming. I glance at Frank and Heather. I can't believe they've agreed to let me crash at their beach house. They've always seemed underwhelmed by me. Some stunts I pulled at family celebrations when I was younger may have left them with the impression that I'm an irresponsible mischief maker. Maybe my recent rescue of their precious son helped to soften their stance?

"Is Cody going to be there?" I ask Mel. Casually. Like, James Bond has nothing on how cool I manage to deliver that question.

"No. He's staying in the city for his piano lessons."

So Cody doesn't need to be babysat when his parents are away, but I do. Slightly unfair, given recent events.

I open my mouth to protest, then shut it. Because three weeks at the beach isn't exactly reform school.

I've heard lots about the beach house at Orakahau which has been in Frank's family since his grandfather was a kid. I've always been jealous that my sisters get to trundle off to live at the beach every summer while I'm stuck in the city begging rides off people to go surfing.

There's awesome surf on that part of the coast. And although she likes to talk tough, Mel isn't a jailer. I'm certain I can convince her to let me invite some friends out to crash for a few nights.

Surfing every day and partying every night. Not a bad combination.

My gaze snags on Cody. There's always a possibility he could come out to the beach house during the weekends.

My stomach flickers as I imagine spending time with Cody. A whispery shiver tickles its way down my spine.

My summer just became a whole lot more interesting.

Chapter 3

All those years when my sisters disappeared off to the beach house, I'm glad I didn't know where they were going. Because I would have exploded with jealousy if I'd realized what I was missing.

The house is hunkered down right on the beach. Although it's an old man compared to some of the flashy homes around it, inside it's been modernized with a new-ish kitchen and living space, yet still has a relaxed vibe.

The best thing is it's a mere fifty-foot stroll from the front door through the sand dunes down to the waves. Leaving Mel to finish unpacking, I make that stroll within an hour of arriving. I paddle out on my board through the surf, the salty tang saturating the surrounding air. I catch the first wave as I try to relax into the zone. My only focus is riding the wave. Everything else slides off into insignificance.

Two hours later, I'm humming a happy tune as I head back to the house, sand caking my wet feet.

My smile fades when I open the back door to the

kitchen and discover Mel's not alone. Cody is sitting at the breakfast bar.

He turns to look at me with those big blue eyes as I stand dripping in my wetsuit.

"Next time you should probably take your wetsuit off outside," he says. "Dad freaks out about water messing up the floorboards."

My shoulders stiffen. Is this Cody marking his territory, reminding me I'm a guest here? And not a particularly welcome one at that.

"What are you doing here?" The words sound too abrupt, but I can't take them back.

He raises an eyebrow. "My piano teacher broke her arm, so my lessons have been cancelled for the next few weeks. I thought I'd hang out here for a while."

"Lucky me. I get to spend time with both of my brothers." Mel directs most of her smile at Cody.

"I'm having a shower," I mutter.

The warm water beats down on my tired muscles as I try to decide how I'm feeling about this recent development.

I'm pissed off. With just Mel here, I didn't feel like an interloper. Now, with Cody, I'm the outsider. But there's something else bubbling underneath the annoyance. Excitement at the idea of spending time with Cody.

Pissed off excitement. That's a new one.

Because I'm me, I haven't thought to bring any clean clothes into the bathroom. I grab a towel off the rail and wrap it around my waist. Pushing open the bathroom door, I find Cody standing in the hallway. He looks me up and down. I brace myself for him to tell me I've used his grandfather's heirloom towel or something, but he simply swallows and continues to stare.

"Hey," I say, just at the point where the silence is about to tip over into an awkward zone.

Cody clears his throat. "Hey…I just wanted to say sorry for crashing your time here with Mel. I hope it won't be weird with me here."

Damn, do I have to add mind reading to my list of Cody's talents?

"Seriously, dude, it's your family's place. You don't need to apologize for being here."

"I don't want to cramp your style."

"Well, you might curtail all the hair braiding and making friendship bracelets that Mel and I had planned, but I'll live."

A faint blush creeps up his cheeks. He hesitates, then speaks again. "It might be good for us to get to know each other better. You know, since we're both about to become uncles to the same kid."

I haven't even thought about Kate's pregnancy in that light. When she first told us, I had to cope with Mum lurching between her disappointment at Kate having an unplanned pregnancy, her excitement about becoming a grandmother, and her concern about whether Kate and her fiancé Chris knew what a big life change having a kid meant. But now I realize what it means for me. Uncle Ryan. Uncle Cody. Another arena for Cody to show me up in. Awesome.

Cody's studying me, wearing a curious expression. I have no idea what he's seeing on my face, but I quickly shutter it.

"I'm all for heart-to-hearts, but do you think we could continue this when I'm not standing here naked?"

He's definitely blushing now. "Yeah, okay. Sorry." He hurries to get out of my way.

I walk past him to my room. After I've thrown on some

clothes, I unpack. I'm just shutting the closet door when I notice it's painted a light purple. Mum's favorite color. I guarantee she was the one who painted the door back when she and Frank were married and they used to come here together with Kate and Mel.

As I head downstairs, I wonder what other leftovers of Mum are in the house. It's weird to think she once spent time here, before I existed.

Mel's in the kitchen making dinner, so I start to help her. Earn my keep and all that. While I'm throwing together a salad, piano music trickles down from upstairs.

The music swells, and I swallow. I mean, I know Cody is an amazing musician. I'd heard details of his achievements over the years. I've never been a fan of classical music, despite how many of Kate and Mel's concerts they have dragged me to. But this. This is something different.

It's not just the incredible music, but it's the feelings the music causes to swell up inside me. Longing. Yearning. Melancholy. All combining into a weird kind of ache.

"Is there a piano here?" I ask the stupid question.

"In Cody's room. Heather and Dad put one there so he could practice here too."

"'Cause it sounds like he needs the practice," I say.

Mel just stares at me. She has blue eyes like Cody, although they're a lighter blue similar to the pale part of a summer sky. But that blue is deceptive, because I'm all too aware of how they can turn thunderous in a moment. Like the time she discovered I'd shared the photo of her drooling in her sleep on all my social media accounts.

"It's good that Cody's here," she says finally as she goes back to cutting up potatoes.

"Good? In what way?"

"I think you guys hanging out together will benefit both of you."

"Benefit us?" It appears my role in this conversation is just to repeat Mel's words back to her. A well-trained parrot could sub in for me.

"Yeah, Cody's always been so intense, and you're so laid back you're almost horizontal. It might be good if you rub off on each other."

Because I can't resist taking it to that level, I raise an eyebrow. "Did you just encourage me to rub off your brother?"

She shoves me. "Don't corrupt him, okay?"

"Sweet, innocent Cody," I mutter. "Aren't you worried he might corrupt me?"

Mel just laughs at that.

"THAT SONG WAS AMAZING," Mel gushes when Cody comes down and takes a seat at the table.

"Thanks." He ducks his head.

An awkward silence fills the space where my compliment should be. Damn, I shouldn't be this petty.

I huff out a small sigh. "Dude, that was insane."

Cody meets my eyes, and a slight smile tracks its way across his face.

"Just something I'm working on," he says.

"You wrote that?"

"Yeah."

"Wow." I don't know what else to say. To be talented enough to even get a piano to produce that standard of music is one thing, but to have created the music out of nothing? It's hard to comprehend.

"Dig in," Mel says, nodding at the meal.

I never need a second invitation to eat. I pile my plate high.

As we eat, I notice Cody picking out every raisin from the salad I made, but leaves behind the grapes.

"Still got your raisin vendetta, I see," I say.

"I'd say it's more of an enduring grudge than a vendetta."

"I don't get it. You like grapes, but you don't like raisins?"

He leans back in his chair. "It's more about the texture of raisins than the taste."

"So, you're biased against shriveled up old things?"

"Play nice, boys," Mel warns.

I roll my eyes and look over to see Cody's rolling his eyes too.

"It's a bit rich, you lecturing us to play nice. Think of all the ways you tortured Kate over the years," I say.

"I never tortured Kate."

I snort. "What about the time you hacked her Facebook page and announced to the world she had a crush on Timmy Jones?"

"That's because she'd just broken my hair straighteners. It was fair retaliation."

"Remember when you set Kate's alarm to go off at two am the night before prom?" Cody pipes up.

I whip my head around to look at him.

"I didn't know that one," I say, delight in my voice.

Cody smiles, and his face transforms.

"And you totally stole that idea from me, from what I did on the camping trip to Taupo," I say to Mel.

"I did not steal any idea from you," Mel says stiffly.

"Oh, and now you're pulling your Oscar the Grouch face!"

"Oscar the Grouch?" Cody's eyebrow quirks. "I always thought of that face as her Grumpy Cat impression."

I can't help spluttering out a laugh, and Cody joins in. Our laughter intertwines while Mel continues to scowl.

Hmm.

All my life it's been the Kate and Mel show. Not only have they always done the big sister thing and ganged up on me, but so much in our family has always been based around them. Plans changing to fit with their schedules. Major holidays postponed until they can join us.

I flick a glance at Cody. Who's still grinning. At me.

Maybe this summer it's time to change the channel.

Chapter 4

The next day I'm out surfing early. The waves are gentler today, and while the rides aren't as intense, it's crazy-cool being out with the early sun glinting off the water and the fresh salt air giving my nostrils a spring clean.

I'm about to head in when I notice a lone runner on the beach. As the figure draws closer, I recognize the lean build and curly hair.

Okay, so maybe I time my exit from the water so I intercept him. But hey, it's a long, lonely fifty-feet walk back to the house. It's natural to want some company.

Cody stops at the start of the path, leaning forward to rest his hands on his legs as he recovers his breath. He's wearing a close-fitting T-shirt that shows off his biceps.

"Hey." Yep, I should win awards for the most original opening line. I stand there, dripping in my wetsuit, sand caking my feet.

"Hey," he pants. He straightens and pulls up his T-shirt to wipe his forehead, giving me a view of his muscled, tanned stomach.

"Heading back to the house now?" I keep my voice casual.

"Yeah."

"I'll be your security detail if you want."

"Thanks, there are lots of bandits in the dunes," he says in such a deadpan voice that it takes me a few seconds to realize he's joking.

"Gotta watch out for those bandits." My reply is a few seconds too late and a few levels too feeble as I step into stride next to him. The sandy path cuts through the dunes.

"So, do you surf?" I ask.

"Nah, I've never learned."

"You spend your summers here, and you've never learned to surf?"

"I bodyboard."

I snort. Making sure as much derision as possible is contained in the snort.

Cody raises his eyebrow. "Bodyboarding doesn't cut it with you?"

"Nah. It's like saying Jimi Hendrix and Justin Bieber are both equal musicians. Or… like Mozart and whoever was the crappy but popular composer back in his time."

"I get the Jimi Hendrix/Bieber comparison," Cody says. "You don't need to put it into classical music terms."

"That's good, because I don't know shit about classical music," I say. "You dig Hendrix?"

"I play a few songs of his. Mainly on the guitar."

"You play guitar as well?"

"Yeah. You ever played an instrument?"

"Does the recorder in third grade count?"

He flashes me a smile. "Kind of like bodyboarding counts as surfing."

"Fair point."

We've reached the house now. The sun is hitting the

front windows, turning them into gleaming pools of gold light. But the yard is still in shadows.

"Wetsuit off, right?" I say.

"Yeah, there's a hose around here somewhere you can use to wash down."

He rummages around by the side of the house and emerges holding a hose.

I strip my wetsuit off. If there's one thing it's impossible to look coordinated doing, it's removing a wetsuit. Luckily, I've got board shorts on underneath so I'm spared the indignity of possible shrinkage on full display.

"Damn, that's cold." I spray myself with the frigid water.

Cody's standing there, immobile. He studies the ground, not looking at me.

Because I'm in control of the hose, I can't help flicking water in his direction. He raises his gaze to mine, his eyes narrowing.

"You looked like you needed to cool off," I say.

"Thanks," he replies dryly.

I turn off the hose.

"Race you for the first shower," I say, taking off through the door.

I'm not expecting Cody to engage, but then I hear footsteps on the floorboards behind me in the kitchen, and he's right on my tail as I streak through the living room.

We're side-by-side on the stairs, jostling each other with our elbows.

He slips ahead when we reach the hallway, but I tackle him to slow his momentum, and we both crash into the bathroom door at the same time and slide down it, laughing through our panting.

"What's with all the noise?" Mel emerges from her

room, squinting down at us. The front bit of her hair is tufted up like it's been in an electric storm.

I stand up, putting a hand down to help haul Cody to his feet. He accepts my hand but lets go as soon as he's standing.

"Sorry we woke you," he says to Mel.

"Don't worry. I had to get up soon, anyway. The painters are arriving this morning. Have you been for a run?"

I can't help rolling my eyes at how polite their interaction is. What are we, in a remake of *The Brady Bunch*?

"Yeah, and Ryan's been for a surf," Cody says.

Mel eyes me with amusement. "Out of bed before midday? That's impressive for you."

I give her a withering glare in reply. Then I turn to Cody.

"So, I think it was a tie. Does that mean we have to shower together?" I raise an eyebrow suggestively.

"Uh… no…" Cody backs away from me.

I put my hands up, all innocent. "Just kidding."

Mel rolls her eyes. "Don't mind Ryan. He missed out on any social etiquette genes."

"Nah, it's okay. You can have the first shower." Cody doesn't meet my eyes.

I'm not going to argue. Goose bumps prickle my skin, and the floorboards are like ice under my feet. I go into the bathroom and strip my board shorts off quickly then jump under the sweet, sweet warmth.

While I'm soaping myself, I push away all thoughts about the way Cody's body felt pressed up against mine. After his reaction to my joke about showering together, I'm guessing he's straight. It shouldn't matter to me either way, because as cute as he is, I will never go there with my sisters' other brother. But I can't pretend I'm not curious.

I've never heard Mel or Kate mention Cody having a girl-friend. Maybe I should just ask Mel casually if she knows what way he swings? Say I'm asking for a friend?

I can't help snorting as I imagine Mel's reaction to that. Mel and Kate barely blinked when I told them a few years ago I was into both guys and girls, but I can imagine their laid-back attitude might change if they think I want to hook up with Cody.

As I turn off the water, my mind moves on to how Cody apologized to Mel for waking her. Have I ever apolo-gized to my sisters without being forced to by a parental unit? If it had just been me here, I would have come up with some smartass reply. And Mel would have responded and it would have descended into one of our usual broth-er/sister battles that we excel at.

My mind runs through the conversation that would've happened in the alternative reality where Cody wasn't here.

Mel: What's with all the noise?
Me: What's with the Wicked Witch of the West impression?
Mel: At least I'm not the brainless Scarecrow.

There's a funny feeling in my stomach as I get out of the shower. I mean, I've always known Cody has a better relationship with our sisters than I do. But it's still weird to observe it at close range.

AFTER BREAKFAST, Cody retreats into his room, and the sound of the piano drifts down the stairs. While I could probably spend my morning hovering in the hallway listen-ing, it might disturb Cody to discover me there.

The painters turn up and start putting up scaffolding so they can paint the top level of the house. 'Cause I've got nothing else to do, I offer to help them.

Maybe I should consider house painting as a career option? I'd get to be outside lots, which is a big bonus. Although my parents would probably moan I'm not using my brain enough. And painting might get repetitive after a while.

When the painters take their morning break, I'm about to head inside for a snack, but then I realize the piece of scaffolding they've just set up looks directly into Cody's room.

I climb it carefully, inching my way over to Cody's window. Then I do my best bullfrog impression, pressing my face up against the glass and puffing out my cheeks.

Cody's sitting at his piano. He's not playing, just studying the keys. Then he puts out one hand and plays a few haunting notes. He stops abruptly and reaches for a notepad, writing something down. Then he goes back and plays a few more keys.

I can't tear my eyes away. He's so intense, so absorbed in what he's doing. The look on his face, it's like everything else has melted away, and the only thing that matters is the piano and the sounds he's creating. He bites his lower lip in concentration, and a flash of... admiration swirls inside me. Have I ever been so focused on anything? Ever?

My cheeks begin to hurt. But I'm the person who once posed as a teapot from the "I'm A Little Teapot" song for over an hour on a dare, so I've had practice suffering for the sake of ridiculousness.

When Cody finally looks up and sees me a few minutes later, it's worth the sore cheeks. The look of surprise on his face is like a cartoon character—mouth falling open, eyes bulging.

I laugh so hard I almost fall off the scaffolding.

When I finally recover, Cody's trying for a glare, but his bottom lip is twitching.

I give him a cheery wave then climb down. Mission accomplished.

"SO, you've got a thing for watching people through windows?" Cody asks when he comes into the kitchen at lunchtime. I'm getting out some bread for the start of an epic sandwich-making operation.

"Yeah, I think I might stalk you permanently. Could be a fun hobby."

Cody pulls up at the counter, resting his elbows on the top as he looks at me. I have a sudden flashback to Cody and me when we were little. I think it was Kate's tenth birthday party, so Cody and I would've been around five. I'd scooped up a bowl of M&Ms and crawled under the dining room table where the long tablecloth hid me from view. Somehow Cody found me and wiggled his way in, and we sat there munching M&Ms together in a conspiracy of silence.

I remember his warm, chocolaty breath and the same intense stare.

"Do famous classical musicians really get stalkers?" I ask, breaking eye contact to butter the bread.

"Sure. Nicola Benedetti had a stalker."

"Who's Nicola Benedetti?"

"A famous violinist."

"Oh. Right." I've already confessed to my complete ignorance of classical music, but I still feel stupid. "You want a sandwich?"

He blinks. "Um… sure."

"Cheese and tomato?"

"Sounds great."

As I turn to the fridge to grab the ingredients, an evil

idea creeps into my brain. And like all evil ideas, this one deserves some indulgence.

Mel comes into the kitchen as I finish making Cody's sandwich.

"Bon Appetit," I say, sliding the plate over.

"Thanks." Cody flashes a genuine smile which gives me a pulse of guilt about what's currently lurking in his sandwich.

I watch him out of the corner of my eye as he and Mel chat about some neighbors who've just arrived at the beach.

Cody's halfway through his sandwich when his expression suddenly morphs into a frown. He slows his chewing, gulps something like he's swallowing glass, and then whips the top off his sandwich to inspect it.

He flicks his gaze up to mine. "Did you put raisins in my sandwich?"

"Maybe."

His eyebrows quirk. "Maybe?"

"You know what people say is the best treatment for phobias. What's it called? Immersion therapy? Be thankful you're not scared of spiders or snakes."

He shakes his head, but I can see he's hiding a smile as he picks the rest of the raisins out and chucks them into the garbage disposal.

Mel's shaking her head too. "It's nice to see you don't just contain your torture to people who are related to you."

I shrug. "What can I say? I've got to share my talent around."

I HEAD out surfing for the afternoon. The sun has changed its setting to baking, so even after the short trek home across the sand dunes, washing myself down with a cold hose is a relief.

I hang my wetsuit over the edge of the deck to dry (because nothing sucks more than having to pull on a damp wetsuit on a cold morning) and then duck inside.

Cody's on the couch in the living room reading a book.

"Where's Mel?" I ask.

"She's gone into town to get some groceries."

"I hope she remembers ice cream." With that thought, I grab my phone out of my pocket and send a quick message. I don't want to take any chances of her forgetting when the consequences are so dire.

When I glance up, Cody's ignoring his book in favor of watching me.

"You want a game of ping pong?" he asks.

"Do you have a ping pong table?" I scrunch up my face.

"No, I was just planning to play it by bouncing the balls off our heads."

I wrestle down the corners of my mouth. "That might be a thing at Appleton, but not in the real world."

Cody goes to a fancy private school, and it's fun to give him shit about it. Of course, I go to my local public school like the rest of the unentitled majority.

I'm sure he's biting down a grin himself. "You want to play or not?"

"Sure, I'm in."

The ping pong table is in the garage, along with a dartboard and a parked jet ski. They really do have all the toys here.

I'm no slug at ping pong, having spent many hours honing my skills at Harvey's place. But Cody slaughters me. Like my carcass is hanging off a meat hook in an abattoir kind of slaughter.

"Do you ever get sick of being so good at everything? I mean, it must get boring, right?" I ask after he aces me for the umpteenth time.

Cody serves again. I manage to get the edge of a paddle to it, but it ricochets off and bounces against the wall.

"Nope, not really." His grin has a cheeky element to it. I fight the matching one that for some reason wants to plant itself on my face.

As if to emphasize my point, when we go back inside, Cody grabs a guitar in the living room and picks away at the strings. I recognize Neil Diamond's "Sweet Caroline."

I slump down on the couch opposite and watch him play. One of his curls hangs over his eye as he strums. He doesn't sing but hums along instead.

"Can you teach me to play guitar?" I ask.

His eyebrows almost fly off his forehead.

I'm as surprised as he is at the words out of my mouth.

I've always wanted to learn to play the guitar, wanting to be one of those guys who can lead a sing-along around a beach campfire. But I've shied away from doing anything musical, because competing with the natural talent of my sisters and Cody feels pointless.

But it strikes me now that maybe music doesn't have to be something you do to compete with other people. It can be something you just do for yourself.

Cody continues to stare at me. I feel like our dog Jett when he rolls on his back and exposes his soft underbelly to the world.

"I'll teach you the guitar if you teach me to surf," he finally says.

Relief floods through me. "Deal."

"Great," Cody says.

Our gazes clash, and there's something in his I can't identify.

"You want to start now?" He brandishes the guitar towards me. I lean back like touching it might scorch me.

"Nah, my brain's fried. We can start both lessons tomorrow."

Cody shrugs. "Suits me."

There's a method to my madness. I like the idea of teaching Cody to surf first, before I expose my ineptitude on the guitar. Plus, I plan to spend a fair portion of tonight watching Guitar for Dummies YouTube clips so I have a head start.

I stand up. "Surfing lessons begin at six thirty tomorrow." I waggle an eyebrow. "Don't be late."

Chapter 5

The next morning Cody and I stand on the flat, firm sand above the low tide mark while the seagulls greet us with their shrill squawks. Our surfboards are on the sand next to us. Cody's got a board he borrowed from the neighbors, which is a bit long for a beginner, but will have to do.

The sun is just rising over the horizon, sending tentacles of fiery red across the water. Unfortunately, the sunrise is not the most attractive thing on the beach this morning because, girls and boys, Cody is in a wetsuit. There should be a law that anyone with a body like his must cover it with more than a quarter of an inch of neoprene.

I'm not lusting after him, because that would be weird and awkward. But I can't help the fact that I have eyes.

"I don't know why, but I imagined learning to surf would involve me being in the water." Cody looks down at our boards.

I roll my eyes. "You've got a lot to learn before I'll let you loose in the ocean, my friend."

I grab a stick and trace a line in the sand around the outside of his board.

"Um, what are you doing?" Cody asks.

"You've got to practice popping up. You know, going from lying down to standing up."

Once I've finished tracing the outline, I haul his board out of the way and draw a line down the center of the shape.

Cody looks at it dubiously. "Isn't it better if I practice on the board?"

"Nah, you can damage the fins. This works better."

He folds his arms across his chest as I finish drawing another outline, this time of my board.

I look up and see the skeptical look on his face. The little hum of nerves that's been present in my stomach since we agreed to this arrangement flares up. I want to do a good job.

"Right, our sand boards are complete. Mine's a JS board, of course," I say.

"What's a JS board?"

"The best surfboard available."

"What about mine?" Cody looks down at the drawing in the sand in front of him.

"Yours is from Kmart."

Cody snorts. "Okay, now we've established what brand our imaginary surfboards are, can you tell me what I'm supposed to be doing?"

"Sure. Watch me."

I lie down on the board outline then use my hands to push myself up and bring my legs through so I'm standing.

"The key is to lift your chest first, because it's so much easier to get your legs in the right position." I demonstrate again.

"You want your legs to be about shoulder-width apart when you finish." I complete my instructions. "That gives you stability."

"Like this?"

Cody's like a cat, lithe and springy, as he whips up to get into a crouch.

I move closer to inspect him. "Yeah, that's almost right, just drop your right leg back a fraction." Without thinking, I reach out and touch his hip. He jerks away like I've scorched him.

I take a step back. His chest rises and falls rapidly, and he doesn't meet my eyes.

"Sorry," I say.

"No, it's okay. You just took me by surprise." He puffs out a breath. He looks down, moving his leg back half an inch.

"Is this right?"

"Yeah, that looks better."

Cody practices a few more times while I watch critically, keeping my instructions verbal.

Of course, he gets the hang of it quickly. I wouldn't have expected anything less.

"You ready to have a try out there?" I ask.

"Have I graduated off the sand?"

"Yeah, your graduation certificate and gown are in the mail."

Cody turns his gaze to the waves. "What do I need to know before heading out?"

"Not much. The key is to find the sweet part of the board to lie on when you're paddling out. You need to experiment with that a bit."

"What about catching a wave?"

"You need to nail a white water takeoff before you try to catch a wave. These foamy waves are perfect." I nod at the surf.

"Okay, lead the way."

Carrying a surfboard through the shallow water is

always awkward. I feel like an uncoordinated penguin. But when the water gets deeper, I lie down on the board and start paddling. Much better.

My breathing always slows on the ocean, and I'm sure my heart rate does too.

Because Cody's just learning, we don't go too deep, just to where there are some frothy broken waves streaking their way onto shore.

And he sees the method in my madness. Because it's a lot easier to practice popping up when you're on something stable. Doing it on a moving board is much harder.

He manages to get to his feet on his fourth try, and he sends me a triumphant smile for the three seconds he's standing before he tips off.

I paddle over to him as he emerges from the water, his hair plastered to his skull in dark curls.

The water is only waist deep here, so he stands up, grabbing his board.

"Damn, I screwed up at the end." His face twists in frustration.

"Relax, you're just starting. You'll get the hang of it."

"I just want to get it right," he mutters, holding on to his board as another wave comes through.

"Dude, you need to chill. You're stressing about surfing. It's like an oxymoron or something."

"Oxymoron?" Cody raises his eyebrow. "You're secretly really smart, aren't you?"

"Yeah, I'm Einstein's clone. Or maybe I just remember anything that has the word moron in it, because it's bound to be useful in life."

He tips his head back and laughs. It's so unexpected, the chuckle reverberating through his body, that I can't help joining in. If anyone was on the shore, we'd look like idiots, standing in waist deep water with our surfboards bobbing around us, laughing together.

After his laughter dies away, his gaze on me is so warm that I have to glance away.

When I look back, he's jutted out his jaw. "Right, let's try this again."

He gets on his board and paddles purposefully through the waves.

He doesn't make it to his feet on the next wave, but the one after that he pops up perfectly and stays on his feet all the way to where the wave dies out in the shallow water.

I give him the thumbs-up, and he grins widely.

Cody continues to practice. I can see some of the traits that make him such a talented musician. Concentration. Perseverance. The willingness to ask for help when he needs it. He really is the perfect student.

The sun is just starting to have some heat in it when we finally head back onto the beach. By unspoken mutual agreement, we don't head straight back to the house but spread ourselves on the sand to warm up in the sun.

The beach is filling up now. A group of girls have set up camp twenty feet away from us and are providing some awesome scenery by stripping down to itsy-bitsy bikinis.

But Cody ignores them as he props himself up on an elbow and looks at me.

"Tell me what you love about surfing," he says. The intensity in which he looks at me is typical Cody. When he's staring at you, he really focuses, like no one else in the world exists.

"It's cool," I say.

Cody raises an eyebrow, his expression unsatisfied. "Cool?"

He continues to watch me, waiting. I don't know what

he wants, but when I open my mouth, the words tumble out without me thinking.

"I don't know. I just love being out there on the ocean. Everything is simple, you know? Like, it all boils down to whether or not you catch the wave, so all the other crap disappears. And it's so peaceful. Like, there's this big adrenaline surge when you catch a good wave, but most of the time it's incredibly chill. And you're so close to the ocean, it's like you're part of it."

My voice curls up in embarrassment near the end. I feel naked, like I've just exposed too much of myself. Actually, screw that, because I'm way more comfortable flashing people my junk than I am being under the scrutiny of Cody's blue eyes as he stares at me now.

"That's kind of… beautiful," he says finally.

"Beautiful?" The scorn in my voice is heaped high.

Cody blushes, but his gaze doesn't waver from mine. "Yeah, it's beautiful."

I stare back at him, and his amazing eyes capture mine. We stare at each other for a good twenty seconds before Cody looks away. I blink. What the hell?

Cody gets to his feet. "We better head back. And after lunch, it's my turn to be the expert and your turn to be the beginner."

"I don't think beginner is the right term for my music skills, actually. I'm more like pre-beginner. Before novice." I say as I jump up.

"I like a challenge," Cody replies.

MEL'S in the kitchen unloading the dishwasher when we arrive back in the house.

"What have you guys been up to?" she asks.

"Ryan just taught me to surf, and after lunch I'm teaching Ryan how to play the guitar," Cody says.

"*You're* going to learn to play the guitar?" Mel looks at me, her eyebrows rocketing off on a journey to the moon.

"What's wrong with that?" I say defensively.

"No offence, Ryan, but you're one of the least musical people I know. Remember how in preschool you couldn't even clap in time properly?"

I fold my arms across my chest. "I have progressed since kindergarten, you know."

Mel snorts. "That's up for debate."

"I'm really hoping that Ryan is completely tone deaf so I can show off my amazing teaching skills," Cody says.

I turn my attention to him. "You need something else to feel good about?"

Cody shrugs. "Any boost to the ego."

"I'm always up to help you find ways to stroke your… ego." I flick him a wink.

I'm trying to freak him out, gain back the upper hand after our conversation on the beach, but Cody just laughs while Mel rolls her eyes.

"What are you doing?" I ask when it occurs to me that Mel is looking far more dressed up than a lazy day at the beach requires. Her hair is in a topknot, and she's wearing a white shirt and navy blue skirt.

"I've decided to do a course this summer," she says.

"What kind of course?"

"Design."

My eyebrows shoot up. "How does that go with law?"

Mel shrugs. "It's just something I want to try. It's being run by the polytech, so I'll be commuting back into the city most days."

"That's fine. We don't need to be babysat," I say.

Mel snorts. "That's another matter up for debate."

Both Cody and I roll our eyes at that.

Mel departs soon after lunch, leaving the house to Cody, me, and the painters.

I'm trying to gulp down my apprehension as I follow Cody into the living room and he hands me his guitar.

It feels foreign and awkward in my hands. The way Cody handles it, it's like it's a friendly dog. I'm treating it like it's a rabid porcupine that will attack at any moment.

I adopt my best who-gives-a-shit face. It's one I've perfected over the years for times like this when I'm out of my comfort zone.

"Okay." Cody clears his throat. "The first thing I'll do is teach you *G* chord. So, it's in the second fret and third fret."

It occurs to me that Cody is nervous about this too. And that relaxes me as I try to follow his instructions.

It's not quite the train wreck I was envisioning. Instead, it's more like a narrow avoidance of a collision between two trains but with the full noise of shrieking brakes and angry yelling.

I've never really contemplated the width of my fingers before. But it turns out my fingers are quite broad, which makes it more difficult to pin down one string and not brush up against the others.

Luckily, Cody is a patient teacher. His face lights up when I'm finally able to get the chord correct. He shows me a few other chords, and I manage not to mangle them too badly.

"Man, those strings really bite your fingers." I shake out my hand.

"Yeah, I know. If you play for a while, you'll get calluses, which makes it easier."

Cody shows me his fingertips of his left hand, where

the skin is roughened at the top. I grab his other hand, his playing hand, where the fingertips are completely smooth.

"That's insane," I say.

Suddenly I realize I'm holding his hand. I drop it abruptly.

Cody runs his hands through his hair. "We can stop now, if you want? I'll show you more chords tomorrow."

"Yeah, okay."

Cody takes back his guitar and starts to strum.

"Is that one of your own songs?" I ask.

He stops playing. "Yeah, just something I'm mucking around with."

"How do you make up songs?"

Cody looks uncomfortable. "What do you want to know?"

I shrug. "I don't know, the process, I guess. Like, how do you decide what to play?"

"It's like, sometimes you get a feeling, and you can't find the words to describe it. Like words can't do it justice. So you try to produce music that makes people feel the same."

"So, it's really all about musically transmitted feelings?" I say.

Cody flashes me a smile, showing off a dimple. "Yeah, that's one way to put it. Say, if you wanted people to feel loneliness, you'd play something like this."

He strums a few notes on the guitar, and suddenly the first prickle of an ache of loneliness starts in my gut.

"That's insane. It's like you're a wizard or something."

It's weird I've never thought about it before. I mean, I know some songs make me feel different things, but I've never thought about how the songwriters deliberately set out to manipulate your emotions.

"And if you wanted people to feel happy, you'd play something more upbeat like this."

He's in instructor mode again. It's incredibly cute.

Cody's halfway through playing an upbeat, happy song when his phone rings.

He puts down the guitar and picks up his phone.

His expression darkens, but he presses to answer the call.

"Hi, Dad."

He stands up, moving away towards the kitchen.

"Yeah, everything's good here. How are you guys?"

He chews on his lip as he listens to whatever monologue is happening on the other end of the phone. He murmurs a few generic "That sounds like fun" type comments.

I can tell when the conversation shifts because suddenly tension travels up Cody's body, stiffening his shoulders and furrowing his forehead. His voice takes on a defensive edge.

"Yeah, I've already made a start on learning the Tchaikovsky piece. It's going okay. The fingering is tricky, but I'm getting there… Yes, I'm putting in the hours… Yes, I know there's no substitute for repetition."

Finally, he hangs up, placing his phone on the counter carefully. He walks back towards me, his expression tight.

"You okay?" I ask.

"Yeah, it's just my dad." He shrugs, but his shoulders are still tense. He sits back down on the couch and picks up the guitar. "Sometimes I think he wants me to have a career in music even more than I want it."

Damn Frank. The phrase pops into my head so naturally, in a maternal voice. I may have heard my mother utter this phrase once or twice. A week. For my entire life.

"He's very musical, right?"

"Yeah, I mean, he was on the cusp of making it professionally. I think he'd just made it into the philharmonic orchestra, but then Kate came along, and he had to find a better paying job."

Oh, that's right. When my mum seduced the poor musician, got pregnant, and forced him to give up his dreams. It's an awesome bedtime story. I'm surprised Hallmark hasn't made it into a movie yet.

Cody continues, running his hand up and down the neck of the guitar as he speaks. "He gets pissed when I spend too much time mucking around with my own compositions rather than learning my concert pieces."

He looks so bleak in that moment I have an urge to cheer him up.

"You know my philosophy when it comes to parents?" I ask.

"What's that?"

"What they don't know won't hurt them."

Cody cracks a grin. "Thanks. I'll remember that."

Chapter 6

"So, you survived teaching Ryan the guitar?" Mel asks Cody that night at dinner as she helps herself to more of the salad.

"Did you not expect me to survive?" Cody asks.

"I expected to come home and find you rocking in the corner. I think there's a support group for Ryan's teachers. I can get you the number if you want."

"Better than the support group for all the people who've been on the receiving end of your humor," I mutter. "Now that's a trauma no one will ever recover from."

Mel goes to kick me under the table, but my reactions are too quick, and she kicks the chair leg instead.

Cody levels her with a gaze. "Actually, he was good. He's a fast learner."

Good is probably stretching it somewhat. Still, a warm feeling flows through me at his praise.

"Cody picked up surfing really fast too," I say, and a shy smile stretches across Cody's face.

Mel looks between us, her eyebrows raising.

We eat the rest of the dinner with only minor bickering between Mel and me. I don't know what it is with my sisters, how we manage to bring out the twelve-year-old versions of each other. It's a bit embarrassing having someone external here to scrutinize our interactions. Especially Cody.

"Oh, I almost forgot. When I was in town today, I got us a surprise." Mel's tone is so nice I look up from where I'm scraping the remains off the plates into the garbage disposal. Generally, if one of my sisters uses that tone on me, they're either sucking up because they want something or trying to conceal that something nasty is heading my way.

But of course she's not talking to me. She's talking to Cody.

"What kind of surprise?" Cody doesn't look nearly as suspicious as I would in the same circumstances.

Mel reaches into a shopping bag that's propped up by the side of the couch. "A whole book of cryptic crosswords. I found it in the bookstore in town."

I snort. I'm waiting for the rest of the joke, but a genuine smile spreads over Cody's face.

"Cool," he says.

"Cryptic crosswords?" I coat my words in so much derision it's surprising they don't sink to the floor the moment they leave my mouth.

"Yeah, our family kind of has an addiction to them," Cody says.

This is what I've always been up against. The guy does cryptic crosswords with his sisters, for Christ's sake. How can anyone compete with that?

"Nerd alert, nerd alert," I chant.

"Don't mock what you can't do," Mel replies.

I narrow my eyes. "I can so do a cryptic crossword."

"You want to bet?"

"Sure. What are the stakes?"

Mel looks at me evaluatively. "Whoever loses the bet has to clean the bathroom for the entire time we're here."

I nod slowly. Decent enough stakes. But there's room for improvement.

"Loser also has to publish the winner's choice of a post on all of their social media accounts," I suggest.

Mel's eyes narrow. "You're on."

Okay, so I've never done a cryptic crossword before. I don't actually think I've ever completed a normal crossword. But a key part of winning is never letting your opposition see fear.

"Done." I smirk, stretching out my hand to seal the deal.

"You need to complete the crossword by yourself, and no googling," Mel says as she shakes my hand.

"Of course."

OKAY, so it turns out that cryptic crosswords are really hard. After I clean up the table, Mel rips one out of the book (randomly, to ensure she's not giving me the most difficult one, I have lots of experience with my sisters and bets).

I sit down at the table and read the first clue. *Going up or down, it goes round and round. Five letters.*

What the hell?

The next clue, *Type of lies told by those cleanly shaved. Nine letters* is not much better.

Mel and Cody begin their own cryptic crosswords just for fun. Because, you know.

Half an hour later, I'm grinding my pencil into a large hole in the page.

"How's it going?" Mel throws me a smirk as she pushes her chair back and heads to the kitchen to grab herself a drink of water.

I use my hand to cover my quarter-complete crossword as she goes past.

"Awesome," I say.

Cody flicks a look at my page, then looks at Mel.

"Can you please grab me a Coke while you're up?" Cody asks.

"Sure."

While Mel has her back turned to us, fishing a Coke out of the fridge, Cody slides me his completed crossword, taking mine in return.

I stare at him.

He stares back, a faint smile lifting his lips.

I glance down at his completed crossword, my mind swirling.

Okay, so it turns out I'm totally not above cheating on this.

I scrunch over Cody's crossword and pretend to write in the answers as Mel returns to the table and hands Cody his coke. Cody takes an absentminded sip as he fills in the blank spaces in my crossword.

"And done!" I lay my pencil down triumphantly five minutes later.

"You know you've got to get the answers right to win the bet. You can't just have filled in any random words," Mel says.

"Ask me the answers."

Mel grabs the book and flips to the back, where the answers are. "What crossword did you do?"

I check the top of Cody's crossword. "Number forty-five."

"What's the answer for two across."

"The answer for *Keep the Jam*? It's *preserve*." I smile winningly at her.

"What about fourteen down?"

"*Ladder*."

Mel squints at my page. "Why does that look like Cody's handwriting?"

"You don't know the difference between your brothers' handwriting? Shame on you, Mel." I shake my head in mock horror.

Cody keeps his face neutral, though there's a flush creeping up his neck.

Mel's gaze darts between us, but I stare back at her with a completely innocent expression. I've had a lot of practice with this particular look. I can see the suspicion on her face, but obviously she decides that Cody is far too pure and good to be involved in a cheating scandal.

I lean back. "I'm sure you remember the lecture Mum used to give about being a good loser."

"I can be a good loser," Mel says stiffly.

AROUND TEN THIRTY THAT NIGHT, I pad into the kitchen to make myself a late-night sandwich. Baloney and cheese. You can't beat that combination.

While I'm standing at the counter, eating with one hand, I grab my phone so I can admire Mel's post from earlier this evening.

I am in absolute awe of my brother Ryan. I aspire to be like him in every aspect of my life. If only I could be as good-looking, talented, and charming as he is.

It's garnering a lot of likes and comments. Although for some reason, people are suggesting I've hacked her phone. Such suspicious minds. For the record, Kate has gone with a mocking *Bahahaha* with a crying/laughing emoji.

There's a noise of footsteps on the stairs. I glance up as Cody emerges into the living room.

He looks startled to see me. I'm only in a T-shirt and boxers, whereas he's got on proper pajamas.

I squint as he comes closer. His pajamas have musical notes on them. I bet they were given to him by Kate last year for Christmas at the same time she gave me pajamas with surfers on them. And while my pajamas were stuffed into a back drawer and forgotten about, of course Cody wears his like the excellent brother he is.

An irritational surge of annoyance flows through me as he comes into the kitchen and pulls out the milk from the fridge, pouring himself a glass.

When you think about it, even helping me out was just showing me up yet again. Is there anything about the guy that isn't perfect?

I slide a glance at him now to find him watching me.

"Couldn't sleep?" he asks.

"Yeah, doing cryptic crosswords gave me an appetite." I polish off the last of my sandwich.

He grins. And luckily doesn't point out that actually he was the one doing most of the cryptic crosswords tonight. Which I realize I haven't acknowledged yet.

I clear my throat. "Uh… thanks for helping me out earlier."

"No problem. It's worth it to see Mel's face." His smile grows even wider.

"Yeah, I wish I'd taken a picture," I say. "It would've made an awesome screensaver."

He chuckles. "Yeah."

He rinses out his glass and puts it into the dishwasher.

There's something about the dim light and the silence that lulls me into asking the next question.

"Why did you help me?"

The amusement fades from his face. He holds my gaze for a few seconds before he speaks. "I don't know. I just thought it might be good to surprise Mel."

I squint at him. "Why?"

He shrugs, looking down at the sink. He reaches out to adjust the dishcloth, so it's sitting completely square. "Families are… weird," he says finally. "It's like, sometimes you get locked into these positions, and it's hard to change people's minds."

I swallow. The noise is audible in the quiet. "Yeah, I get what you mean."

He tugs at the collar of his pajamas as he heads to the bottom of the stairs. He raises his gaze to mine.

"I'll see you in the morning. Six thirty again for surfing?"

"Yeah, see you then."

Chapter 7

It takes the painters two weeks to paint the upper story of the house.

In those two weeks, Cody learns to surf, and I manage to progress from "Three Little Birds" to "American Pie" on the guitar.

And we become friends.

It happens so slowly I almost miss it. Like that old story about how if you put a frog in a pot of boiling water it will jump straight out, but if you slowly heat it, then the frog will stay there until it boils to death.

By the time I realize that any hostility I have toward Cody has completely faded and now I'm boiling in a pot of friendship, I don't care. I'm definitely staying in the pot.

Because as much as I don't want to like the guy, I can't help it.

It turns out the Cody I've observed in the past was just the performer.

Real Cody is an intoxicating mixture of capable brilliance and shyness with a sprinkle of dry humor that somehow ties the whole thing together.

Real Cody chews his bottom lip when he's concentrating. His real smile is a slow burn that starts with just a lift of his upper lip then dances its way across his mouth to the opposite corner. His real laugh is unexpectedly deep, and when he finds something especially funny, he throws his head back and shares it with the world.

Okay, okay, so I'm attracted to him. But I've been attracted to assumed-straight guys before, so I know how to handle it. The key is to put those feelings in a box and solder a steel lid on top to keep it shut. Make sure my attraction doesn't ruin our friendship.

And with Cody, it's easy to kill my libido. I just imagine my mum and dad, Frank and Heather, all staring in judgement at us. And that always does the trick.

Mel's away at her course most afternoons, so I fall into the habit of cooking, because that's when Cody practices. I cook and fry and stir and strain all to the background of soaring music that floats down the stairs.

Mel arrives home one day just as Cody comes down.

"Perfect timing," I say as I hand them a plate of nachos each.

Cody takes his plate to the table and immediately digs through his dinner. It's become a game for me to hide raisins in Cody's meals—stashing them away in the middle of mashed potatoes, hiding them under carrots, or in one particularly inspired moment, grated into the sauce of the lasagna.

But tonight, just to mess with him, I haven't put any raisins in. It's hilarious to watch him pick apart his whole dinner looking for the absent raisin.

I'm doubled over on the other side of the table, silently laughing.

"Where is it?" His fork clangs down, one of his lips twitching as he takes in my laughing face.

"I didn't put one in," I recover enough to choke out my confession.

"Seriously?"

"Seriously."

"You suck," he says. But he chuckles, undoing his words.

Mel rolls her eyes at me. "For the right price, I might tell Cody what Kate's nickname for you is."

I stop laughing. "You wouldn't."

"I'm willing to hear what Cody offers, compared to your counteroffer." Mel grins evilly.

I give her my death star laser glare. Unfortunately, it does not melt the smile off her face, which was the effect I was going for.

Cody leans back in his chair, his blue eyes scanning me contemplatively before turning back to Mel. "Dishes for a month."

"What's your counteroffer, Ryan?" Mel asks.

"I won't share that video when you jumped into the pool and your bikini top came off."

Mel sits up straighter. "You told me you'd deleted it!"

"The cloud is a great invention," I reply nonchalantly.

She glares at me. Now that is definitely a melting substances glare. Maybe I should ask her for lessons.

"I'll write you a song," Cody offers.

"I won't write you a song," I reply.

"How is that a bribe?" Mel asks.

"I'm sparing you the trauma of listening to a song I made up. That's got to be worth something."

"Dishes for a month, a song about how great you are, and I'll loan you my portable speaker anytime you want it."

"If you tell him, I will resurrect my pet spider colony, but this time in your closet."

Mel snorts. "Interesting how Cody understands the idea of bribing me, where you go for threats instead."

I shrug. "I guess I'm more of a stick than a carrot type of guy."

Cody laughs. I shoot him a curious look.

"I'm sure there's some questionable way that statement can be interpreted," he says.

"Man, you've been hanging out with me for way too long." I grin at him.

He grins back.

Mel looks between us. "So, this weekend I'm heading back to the city for Kirsten's twenty-first. You guys will be okay here, won't you?"

"How many times have I told you, we don't need to be babysat?" I ask.

"Even when you're in an aged care home, Ryan, you will still need to be babysat," Mel replies.

I manage to stop myself making a joke about adult diapers. We are eating, after all.

AFTER DINNER, I head up to my room. Because I do the cooking, Mel and Cody do the dishes. I usually hang out with them while they're doing it, but I have a stream of unanswered messages from Oz and Harvey that I need to reply to. I've neglected keeping in contact with my friends since I've been at the beach

I'm halfway through catching up with Harvey when my phone pings with a message from Cody.

It's a picture of a rhinoceros dressed in a tutu. Damn. He broke her.

I send back a YouTube clip of someone snorting raisins. It made me gag, so I'm pretty sure it's going to be even worse for him.

He replies with one of a rhino wearing a G-string.

As I'm scrolling through YouTube looking for more raisin grossness, Harvey sends me another message. He's probably wondering why I've suddenly gone AWOL from our conversation.

Suddenly I get an epic idea. I head to Cody's room.

The door is ajar, and Cody's lying on his bed, studying his phone intently. I edge inside. It's the first time I've been inside Cody's room. It's bigger than the spare room I'm sleeping in but looks smaller because of the piano jammed in. It has an impressive view of the ocean though.

"What are you looking at?" I ask.

He flicks his head up guiltily. "I may or may not be watching videos of cute baby rhinoceros."

"Bet they're not as cute as me," I say as I perch on the edge of his bed, wrinkling his bedspread. It's navy with green dinosaurs marauding over it.

Cody's mouth quirks. "Of course not."

"So I was thinking…" I start.

He sits up straighter. "That's always dangerous."

"Mel's heading back to the city for the weekend, so you know what that means, right?"

He eyes me cautiously. "What?"

"It means it's *party time!*"

He continues to look at me. "Yeah, I'm not sure if that's such a good idea," he says finally.

Disappointment surges in me, but I'm not giving up yet. There's a reason why my old English teacher said she saw my future career would be selling sand in the desert.

"Come on. I'll invite a few of my friends, and you invite a few of yours. Breaking down barriers between the private and public education system. Really, it's for the good of society."

"You talk so much bullshit, you know, right?" But a smile has slid up his face.

I can work with that smile. "So, are you in?" I ask.

Cody hesitates. "We keep it small. Like, really small. Like five people each, max."

"Ten," I counter.

He narrows his eyes. "Eight."

"You're a tough negotiator," I say, crashing back on his bed dramatically as I reach for my phone in my pocket.

"Eight. And only people you trust won't trash the place," Cody's voice is firm.

I'm already halfway through typing a message to Oz. "Done."

Chapter 8

Trying to choose only eight friends to invite to the beach is like trying to choose my favorite pizza toppings, Marvel film, or Dr Seuss quotes. A herculean task requiring intense contemplation.

Oz and Harvey are a given. In the end Nico, Eddie, Annabel, Grace, Anika, and Mia also make the cut.

Mel leaves around midday on Saturday. We haven't mentioned our little plan to have people over. As long as everyone leaves by lunchtime Sunday and we clean up properly, I figure she never needs to find out. I extend the parental principle "What they don't know won't hurt them" to older sisters as well.

Oz's rusty beast of a car grinds onto the gravel driveway around four o'clock, and Harvey, Eddie, Anika, and Mia tumble out. I go out to greet my friends with a huge smile on my face.

"Dude, this is a sweet place," Eddie says, looking around, taking in the house and the sand dunes behind. "How did you get hooked up staying here?"

"It's not what you know, it's who you know," I reply as I lead them inside.

Cody's coming down the stairs as we walk in. His hair is still damp from his shower, and he's wearing a tight navy T-shirt and Levi's. He stops at the bottom of the stairs and flicks his eyes at me.

"Hey, this is Cody," I say. "This is his parent's place."

I try to ignore the eyebrow raise that Harvey shoots Oz, or the speculative looks the girls give Cody.

"Cool digs," Oz says to him.

Cody swallows. "Thanks."

"You're the pianist, right?" Mia says. She's cut her hair since I've last seen her, so it's almost as short as mine now. Although she's also dyed hers a vivid red. With the three studs in her left ear and her nose ring, she looks like a Maori punk goddess.

"Um… yeah." Cody looks mildly alarmed that she knows that about him.

"My sister studies with Marilyn Adams too," she explains.

"Oh, okay."

"You in a band?" Eddie asks, studying Cody with interest.

Cody clears his throat. "No. I only play classical stuff."

He's spared more of my friends' interrogation by the sound of another car crunching its way onto the driveway. It's a dark blue, new model BMW.

I don't recognize the car or the bunch of people who emerge from it, but Cody's face lights up, and he heads out the door to greet them.

As he leads his friends back to the house, a knot forms in my stomach. Is it going to be weird having two different groups together? What if Cody's friends are all private school assholes? It occurs to me that this evening could crash and burn spectacularly.

But as soon as they come inside, Eddie recognizes Cody's friend Jake from cricket, and then the next carloads of our friends pulls up pretty much simultaneously, and there're already hellos and banter exchanged between them before they make it inside.

Soon everyone is lounging around the living space while Billie Eilish blares from the speakers.

Oz and I are at the breakfast bar together sorting out the drinks. Oz methodically removes the tops off bottles of Coronas. I'm making a bowl of punch, diluting the alcohol with lots of soft drink. I want our friends to have a good time, but I'm not excited about cleaning up anyone's puke.

Harvey comes over and rests his chin on his hands as he watches us work.

"Cody is your sisters' other brother, right?" he asks in a low voice.

I glance over at the couch where Cody's perched on the edge, having an animated conversation with Jake and Eddie. He tips his head back and laughs his deep laugh, and something stirs low in my stomach.

"Yeah," I say.

"I thought he was a dorky goody-two-shoes who always tried to upstage you," Harvey continues.

I wince hearing the words come out of Harvey's mouth. Because I'm fairly sure they're an echo of something I've said.

"Yeah, I might have been a bit premature with my opinion. He's actually a good guy."

"From what the people you've hooked up with say, it's not the only thing you're premature about." Harvey chortles at his own joke.

I roll my eyes as I squirt some lime syrup into the bowl

and give everything an overenthusiastic swirl. I then grab a handful of mint leaves from the fridge to sprinkle on top, because we've got private school people here, and I'm going for classy.

"Anyone want some punch?" I ask loudly.

"Yes please," Annabel calls out from across the room where she's on the couch next to Eddie.

I ladle some punch into a glass then walk it over to her, trying not to glance at the way her lowcut tank top high-lights her impressive cleavage.

"Now that's what I call hospitality," she says, taking a sip.

"You know me, superior in all dimensions," I say.

Annabel replies with a knowing smirk. I know her mind has probably gone somewhere X-rated. We've done the casual hook up thing a few times. I've never been inter-ested in doing the relationship thing with anyone; they look like more trouble than they're worth. Normally I'd be up for a bit of flirty banter though—along with soccer and surfing, it's a sport that I excel at—but Cody's sitting right there watching our exchange. So instead I glance at him. "You want to try my incredible punch?"

Cody shakes his head, unsettling his dark curls. "Nah, I'm fine thanks."

"So, how do you guys know each other?" Eddie asks, glancing between us.

Cody's shoulders stiffen. He shoots me a look.

"It's complicated," I say.

"Complicated?"

"Yeah. You know my sisters? Mel and Kate?"

"Yeah."

"Well, they're his sisters too."

Eddie's brow crumbles. "So, you're like, stepbrothers?"

"No. My mum and his dad were married to each

other, like, twenty years ago, and they had Mel and Kate. Then after they separated, my mum married my dad, and they had me, and Cody's dad married his mum and had him."

"Right. So. Complicated then," Eddie says.

"Yeah, complicated," Cody echoes. For a second his gaze clashes with mine. I don't recognize the look in his eyes.

From Eddie's expression I can see he has more questions brewing, so I intercept them.

"You want punch or beer?" I nod at his empty bottle.

"Beer, thanks."

I turn and head back to the kitchen and grab one of the beers Oz has opened before trekking back across the room to hand it to Eddie.

"Thanks, man."

"I think I might start the barbecue," I say.

I grab some meat from the fridge and wander outside, trying to work out why I'm feeling so weird.

I was excited to see my friends. But now they're here, I kind of want them to go home so it can be just Cody and me again. I wasn't expecting scrutiny of our friendship. I don't know why I'm feeling defensive. We're allowed to be friends.

The barbecue is on the back deck. Fitting in with everything in this place, it is pushing the boundaries of what a barbecue is. It's more like an outdoor kitchen.

I turn the knob, and the gas flickers to life.

I chuck a bunch of sausages on the grill. They remind me of sunbathers on a beach, all lined up and ready to get burnt to a crisp.

Mia comes out to talk to me as I'm focusing on not burning anything. It involves a very disciplined regimen of turning the sausages and burger patties regularly.

"This is a cool place to hang out for summer," she says, looking around.

Through the gaps in the sand dunes, the sun is just starting to set over the ocean. The whole thing looks like a postcard.

"Yeah, it's been great."

"Cody's friends with Jamie Anderson, right?" she asks.

"Yeah, that's right."

"I thought I recognized him. He's the guy who hooked up with Angie at Jamie's birthday party."

I accidentally stab a sausage. "He hooked up with Angie?"

"Yeah. Didn't you see? They were all over each other."

"Nah. I was late to Jamie's party." Obviously too late to observe the entertainment of Cody and Angie together. Angie Baker is a stunning redhead with an incredible body that she enjoys sharing. The thought of Cody pressed up against her, Cody kissing her, has me jabbing at the burger patties viciously.

Shit.

Mia's watching me, and I know she's clocked my reaction.

"Damn, I thought Angie was saving herself for me," I say.

Mia smirks. "I know. It's hard to believe she's not."

"You want to grab some of those burger patties?" I ask.
"Sure."

As Mia helps me cook, we have a debate about the best barbecue food. I'm giving an impassioned speech on how barbecued corn on the cob is epic, but part of my mind is still caught up on her revelation.

Cody and Angie. The thought sits like a splinter in my brain, growing more and more infected as the minutes tick by.

I dart a look through the living room window at the girls Cody's invited tonight. Beth, Sara, Whitney. Is he hoping to get together with one of them? Am I going to watch Cody hooking up with someone tonight?

I know I shouldn't care.

But I'm fairly sure the hollow feeling in my stomach isn't just because I'm hungry.

As we eat and then head to the beach for a bonfire, I'm watching Cody and the girls closely, trying to work out if something is going on with any of them.

Beth seems like a typical private school snob with straight blonde hair she keeps tossing around like she's some kind of show pony. Whitney's stunning, a Pacific Island goddess with a mass of black curls and a loud laugh. Sara's more the girl-next-door type, but if you look closer, she's pretty with light brown hair and clear blue eyes. She has a quiet laugh, and when Cody sits on a log next to her, she stretches out her long legs so they line up next to his.

My stomach twists, and I stare at the bonfire. It's growing now, the driftwood crackling and spitting as the fire consumes it.

To distract myself from the thoughts that seem intent on consuming my brain, I grab the guitar Cody's brought and strum "Wagon Wheel."

After a minute, I'm aware the conversation amongst my friends has completely died. When I glance up, Oz's mouth is literally hanging open. He could take a stroll out in the ocean and catch sharks in that thing.

I stop strumming.

"Since when do you play the guitar?" Oz asks.

"Since recently," I reply. "Cody taught me." I nod across the bonfire in Cody's direction, and my gaze catches on his expression.

Pride.

A knot forms in my throat. Because the idea that Cody is proud of me stirs up feelings that I can't cope with.

Annabel shifts closer to me. The cloying, clinging scent of her perfume mingles with the smell of smoke. "I didn't know you were musical."

I rip my gaze away from Cody.

"I'm full of surprises." I flash her a smile as I return to playing.

HALF AN HOUR LATER, the wind kicks up and the swirling smoke stings everyone's eyes, so we retreat to the house. Once we're inside, I plant myself on the couch and use the reflection of the window to keep an eye on Cody who's sitting on the arm of the chair talking with Beth and Jake.

Our eyes meet in the window. He's watching me too.

I glance away, only to notice Eddie and Harvey have started a wrestling match on the mat by the bottom of the stairs. Harvey pins Eddie down, and Eddie kicks out his feet to hit the base of the lamp, which wobbles but luckily doesn't topple over.

Cody stands up from the chair and moves toward the wrestling arena, his eyebrows drawing together, his mouth pinched. He stops a few feet away from them and shoots a look at me.

Shit.

Normally I'd be joining in and insisting loudly that jackknife power bombs are legal, but not tonight.

Before I know it, I'm on my feet and heading over to them too.

I loom over them and try to mimic the tone of every teacher who has told me off for doing something stupid. There's a few to choose from.

"Hey, knock that off, you guys. You're going to break something."

Eddie and Harvey both stop, looking at me with identical quizzical expressions. It's almost funny seeing them frozen in mid-action as Harvey has his legs wrapped around Eddie's hip and Eddie has a chokehold on Harvey.

I work hard on keeping my face serious.

"Since when did you become the fun police?" Eddie asks as he slowly disengages himself from Harvey.

"Since they gave me the official handcuffs to play with," I reply.

Eddie smirks. "The fluffy kind?"

"Definitely. Pink and fluffy. With yellow polka dots."

"You seriously want us to stop?" Harvey cuts through Eddie's and my random shit.

"Yeah, we don't want anything to get broken."

Harvey slides a look to Cody, who's standing there as an unmoving witness to our conversation.

"Okay," he says slowly, standing up and pulling down his T-shirt. "I'm going to grab another beer."

"Don't drink too much. I don't want to be cleaning up your barf either," I warn as I follow him out to the kitchen.

"Shit, you really have had a personality transplant this summer," Harvey mutters.

"It must be all the salt air," I say casually, watching him as he grabs a beer out of the fridge.

He turns back to me and gives me a look that I can't interpret before he heads back to score one of the beanbags to sit on.

I don't follow him, instead remaining in the kitchen where I survey the party.

It's that coupling up part of the evening. Beth and Jake start making out in the corner. Cody's friend Marco seems really into my friend Grace. He's been hanging around her the same way the bonfire smoke is now clinging to our clothes. Grace is a cool customer who normally keeps her cards very close to her chest, so the fact that she's laughing at something Marco said means she's interested too.

Cody thankfully doesn't appear to be looking to make out with anyone. He comes to stand with me in the kitchen.

"Thanks for that," he says in a low voice.

"No problem."

"You having a good time?" Cody asks.

"Yeah," I say automatically.

His arm brushes mine as he moves past me to the fridge. My skin automatically pricks into goose bumps where he touched me. I rub my hands over my arms, pretending that there's some phantom breeze that's responsible for my skin's reaction.

I glance over at the beanbag and see Harvey's watching me. I cock an eyebrow in the universal *What?* expression, and he glances away.

After Cody closes the fridge, I notice what's in his hand.

"Switching to Coke already?" I'm fairly sure he's been nursing one beer most of the evening.

"Yeah. You know better than anyone I can't really handle my alcohol." He gives a rueful smile.

Oz drifts over to us before I have a chance to reply.

Annabel, Eddie, and Anika have started a game of poker around the coffee table.

"Come on, Ryan. Come play with us," Annabel calls.

"Uh, no thanks."

"It's strip poker." Annabel raises an eyebrow suggestively.

"Tempting, but still no. I'll just enjoy the view you guys provide instead."

She pouts. "Suit yourself."

She deals the cards out amongst the players before sending another flirty grin in my direction.

Oz grins at me as he pours himself some punch. "You two looked like you were getting cozy earlier."

"What?"

"You and Annabel. At the bonfire. You're not going for a repeat, are you?" Oz asks.

I snort. "Nah, definitely not."

Oz drifts away, leaving just Cody and me again.

"You hooked up with her?" Cody is staring at Annabel, who's just lost the first hand and is pulling off her top to wolf whistles from the guys. I have to admit, she fills out a bra spectacularly.

"Yeah. I've hooked up with her a few times," I admit.

He continues to stare at Annabel. I don't know whether Mel or Kate have ever mentioned my sexuality to him, but after the news Mia gave me earlier, I suddenly decide to share something else with him too.

I nod toward where Nico is sprawled on the couch looking half asleep as he messages someone on his phone. "I've hooked up with him too."

Cody spins around so fast he's tempting whiplash. He sees Nico lounging on the couch, and his eyes widen. "You hooked up with a guy?"

Okay, so it appears my sisters have never shared that particular Ryan fact with their other brother.

"Yep."

He blanches. "You're… bi?"

"I'm bi, pan, whatever. I don't like labels. I don't like ruling anything out either. Takes too much effort." I flick him a grin.

Cody continues to look like he's about to throw up.

And suddenly a hole opens up in my stomach. Shit. I

know his mum goes to church, but he's never struck me as a bigot. Mel and Kate would have beaten that out of him, surely.

"You cool with that?" I ask cautiously.

He gulps. "Yeah, I'm cool."

He gives me a tight smile that doesn't reach his eyes. Crap. Maybe outing myself to him wasn't the best idea. Will this make things weird between us? Will Cody figure out I'm attracted to him? In typical Ryan fashion, I really didn't think this whole thing through.

Shit. Shit. Shit.

IT'S two in the morning. Nearly everyone has crashed for the night. Sleeping bodies are strewn on the couches and floors throughout the living space.

I sit on the steps of the back deck. It's freezing out here, but I'm too amped to sleep. Jumbled images of the evening play through my mind. I keep circulating back to Cody's face when I told him I'd hooked up with Nico.

The noise of the sliding door opening shatters my quiet thoughts.

I turn. I don't realize hope is rising in me until it's dashed when I recognize the person.

"You'll freeze your tits off out here," Harvey says as he comes to sit next to me.

"It's a bit fresh," I agree.

We sit there in silence for a few moments. Which is practically unheard of from Harvey.

"So, you and your stepbrother, eh?"

Shit. So that's what he's been brewing up. I deliberately keep my face neutral.

"He's not my stepbrother. He's my half-sisters' other brother. He's nothing to me."

Harvey snorts. "Doesn't look like he's nothing to you."

My shoulder's tense. "What do you mean by that?"

"I don't know, just the way you two act around each other." Harvey shrugs.

"I told you we've been hanging out this summer," I say carefully.

"So, you're just hanging out together?" There's a challenge in his voice.

"Yeah, we're just hanging out."

"Cool, 'cause you know the saying, don't screw the crew?"

A ball lodges in my throat. I'm fairly sure I know the direction this conversation is going. "I'm familiar with it, yeah."

"Good. Because I think it definitely applies in this case."

"Thanks for that insight." My voice is as cold as the wind whipping off the ocean.

Chapter 9

We get rid of all the interlopers by ten the next morning and then spend the next two hours erasing all evidence of the party.

I drive two trash bags containing all the bottles from last night to the recycling center. We straighten furniture and cushions, vacuum up the remains of spilled popcorn and chips, and I even clean the grill on the barbecue.

When Mel waltzes in, Cody and I are standing at the breakfast bar in the pristine kitchen, admiring the immaculate living space. We should write the handbook on how to have a secret teenage party and get away with it.

"What are you looking so smug about?" Mel asks me, her eyes narrowing.

"This is my pleased-to-see-you expression. Didn't you recognize it?" I ask.

Mel puts her handbag on the counter, her suspicious expression not wavering.

"How was the party?" Cody asks.

"Great. She held it at the Juggernaut, which I thought

was a weird choice, but it turned out to be a great venue. They have this massive deck…"

Shit. As Mel's talking, I spot a bottle cap lying under the corner of the living room rug that we've somehow missed.

Cody asks more follow-up questions, and I let the perfect brother run interference as I casually stroll over and pick up the bottle cap, stashing it in my pocket. I keep my face completely nonchalant, but Cody gives me a strange look.

"You want to head out for a surf?" I ask Cody.

"Sure."

On our way through the dunes, the sand warm on our feet, Cody glances at me with a grin. "I know you're still trying to figure out what you want to do with your life, but I'm thinking a career in acting might not be your thing."

I don't have a suitable reply, so I go with the tried and true. "Jackass." I give him a mild shove with my shoulder.

He shoves me back, and we stroll along like that, giving each other little shoulder bumps until we reach the water.

The surf is immense today. It's one of those days when I catch every wave I go after and get a great ride after ride. Cody's doing awesome too and grabbing some sweet waves.

I've just caught a great wave when he catches an epic barrel that cuts towards the shore in a perfect line.

I watch as he pulls out of the wave and jumps off his board.

"That was unreal," Cody says. He's standing in the thigh-deep water, his hair plastered to his head, grinning triumphantly. The black of his wetsuit makes his blue eyes stand out even more. His eyes that match the sky perfectly.

My breath leaves me.

"Yeah, unreal," I echo.

Something in my expression must be weird, because he gives me a puzzled look.

I try to quickly morph my face back into the dudes-hanging-out-surfing-together realm. I'm not sure I'm succeeding, because the curious frown line stays wedged between his eyebrows.

Just as my brain is scrambling for something light-hearted to say, a scream pierces our little bubble. It has a different, desperate edge to the usual shrieks of beach-time happiness.

I whirl around.

Standing on the shoreline twenty feet from us is a woman wearing an oversized sweater and a long dress that the wind whips around her knees.

"Help! Help! Please… my son." She wades into the water, flapping her hands in distress.

I spin in the direction of her gaze. In between the waves there's a flash of unnatural red in the water sixty feet out. The red object is being buffeted by the waves but doesn't appear to be moving by itself.

My stomach falls away.

Shit.

Before I have time to think, I'm moving. I whip around and splash through the surf a few steps before I jump onto my board. Salty spray hits my face as I paddle as fast as I can.

Holy Crap. Is this happening? My brain struggles to catch up as my breath comes in short pants, and my arm muscles burn as I plough through the water.

The large waves I was so happy about a few moments ago? I'm now cursing them, because I keep getting pushed back and it's taking me longer to get out there.

I wipe one of my hands over my face, trying to get rid of the water spray so I can see better.

Where is he? Am I even heading in the right direction?

Bridging the top of the next wave, the flash of red is right in front of me. A kid around eight or nine wearing a red and black wetsuit. The brief burst of happiness at finding him vanishes when my eyes focus in. Because he's facedown in the water.

Holy, holy crap.

Panic and adrenaline surge through me. I paddle toward him frantically, my arms screaming in protest.

Terror claws inside my throat, trying to escape.

I did a surf lifesaving course last summer, but I'm scrambling now, my thoughts flying in all directions as I try to remember what I'm supposed to do. There's only one consistent thought my brain is clinging to. I can't screw this up. I can't screw this up.

When I reach him, I stretch both arms out to grab him.

His body is like a dead weight, like a floppy fish on the end of the line, and it takes all my strength to turn him over onto his back. I can hardly hear myself think above the noise of my own breathing.

Holy hell.

Flipped on his back now, his eyes are closed, his face pale, and he has two stripes of orange and black zinc across the bridge of his nose. Like his mum carefully drew tiger stripes on his face this morning, getting ready for a day at the beach.

When I see those stripes of zinc, it's like something clicks in my brain. The voice of the instructor Rick comes back to me, his calm tone echoing in my head like he's right there, reminding me what I need to do.

Jumping off my board into the water, I put my surfboard between us and grab his limp hands, pulling them onto the edge of the board. Then I tug the board towards me, and it rolls over, lifting him up so his armpit and head are out of the water. When I pull the board over again, his body moves onto the board.

"Can you hear me?" I ask. Shit, my voice doesn't sound like my own. It's high pitched and shaky.

No response.

Damn. I've got to get him back to the beach.

"It's okay, buddy. I've got you."

Grabbing his arms and yanking him around so he's lying lengthwise on the board, I jump on behind him.

I reach forward to touch his chest.

Shit. Shit. Shit.

I don't think he's breathing.

I turn the board around and keeping one hand on the boy to make sure he's not going to fall off, riding the waves as much as I can on my knees. This time the swell is my friend.

Forty feet to go. Thirty. Twenty. Ten…

I jump off the board to hold on to him as we come through the choppy white water.

The water churns around my legs, trying to whip them out from under me. I concentrate on plowing through the ocean as fast as possible toward the beach.

When it's knee deep, I grab him under his arms, hauling him through the water to the wet sand at the edge. Placing him down as gently as I can, I drop to my knees next to him.

He's pale and clammy, his face puffy and dripping.

I'm vaguely aware of people pressing around me and the ragged cries of the boy's mother, but I ignore them as I go through the basics. DRS ABC. Danger, Response, Signal for help. Airway, Breathing, Circulation.

He's out of dangerous water, but he's not responding.

"Someone call 9-1-1," I say as I tilt his head back to

make sure his airway is open. Then I lean forward, putting my ear to his while looking at his chest.

Shit.

The kid is definitely not breathing. Holy hell.

There's only one thing to do.

I start CPR.

Our instructor played the Bee Gee's 'Staying Alive' song when we were doing chest compressions, giving us the timing we should press down for.

At the time we mocked the music, but now the song circulates in my head like it's on spin cycle, and I force everything else out.

My focus is solely on the boy. Noise is pounding all around me, people are trying to speak to me, but I ignore them all. Nothing else matters but my hands on his chest, the heel of my hand pushing into his chest, my other hand on top, elbows locked, arms straight. Fear chokes my throat as I bear all my weight down on him. I know the principle, that you've got to press down hard to make a difference. It feels wrong to manhandle a kid like this. But as Rick said, a dead person doesn't worry about broken ribs.

I can't remember the exact ratio of breaths to compressions, so after twenty I stop and close my mouth over the kid's. His lips are cold and clammy, and there's this weird froth at his mouth, but I ignore all that and breathe a mouthful of air into his lungs.

Then I go back to my Bee Gee compressions.

The boy stays immobile under my hands.

I stop to give him another breath, then twenty more compressions. Another breath. Twenty more compressions. Breath. Twenty more.

He doesn't respond.

No. No. This can't be happening.

My arms are aching, but I'm not taking my hands off him.

Then suddenly, just after I've given him another breath, he gives a little cough and then barfs, gushes of vomit streaming out of his mouth.

Instinctively, I turn him on his side so the vomit flows onto the sand. The bitter smell hits my nostrils, and I almost gag.

Regardless, I scoop into his mouth to make sure there're no chunks obstructing his airway.

He gasps and coughs, the most awful sound, and some vomit-stained water dribbles out of his mouth.

I'm vaguely aware of a piercing noise. Sirens. Close by.

I rest back on my haunches as a woman in a para- medic uniform pushes past me to reach the boy. I watch with blurred vision, lightheaded, as she and another para- medic examine him then strap an oxygen mask to his face.

"You did good, kid," someone says to me.

I stagger on wobbly legs a few feet away and collapse on the sand while the paramedics take over.

I'm shaking. Full body tremors, like my body has decided now is the time to stage a 9.5 earthquake.

A towel is placed around my shoulders. I look up. Cody is standing over me, his face pale.

Hugging the towel around me, we both watch as the paramedics move the kid onto a stretcher then race the stretcher to the ambulance, his mother running beside them. The ambulance pulls away, the sirens at full noise.

I'm aware some other bystanders are saying stuff to me as the crowd disperses, giving me praise, but I don't really hear it. I'm trying to calm my breathing and stop the godforsaken shaking.

Cody drops to his haunches next to me. "You okay?"

"Yeah," I manage to reply. My voice doesn't sound like mine. It sounds like a strung out version of mine.

I wipe a hand across my forehead then realize my hand smells like vomit. Standing, I lurch to the water's edge and crouch down to rinse my hands in the water.

Cody's right there by me as a wave comes in, washing over my ankles and wrists.

Another wave rolls in. And another.

I remain hunched over, still trying to process everything that happened. It feels like a surreal dream.

"Come on, let's get you home," Cody says finally. He reaches down a hand to me, and I take it, letting him pull me to my feet, shuffling up the sand with him to where our boards lie abandoned on the beach.

Picking up my board, I take a deep breath, straighten up, and clear my throat.

"Well, that was quite the adventure," I say when we hit the path. I'm trying for a casual, cool tone and a matching expression, but it withers when I meet Cody's intense gaze.

"You…" Cody begins, his eyes dropping to study the path in front of us.

"What?" It's like the events of the afternoon have destroyed my filter, so I can't hide the neediness in my voice.

"You were incredible," he says the words in a half-whisper as if he's telling the sand some incredible truth. He lifts his gaze to mine and speaks again in a stronger voice. "You were absolutely incredible."

My entire body tingles at his praise. I take a deep breath before I answer him.

"I just did what I had to," I say.

He doesn't speak as we walk the rest of the path.

When we reach the house and start stripping off, I suddenly realize how tired I am. My arms feel like dead-weight as I reach behind me to grapple with the zipper of my wetsuit. I can't quite tug it at the right angle to get the zipper moving.

"Let me," Cody says gently.

"Thanks."

The puff of his breath against my neck causes the hair there to rise. He carefully unzips my wetsuit, and I step out, shuddering although it's not cold.

I'm feeling a deep, existential tiredness that I've never felt before.

As soon as we make it inside, I stumble to the couch.

Cody heads straight to the fridge then returns to me.

"You need sugar," he says, handing me a can of Coke.

"What happened to you?" Mel rolls her eyes as she sorts junk mail on the counter.

Cody fixes her with a glare. "Ryan just saved a kid's life."

Mel stops still, her eyes widening. "What?"

"He saved a kid from drowning. Rescued him on his surfboard and gave him CPR and everything until the paramedics arrived."

Her mouth drops open to match her eyes. "Seriously?"

"He was amazing," Cody says quietly. "A total hero."

Mel insists on calling Mum to tell her what happened, and I have to deal with my parents confused praise. I'm guessing when they realized Mel was calling them about me, they were expecting I'd pulled off some prank, not heroics.

Mel takes the phone and retreats to the kitchen. She tells them how I've been great, cooking dinner nearly every night and helping with stuff. I can hear the surprise in my mum's voice from my position sprawled on the couch.

Cody's watching me closely. "You okay?"

"Yeah, just a bit of a delayed reaction," I say. I take

another swig of my coke and swallow before continuing, "I think that was the scariest thing I've ever done."

"You looked so confident, in control. Like you knew exactly what you were doing."

"I was shitting myself," I confess.

Cody runs his hands through his curls. "This kid from my class, Jason, once had an epileptic fit right in front of me. He was thrashing on the ground, and I just froze. And what's worse, we'd been given this training only a few months before about what to do if Jason had a fit, how to keep him safe, and I couldn't remember any of it."

"It was kind of the opposite for me," I say. "Like my brain regurgitated all this stuff that I'd learned ages ago and didn't think I would remember."

"You should think about becoming a doctor or nurse or something."

I snort. "I don't think I could get through all that study."

Cody just gives me one of his looks. "Seriously, keeping calm under pressure is something no one can teach. You either have it or not. And you definitely have it."

I try to school my face so I don't reveal how much his words mean to me. Would I like to do something like that? Maybe. The idea of doing a job where you're not stuck in an office, a job where you get to help people definitely appeals. But I don't know if I'd want to be stuck inside a hospital either.

Mel finishes her conversation and comes back over to us.

"Mum and Max are coming home on Saturday," she tells me.

Saturday. Two days away. The buzz I was feeling from Cody's praise drains away.

"Oh, okay," I say. "That's earlier than expected."

"Yeah, so you can head home Saturday morning if you want."

If I want. Yeah, it's actually so far from what I want, it's not even on the same continent.

"Why don't you stay here a bit longer, hang out?" Cody suggests, not meeting my eyes.

"Surf forecast is good for the weekend. I might hang around for that," I manage.

As I take another sip of my coke, my chest tightens, and I don't think it's anything to do with the rescue.

Instead, it's due to something I've been trying not to think about.

My time with Cody is ending.

Chapter 10

That night I'm surfing with Cody when he falls off his board and starts to sink.

I desperately try to reach him, but he moves further and further out of reach. He slips under the water, and I dive down, but he's sinking so fast, and my lungs scream for air. I know if I go back to the surface, he will sink by the time I dive back down. Panic surges through me, my lungs are on fire, but I refuse to go up. I can't leave Cody…

"Ryan." Someone is gently shaking me.

I open my eyes. It's Cody sitting on the edge of my bed.

Oh, thank God. He's here. He's safe.

I don't think. I sit up and lean into him, shuddering as I try to get my breath back. My heart pounds in my ears, a rapid, frantic beat that shows no sign of slowing.

Cody's hand goes hesitantly to my back. "It was just a nightmare."

"Someone was drowning… and I couldn't save them." My breath still comes in ragged gasps, the suffocating, choking feeling smothering my throat. My body is taking a long time to get with the program and realize I'm not drowning.

"It was just a nightmare," he repeats.

I concentrate on filling my lungs, trying desperately to smooth my breathing.

Finally, my frantic need to fill my lungs fades, and I become aware of Cody's proximity. The heat of his hand through my T-shirt. I've got my forehead pressed against his shoulder, and he smells of soap and salt and something else that is just Cody.

I pull back before my traitorous body can react in an inappropriate way.

Cody's hand drops to his side.

"Thanks." My voice is all croaky.

"You okay?"

"Yeah." I rake a hand over my face.

Cody left the door partially open, so the light from the hallway is spilling in. He's watching me, concern etched on his forehead.

"Sorry," I say.

"There's nothing to apologize for." Cody's tone is soft. "It's not surprising you had a nightmare after what happened."

"Yeah, I guess."

I don't want to dwell on the particulars of my dream. You don't have to be Freud to work out where it came from.

"I should head back to my room," he sounds unsure.

"Stay. Please," I respond without thinking.

I see him swallowing. "Okay."

He gets up to shut the door then climbs into the other side of the bed. He lies on his back, motionless.

"You okay?" I ask.

"Yeah."

"Was I making lots of noise before? You know, to wake you up?"

"Yeah, you were kind of yelling and…"

"And?" I prompt, propping myself up on my elbow to look at him because I can tell from his voice there's more to say.

"And you were calling out my name."

Oh. I lie back down, facing the ceiling.

"I dreamed you were drowning and I couldn't save you." It is easier to whisper the words in the darkness when I can't see his face.

Cody says nothing for a while. "I hope you're not good at predicting the future," he says finally.

I huff out a laugh. "I'm fairly sure I have zero psychic abilities."

"That's good to know."

The silence thickens between us. Eventually Cody's breathing evens out.

I lie there, letting the sound of him sleeping next to me soothe away the last of the panic from my dream.

Cody's here. He's safe.

THE NEXT MORNING, I roll over as I open my eyes, and Cody's right there. He's turned to face me in his sleep, his curls spilling over the pillow.

Shit.

What felt so right last night, asking him to stay with me, now seems strange in the gray light of the morning.

Or maybe my strange feeling is because of how it doesn't feel that weird? How finding Cody curled up next to me seems such a natural thing.

I have to recite times tables backwards and remember the exact snaggle of my third grade teacher Ms. Finlay's teeth and the ten hairs she had on her chin to stop my body having a natural reaction to waking up next to Cody.

When Cody opens his eyes a few minutes later, he doesn't look like he thinks it's a natural thing. He looks freaked out.

"Keep your morning breath away from me," I say.

A hesitant smile blooms on his lips.

"You sleep okay?" I ask.

"Yeah, really well. You? No more bad dreams?" he asks, stretching. The act of stretching causes the duvet to slip off his shoulders.

"No." I tug the duvet back down around me. I change tack. "Thanks for coming to my rescue last night. Rescuing me like a maiden in distress. You're my loyal knight in shining armor. Sir Cody of the Round Table. Actually, you'd look good in those tights they used to wear."

Cody doesn't laugh like I expect him to. Instead, his eyebrows knit together. "Why do you do that?"

"Do what?"

"Cover everything up with a joke."

My stomach tightens. "I do not."

"Yeah, you do. You're allowed to be freaked out by what happened yesterday. It's perfectly normal."

"Sometimes it's easier to laugh rather than the alternative, okay?" My voice is strained.

Cody pins me with his stare. I'm like an insect stuck in one of those collection boxes. "What's the alternative in this case?"

"I don't know… I guess the alternative is thinking about how close that boy came to dying yesterday. How freaked out I was that I would do something wrong. I would have felt like crap if he had died, like I'd let everyone down."

Also, I'm trying not to think about the fact that we're going to be apart soon, and my subconscious obviously doesn't like that idea.

"Even if he had died, you wouldn't have let anyone down, Ryan. You'd have tried your best. You'd still be a hero. It shouldn't depend on the outcome."

I let his words sink in, turn them over in my mind. Because Cody's making a valid point. No matter if the boy had lived or died, my actions were exactly the same. I deserve the same amount of credit. It's hard to get my head around that, though.

"If I'm a hero, would I be more Superman or Spider Man?" I ask.

"There you go again." Cody rolls his eyes and climbs out of bed.

"It's a legitimate question," I defend. "Am I more Clark Kent or Peter Parker, do you think?"

Cody throws me a look. "Definitely Peter Parker," he says as he leaves.

THE NEXT MORNING, heading out surfing is charged with a different feeling. After the events of yesterday, I can't look at the ocean in the same way. Yesterday was definitely a reminder that the sea is a dangerous beast that you've got to treat with respect.

Cody seems to pick up on how I'm feeling, and he's more subdued as we surf together. Then after lunch he disappears off to practice while I muck around downstairs doing the other type of surfing on my phone. Because I have ears, I can't help but hear Cody as he practices. Which is hardly a hardship. My opinion of classical music has done a U-turn this summer, diverting from the *God this is as boring as shit* street, to *Sometimes this stuff is pretty awesome* highway.

I've learned to tell if Cody's had a good day by how often he stops and starts while practicing and the deepness of the crease on his forehead when he comes down to dinner.

Today, it's a stuttering day, and I don't even need to look at the crevasse on his forehead when he comes into the kitchen because his whole body is almost vibrating with frustration.

He sits at the breakfast bar cutting avocados into slices while I turn into a one-man comedic show as part of my mission to cheer him up.

Mel comes home when I'm halfway through my repertoire of "Yo mama" jokes. So I immediately turn them into "Yo sister" jokes.

"Your sister is so stupid she thought Dunkin Donuts was a basketball team."

"You realize that "Your sister" jokes don't really work between us, right?" Cody says with a glance at Mel.

"What do you mean? "Your sister" jokes always work." I continue to grate the cheese nonchalantly.

"But you're insulting your own sisters."

"So?"

Mel just rolls her eyes. "Ryan's never had a problem insulting his sisters."

"No. One might even say I'm a natural at it," I say. "But then, you and Kate make it so easy."

"I swear I need to run an intervention between you guys sometimes," Cody says.

"How far away is dinner? I'm starving," Mel takes a seat next to Cody at the breakfast bar.

"Busy day?" Cody asks.

"Yeah. I've got this massive assignment that I'm trying to finish."

"I can't believe you've spent the summer studying when

you don't have to," I say as I assemble the tacos. Tacos are the best invention ever. Easy to prepare components. Easy to put together. Yet somehow they taste better combined than the sum of their individual parts.

"I love design. It's been great to learn more about it," Mel replies.

"Why don't you just study it at university then? Why bother with law?" I ask as I slide a plate of tacos over to her. Mel immediately stands and heads for the table. I've suggested previously that we should just eat at the breakfast bar, but apparently Heather always insists on everyone eating dinner together at the table properly. Cody and Mel feel obliged to continue that even when she's not here.

"Because law is a much more reliable career path than design. But I don't know, I'm hoping I can incorporate both somehow," Mel says as she plops down.

"That's a good idea." Cody takes his plate, following us to the table.

"Law and design, 'cause that's a natural fit." I settle myself in the chair. "Why don't you just follow your passion?"

"Yeah, you don't have our dad," Mel says. "If you think Mum and Max give you a hard time about not knowing what to do, you should see what our dad's like. He's on another level when it comes to planning his kid's futures. He's had my glittering law career planned out since I won that debate competition in year four."

"His approach didn't work for Kate, did it?" I say. Because Kate is someone who got an impressive university degree majoring in finance but has jumped from job to job since, never sticking with anything before getting accidentally pregnant.

"I think that means Dad's just going to try even harder with us," Mel says glumly.

Cody doesn't seem to be paying attention to the conversation. Instead, he's inspecting something hidden under his lettuce in the taco shell.

"Raisins?" he asks as he removes the bundle of grapey goodness.

It's been a while since I've done the raisin thing. "I was feeling nostalgic," I say.

He grins at me, and a spark flares in my chest, bright and sharp.

I crunch down on my taco to distract myself.

"I just want to get the last of my assignment finished. Then I will veg out on the couch," Mel says when we finish dinner.

"Go do it now," Cody says. "I'll clean up here."

"Are you sure?"

"Yeah, no problem."

"Thanks," Mel gives him an affectionate grin.

"God, you are such a suck-up," I say to Cody after Mel heads upstairs.

"It's called being a nice brother. You should try it sometime," Cody says. His comment should sting, but he's said it in a teasing tone, and no maliciousness lurks beneath his words.

"Nah, why change habits of a lifetime?" I start clearing the table.

"You don't have to do that," Cody says.

"I'll help you with the dishes."

"But you cooked," he protests.

"Yeah, it turns out that I'm capable of both cooking and doing the dishes. I know, I know. It's hard to believe so much talent resides in one person."

"You're definitely unbelievable," Cody agrees with a grin.

We clear the plates away from the table and start rinsing and stacking.

Cody steps back from the sink just as I'm heading to the fridge to put leftovers away.

His hip brushes against mine and our legs collide. My stomach flips. We both jerk away like we've been electrocuted.

"Sorry," I say.

"My fault," he murmurs.

His blue eyes catch mine, and I'm trapped, caught in Cody's gaze. We continue to stare at each other.

The spell is broken as Mel thunders down the stairs. We both turn to look at her.

"I thought you were busy studying while we were slaving away." I put some distance between Cody and me. My heart thumps more than doing the dishes usually inspires.

"I was, but Kate's just called. And she's got some news to share."

Mel hits speakerphone and puts her phone on the middle of the counter.

"Hey, Kate," Cody says.

"What's up, Katydid?" I say. Hey, if you're going to dish out nicknames like rhinoceros, you've got to be prepared for retaliation. And it's a toss-up whether a large horny grey mammal or a weird mutant grasshopper is a worse insult.

Cody flicks me a glimmer of a smile, which I take as approval of my nickname-giving prowess.

"I've got some news." Kate's voice is full of suppressed excitement, reminding me of six months ago when she called to tell us she was pregnant. Mum immediately burst into tears.

I eye Mel and Cody suspiciously. Hopefully, there's not going to be any waterworks at whatever this news is.

"Well, don't let us die from the suspense," I say when she doesn't continue. "What is it?"

"I'm moving home!"

Cody's eyebrows shoot up, and I'm sure mine match his.

"Seriously? I thought you loved it in Wellington," I say.

"Yeah, I do love it here. But now with the baby, I thought it would be nice to be close to family."

"That's so great," Cody says.

"I'm assuming Chris also wants to come?" I ask.

"Yes, Ryan, of course Chris wants to move. Do you think I'd make the decision without talking to him?"

Ha. Kate's fiancé Chris is one of the most laid-back guys on the planet. I'm sure he's just continuing his philosophy of doing whatever Kate wants. It's a way to guarantee his peaceful existence.

"When are you moving?" Cody asks. "Are you going to work remotely or look for something here?"

Kate and Cody chat about logistics and maternity leave, and I tune out. I should be pissed that Cody's showing me up as usual. He's got all the right questions to ask Kate, and she's using her affectionate tone with him that I hear once a year if I'm lucky.

But his face is lit up, and he's talking animatedly, so buried under my resentment something else flickers.

Happiness.

Cody being happy makes me happy. Yeah, I don't want to examine that one too closely.

"Ryan, you there?" Kate asks.

"Yeah, I'm here."

"Well, what do you think about the whole thing?"

"I'm just planning all the pranks I will teach your kid," I say. "I hear that's what all good uncles do."

I can almost hear Kate rolling her eyes.

"God help the child if they don't like raisins," Cody says, sneaking me a grin.

"This child has some of my genes. There's no way they'll have such freakish phobias," I reply.

"Are you two getting along okay?" Kate cuts in, sounding like her typical bossy older sister self. "Ryan, are you behaving yourself?"

"He's been remarkably well behaved," Mel says.

"What am I, some pet you're trying to house train?" I mutter.

"You said it, not me," Mel replies. "And yeah, they're getting on fine."

Fine is not the word I personally would have used to describe my friendship with Cody. It's a few levels above fine. But I'm not going to disagree with Mel's assessment right now.

"Did you hear Ryan saved a kid from drowning?" Cody asks.

"What? When did that happen?"

Cody launches into the account of me rescuing the kid, turning it into a dramatic action movie. Seriously, the way he describes it, I'm Captain America, Superman, and Hercules all rolled into one.

"Holy shit, Ryan, that's incredible," Kate says when he finishes up the story.

"All in a day's work," I say.

Cody throws me an exasperated look.

"Anyway, I've still got to finish my assignment," Mel says. "And the boys have got to finish cleaning up the kitchen."

"Ms Bossy Boots," I say.

"Yeah, well, I guess I'll see you all in a few weeks." I can hear the smile in Kate's voice.

"I can't wait," Cody says.

As soon as Kate hangs up, Mel and Cody start an excited discussion about Kate and Chris coming home and how having the baby nearby will be so great. Cody suggests that maybe they could resurrect that three-piece orchestra group they started a few years ago, and they go into some obscure music discussion I can't follow.

Eventually I cut through their chat with a well lobbed dish cloth aimed at Cody's face.

"Hey, this dishwasher isn't going to load itself."

I HEAD UPSTAIRS to my room after we complete loading the dishes.

Kate hasn't lived here since she left for university, so it will be weird having her around again. But it will be great to get to know Chris better, who seems like a good guy. And awesome that I'll get to spend tons of time with my niece or nephew, rather than just seeing them on a screen occasionally.

But my brain decides not to dwell on any of that important stuff as I slouch on my bed. Instead, it's providing me with helpful replays of brushing up against Cody in the kitchen. The look on his face when he found the raisin in his tacos. His laugh.

There's a gentle knock at my door, and Cody pokes his head around. "Mel's finished her assignment and is now hogging the TV watching some chick flick. Do you want to hang out in my room and watch *Lord of the Rings*?"

I hesitate for a second. Right now, close proximity to Cody feels dangerous. But we've only got a few nights left together. I don't have the self-control to say no.

"Okay," I say.

I follow him into his room. He sits down on his bed near the headboard, and I jump next to him. He grabs a pillow to prop behind himself and gives one to me. I notice his pillow has Batman from the Lego movie on it, and I can't help grinning.

Cody settles his laptop between us. "Cool news about Kate, huh?"

"Yeah, it's awesome. I always need another big sister around to give me lectures. It's something lacking in my life."

"It's funny, they're not like that with me."

"Yeah, I've noticed," I reply.

Cody bites his lower lip.

He opens his mouth to say something, but I cut him off. "Nah, it's great. It'll be cool to have a little niece or nephew running around."

"Yeah," he says slowly.

"You realize I'm going to kick your ass in the cool uncle stakes, right?"

Cody raises an eyebrow. "You reckon?"

"Sure. Kids like gross stuff like fart jokes and fake vomit. I will own you."

"I guess I'm willing to concede fart jokes and fake vomit to your superior skill set," he says.

His smile is so warm my skin heats up in response. Shit.

"Anyway, we going to watch this movie or what?" I ask.

"Sure."

Cody presses play, and suddenly we're in the Shire, preparing for Bilbo's birthday.

He sighs happily, "I love these movies."

"You'd make a good hobbit," I say, sliding back and adjusting my pillow against the headboard. "Actually, you do remind me a bit of Frodo Baggins."

The dark curls. The large eyes. Although Cody's cuter than Elijah Woods, but I don't say that.

Cody smirks. "In that case, you can be Samwise Gamgee."

"I'll be Sam to your Frodo." I mean to say it lightheartedly, but somehow the words are weighed down with layers of meaning.

The air crackles between us. He swallows, looking away.

"Although you need hairier feet if you're going to be a hobbit." I nudge his foot.

"Okay, I'll get on to growing foot hair." He keeps his foot resting up against mine.

Suddenly my whole awareness is centered on that slice of skin. As the movie progresses, I hardly see the elves and dwarves and orcs slaying each other. I'm too busy noticing how good it feels to have Cody's skin pressing against my skin.

I'm aware it's pathetic. I mean, they're feet. They're as far from the fun zone as you can get.

I nod off halfway through the third movie. I definitely remember watching Eowyn slaying the Witch-king, but after that it blacks out.

When I wake up, the first light of dawn is creeping through the windows. I turn my head.

Cody is facing me. He's still asleep, his curls messed up. Even now, he has this serious, intense expression, with a line etched between his eyebrows like he's solving global warming or world poverty in his sleep.

Two mornings in a row waking up next to Cody. It's getting to be a habit.

I try to ignore the happiness thumping through me. And the urge to reach over and smooth the line on his forehead and brush the curls off his face.

Damn.

I scramble to get out of bed before I give in to my impulse to touch him.

Climbing out of bed disturbs Cody, because suddenly he's sitting up, his face still crumpled from sleep, his curls sticking out in all directions.

"You want to go for an early surf?" I ask from the doorway.

"Yeah, definitely."

Chapter 11

The waves are dumpier today, which is good because I have to concentrate hard to catch a good ride. I want to focus only on surfing, let the spray of the surf and the salt and the sunlight fill my senses so I don't have to think.

Cody's struggling today, though. He curses as he falls off again.

"I just can't find the right rhythm," he complains. His hair is plastered to his skull, water slicking off his wetsuit. He walks a few steps to where I'm waiting for him so we can paddle back out together.

"Sometimes you've got to stop analyzing and just feel it," I say.

"Feel the ocean?" He looks at me like I've lost my mind.

Which maybe I have. It's starting to feel that way, at least when it comes to Cody. But I still stumble on, struggling to find the right words so he can understand what I mean.

"Don't you ever get that in music?" Another dumpy wave slams into us, trying to wrench our boards away. I tug mine back to me like it's a disobedient pet. "Like, when you get to the point where you stop thinking about technique and worrying about being perfect and just go with your feelings?"

"Yeah, all the time," Cody says as we brace for another wave. "I mean, you can be completely technically correct, but if you don't get what the music is about, the feeling you're trying to portray, then it comes out all robotic."

"It's the same out here. Stop worrying about getting it right. You've got to respond to the wave like its something living."

"Something living?"

"Trust me. Just try it and see."

Cody raises his eyebrow as we jump on our boards, but I can see his normal look of Cody concentration come over his face as he paddles out next to me. We turn around to face the beach, a few feet from each other. I keep one eye out over my shoulder, evaluating the approaching waves.

"Here comes a good one," I call to him.

He nods and paddles frantically to build his momentum.

"Go, go!" I yell as the wave swell lifts me up, then leaves me behind as it barrels on toward the shore.

I give a whoop when I see the wave break, and Cody's still there riding it. He pulls out just before the shallow water and gives me a thumbs-up. I offer a thumbs-up in return, a wide smile on my face.

Now it's my turn to catch one, and somehow it's an even sweeter ride than before.

After another half hour, Cody and I signal each other, and I catch a last wave in to meet him.

Cody waits in ankle-deep water for me. He runs a hand through his hair, shaking out the water.

"Strangely, what you said out there made sense," he says as we start our trek home through the sand dunes, sand caking our feet like another layer of skin. "It's like the difference of treating surfing as an art versus a science."

I roll my eyes as I hitch my surfboard up under my arm. "Only you could turn this into a philosophy thing. You just had to stop worrying about being perfect."

"You're telling me I'm not perfect?" He throws me a grin, his tone teasing.

"I'm telling you that when you stop trying to be perfect and just feel, you're better than perfect."

I walk for another few feet before I realize Cody has stopped and I've left him behind. I slow down and turn back to face him.

He's still standing on the path, staring at me, eyes wide.

I replay my words, and my shoulders stiffen, my cheeks heating.

We stare at each other for a few heartbeats.

"And you claim I'm the philosopher," he says finally, starting to walk again, taking long strides to catch up with me.

My shoulders relax. "You're right. Aristotle must be trembling up in heaven, worried about me eclipsing his legacy."

Cody huffs out a laugh, but the admiring gaze he slides me causes my legs to turn wobbly.

We reach the house.

"Wetsuit off, right?" It's become my habit to ask, a small joke before I strip off. This has to be one of my favorite bits about surfing now. Cody in a wetsuit is one thing, but Cody in only board shorts is a whole other dimension of awesomeness. Of course, I only allow myself sneak peeks.

"Right."

I strip down: the wetsuit releasing my skin in a loud slurp.

Cody strips down too, showing off his tanned skin and taut muscles. He grabs the hose, a smile licking at his lips as he turns toward me.

I recognize the look of calculation on his face… because it's normally on mine. I narrow my eyes. "Do it and die."

He tilts his head. "Nah, see, I'm now approaching all situations with the question, *What would Ryan do?* And I'm sure if you had the hose, you would do this." He lifts the nozzle up and sprays the water at me.

The blast of cold is a shock to my skin, causing instant goose bumps.

"I can't believe you just did that," I splutter.

"Payback's a bitch." Cody's still grinning at me.

His grin fades slightly as I stalk toward him.

He lifts the hose and sprays me again, but I brace myself for the cold and don't let it deter me from my mission. Which is to grab him and try to wrestle the hose off him.

Cody doesn't relent, and so we scuffle. I use my superior weight to pin him against the side of the house. He stretches out his arm, holding the hose as far away as he can, but I clamp down on his hand. I try to twist the hose out of his grasp, but his fingers cling on.

"Let go of the hose."

"Never," he replies. His breath is coming hard and fast. Mine is too.

Our chests are pressed together, and his face is so close to mine I can see a scattering of faint freckles across his nose. My heart rate picks up to match my breathing. I'm sure he feels the frantic thumping where our skin touches, an up-tempo beat.

I drop my gaze down to his mouth for a second, which is a mistake because now all I can think about is kissing him. About how it would feel to have his red, slightly chapped lips pressed against mine. My mouth goes dry.

When I flick my gaze back up to his, Cody's eyes are wide, his smile dimming as we stare at each other. I can't escape the intensity of his blue eyes. I don't want to escape it.

I stay pressed against him, feeling his chest heaving against mine, trapped in his gaze.

The noise of a car crunching gravel on the driveway shatters the moment.

I blink. Cody blinks.

I release his wrists and step back. Desperately swallowing, trying to get some moisture back into my mouth, I look at the driveway.

My stomach dives.

Shit.

It's Frank's car. I recognize it from the night he drove me home.

Cody's chest is still rising and falling rapidly. He drops the hose, walking over to turn the tap off. He doesn't meet my eyes as he walks past me.

Double shit. How much did his parents see when they pulled in? Did it just look like normal roughhousing? Was that all it was?

Cody picks his way on bare feet over the gravel to where his parents are just emerging from the car.

"Mum, Dad." He gives them both a hug. "I thought you guys weren't coming back until Thursday?"

"There was a storm forecast, so we wanted to get home before that hit. We changed our flights." Frank's voice carries to me.

I grab a towel and wrap it around my waist, because just standing there in board shorts makes me feel exposed.

Frank glances over, his eyebrows raising. His expression reminds me exactly of Kate's when I was ten and she caught me gluing her jewelry box closed. It doesn't make the moment any less weird.

"Hi." I give a foolish half-wave that probably looks even stupider than it feels. In the highlights reel of Ryan's dumbest moments, it would definitely make the top ten.

"Ryan." Frank nods in acknowledgement.

Heather tries a little harder, throwing me a wan smile as she grabs her handbag out of the car. "Hi, Ryan, it's nice to see you. I hope you've enjoyed your time here?"

"It's been great," I say.

"Ryan's been teaching me to surf," Cody says.

"I hope you've still been practicing," Frank says stiffly.

"Of course I have."

Tension rises in Cody's spine.

To ease some of the strangeness of us standing there staring at each other, I pick my wetsuit up off the grass and hang it over the side of the deck as normal. I see Frank giving it a sideways glare.

God, this is awkward.

I follow them into the house.

Shit. We're not prepared for the scrutiny of parents. The sun streaming through the windows highlights the baked-on cereal on the breakfast dishes strewn over the counter. The living room isn't too messy, but Cody's and my guitars lie on the couch where we abandoned them after our last jam session.

"Where's Melanie?" Frank asks, glancing around.

"She must have left already. She's been doing a course this summer," Cody replies.

Frank frowns, the lines on his face deepening. He turns to look at me. "Are your parent's home yet, Ryan?"

"Um… yeah. They got home last night."

Then why are you still here? He doesn't say the words out loud, but he doesn't have to. They're written on his face for anyone to read.

"I'm going to go pack my stuff," I say.

As I walk up the stairs, cement has replaced the blood in my body, weighing it down.

I haphazardly chuck my things into my bag. In the three weeks I've been here, I've managed to scatter my possessions all over the room.

I've left my bedroom door open, so it doesn't surprise me when a minute later Cody is there hovering.

"Sorry about my dad," he says, not meeting my eyes.

"It's fine."

"He's not normally such a prick."

"Nah, I get it. He's jet lagged and just wants to relax. I'm sure the last thing he wants is a reminder of his ex-wife around."

"Yeah, I guess."

Cody scrapes his foot against the doorjamb, not saying anything further. It's like we've gone back in time, back to when Cody and I were strangers.

I squeeze past him to go to the bathroom and grab my toothbrush and shampoo.

Cody's still standing in my doorway when I get back.

I move past him, my body too aware of his proximity.

"I'll get out of you guys' hair now, make it easier on everyone," I say as I throw the toiletries into my bag.

"You don't want to wait until Mel gets back?"

"Nah, I'll just send her a message."

Cody blows out a breath. "It's pretty screwed up, this thing between our parents."

"Yeah, our families really put the fun in dysfunctional."
I'm trying for lighthearted, though I'm really, severely not
feeling it right now.

Cody gives me a strained smile.

"Do you think I should change the bedding?" I gesture
to the bed.

"Leave it. I'll do it later."

"Thanks."

Cody and I head downstairs together.

His parents are in the kitchen, making coffee.

I scrounge for my manners. "Thanks very much for
letting me stay here," I say. "It's a beautiful place."

"You're welcome," Heather replies.

"Drive safely," Frank says stiffly.

Cody follows me outside. I grab my wetsuit off the
deck and throw it on top of my stuff. It hasn't completely
dried, so it will get the rest of my gear damp, but I don't
really care about practicalities right now.

I throw my bag onto the front seat of the car and turn
to face Cody.

This is the moment I've been dreading. How do I say
goodbye to Cody?

"I guess this is it," I manage.

He hesitates. I know he's got words brewing, so I wait,
holding the top of the car door.

"I'm glad we got to hang out this summer," he says
finally.

My hand tightens, so I feel the metal edge dig into my
palm. "Thanks for teaching me the guitar."

"Thanks for teaching me to surf."

The words seem too formal between us. Like we're
speaking some foreign language neither of us is fluent in.

Cody swallows. "I'll see you around."

"Yeah." I hold out my hand for a fist bump. He bumps

it back, his knuckles rubbing against mine. Although he's got those slender long pianist hands compared to my larger ones, somehow his knuckles slot perfectly into the groove of my knuckles. Our hands linger for a few moments longer than a standard fist bump.

I pull my hand back and clear my throat. "See you around."

Chapter 12

The last few weeks of summer suck ass. I'm back in the city with the timer ticking down to the start of school like it's a bomb.

Mum reclaims her car, so I'm stuck begging rides off people or donating my scarce cash to Uber and Lift drivers.

I get a few rides to go surfing, but not all the way out to Orakahau.

I think of Cody still at the beach. Surfing in the morning. Practicing the piano in the afternoon. I consider messaging him but decide maybe it's a good thing to let some distance grow between us.

It's like we were in this bubble out on the beach where Cody and I could just be two guys hanging out, getting to know each other, starting to like each other. Then Frank and Heather turned up, and it was like a bucket of cold vomit was poured over everything.

And the vomit continues.

When I got home, Mum had asked me questions about my holiday, her lips pressed thin. It makes me wonder what memories she has of the beach. She must have been happy with Frank at some stage, before everything went to crap between them.

It appears wonderful memories are the last thing on her mind right now though. Because she's on the warpath about Kate's plans to move home.

Apparently Kate's initial plan was for her and Chris to stay with Frank and Heather until after the baby is born, giving them some time to save towards a deposit for a house. But Mum is pissed at the idea of Kate staying with Frank instead of with us.

Even I can see it's more logical for Kate and Chris to stay with Frank and Heather, because there's more room at their place. But I don't point out the logic, because Mum doesn't just have a shoot the messenger mentality right now. She's in a shoot, quarter, and bury the messenger in a shallow, unmarked grave kind of mood.

When I step into the kitchen one morning, she's on the phone to Kate. And you don't have to be a top-level detective to work out from the way Mum's stalking around the kitchen and slamming cupboards that the conversation is not going well.

"When you and Mel were little, I used to imagine what it would be like when you were pregnant, imagined what it would be like to share that experience with my daughters. I certainly never imagined that you would choose to live with your father and stepmother over me."

Oh, she's bringing out the big guns. Emotional blackmail with a side order of guilt.

She listens to whatever Kate says before continuing in the same tone. "So, you're more worried about offending your father and Heather than about my feelings?"

I wince as I grab some cereal and fling it in a bowl. I'm prioritizing speed over taste for my breakfast today, going for a quick exit so I don't get caught up in any of this.

Whatever Kate's reply is, it makes the scowl lines on Mum's forehead deepen.

I spoon cereal rapidly into my mouth and concentrate on maximizing my chewing speed.

The thing is, Kate's quite like Mum in personality. Stubbornness being a major trait they share in common.

"It won't be the same," Mum replies to whatever Kate said. She's loading the dishwasher now, but it's probably the most aggressive dishwasher loading in the history of man. "Visiting someone is not the same as living in the same house. With a newborn, you will not feel like traipsing out and about all the time. And you know I'm not going to feel comfortable coming to see you at your father's house. So basically, I won't get to see my grandchild." Her voice chokes up during the last sentence.

And… that's my cue for my exit. Waterworks are common between my mum and my sisters. However, tears are not simply a sign of emotion, they're used as a weapon. And both my mum and Kate are advanced players in this form of warfare.

Time to get out of the combat zone. I give my half-eaten bowl of cereal a glance of regret. But when it comes down to it, self-preservation trumps hunger.

When I get back to my room, my phone is lit up with a new message.

I open it. It's a picture of a rhinoceros with the caption *real unicorns have curves*.

saw this and thought of you

It's ridiculous how wide my smile is. The joke's not that funny.

A quick search on Google later, I send Cody a picture of a baboon's backside.

funny, I saw this and thought of you

He sends me a gif of someone hysterically laughing, followed by a quick text.

how's it all going?
boring here. you? been out surfing much?
a bit. doing lots of practice but getting out most days.
send me some pics of surf so I can get jealous
will do

And that's the start of a continuous message chain between me and Cody. Nothing major, just touching base with each other every day, sending little snippets of stuff to make each other laugh.

He sends me pictures of the surf every morning out his bedroom window. I send him back a picture of the view out my window of my neighbor's fence. Fairs fair and all that.

THE NIGHT BEFORE SCHOOL STARTS, Mum and Dad sit me down for a serious talk. Mum takes the lead like usual, with Dad the balding supporting act. It's the standard lecture I'd expect— it was my last year of high school, I needed to get serious about the future, live up to my potential, blah, blah.

"You need to decide what you want to do when you graduate. You can't go through your final year completely aimless," Mum says.

I clear my throat, deciding that now might be the time to voice something that has been bouncing around in my head.

"Actually, I've been thinking about maybe… being a paramedic."

"A paramedic," Mum repeats, her voice skeptical.

"Yeah… I mean, I thought it's something I might like."

I keep my voice casual. Cody's compliment about how I stay cool under pressure has stuck with me. I don't want to work in a hospital though but being a paramedic would be cool.

Mum's entire body has joined in the skepticism party. With enthusiasm. Her eyebrows have collapsed towards each other, and she's wrinkling her nose. "I don't know Ryan. I thought you hated science. And you'll have to take things seriously, you know. People's lives will be in your hands."

Well, ouch.

"I can take things seriously when I have to."

Mum still looks doubtful.

Gee, way to go about the parental encouragement. She should give out lessons or something.

"If you're serious about being a paramedic, you need to find out what training paramedics need and what subjects you need to do," Dad speaks up.

"I will." I fold my arms across my chest.

"Ryan, we know you can achieve whatever you set your mind to. You just need to be prepared to put in the effort," Mum says.

Weirdly, Cody flashes into my mind as Mum's words settle.

Though I'm not sure if she wants the concept extended to me building a friendship with her ex-husband's son.

Chapter 13

First week of school and I'm determined to turn over a new leaf. Hell, it's more than that. I'm really creating a whole new tree. Changing from being a spindly poplar to a mighty redwood in the world of academia.

Ms. Brenton, my guidance counselor, is as skeptical as my parents when I tell her I want to be a paramedic, but to her credit she tries harder to hide it than they did.

"You don't have the prerequisites for doing senior biology or chemistry, but I know you're smart enough to do it, Ryan, if you put in the work. Don't let me down."

Unfortunately, my biology teacher is none other than Mrs. Steinberg, who taught me for year nine science. I think I'm still the record-holder for the number of detentions she's given out in one year. Our reunion is not the stuff of Hollywood movies. Unless you're talking about horror movies.

Mrs. Steinberg stands at the door greeting students when we arrive. Her welcoming smile quickly morphs to a scowl when I walk in.

Grace and Mia, who I haven't seen since the party at the beach house, are sitting at a bench at the front. I head to them, pretending not to see Eddie waving at me from near the back. If I'm going to do well in this class, I need conscientious lab partners, not someone who will be eagerly expecting me to lead them astray.

Before she starts the class, Mrs. Steinberg makes a beeline to our bench.

"I'm not interested in people who are here to muck around," she tells me.

"I'm not a poplar anymore. I'm a redwood," I reply.

From the look on her face, she totally doesn't get my tree metaphor. And she calls herself a biology teacher!

"I mean it. If you distract other students, I'll have you removed from this class."

"Wow. She really told you," Grace whispers as Mrs. Steinberg moves away.

I shrug, pretending not to care, although I feel the tips of my ears heating up.

I'm determined to prove Mrs. Steinberg wrong. But it's hard. The first lesson is genetics, and anything I learned in previous years appears to have evaporated out of my head by the summer sun.

Plus, the word mutant is a joke waiting to happen. No one else steps up to claim it like they should. I have to pretend my lips are super glued together to stop myself saying anything.

I take notes furiously, although I don't really under-stand half of what I'm writing. Shit. I will seriously need help to pass this class.

"How are things going with Marco?" I ask Grace as we pack up. Surely the amount of flirting that was on display at the party has to have led to something more.

"Good." She bites her lip, a tinge of pink trekking up her cheeks. "He's invited me to a party this weekend, actually."

I raise my eyebrows. "An Appleton party? Get ready for the caviar and champagne."

"Hey, you should come too."

I concentrate on stuffing my notes into my folder, my heart rate speeding up at her words.

"Nah. I don't think it's my scene."

"Please. It will be less weird for me if you're there. And you're friends with Marco's friend Cody, right?"

"Yeah, we're friends." I keep my eyes on my folder instead of meeting her gaze.

"Then come hang out."

I keep my voice casual. "Okay, I might tag along."

"Great, thanks." Grace gives me a bright smile, which makes me feel shitty. Helping her out isn't exactly my primary motivation for agreeing to go to the party.

"You coming to the cafeteria?" Mia asks me as we stand up.

"In a sec. I want to talk to Mrs. Steinberg first."

Mia raises an eyebrow but doesn't say anything.

I walk to the front of the class where I hover around Mrs. Steinberg's desk until she finally decides to acknowledge me.

"What can I do for you, Ryan?"

I scratch the back of my neck. "Uh… because I didn't really focus last year, I need to do some catching up so I'm prepared for this year's course."

Mrs. Steinberg's eyebrows shoot up. She grabs a textbook and slaps it down on her desk with an ominous thud.

"I think you'll find this is an excellent place to start."

GRACE PICKS me up for the party in her funky pink beetle. She's dressed in jeans and a green halter top that's almost exactly the same shade as my *Ninja powers loading* T-shirt.

"Snap," I tease.

She looks down at her outfit and laughs.

We discuss school stuff as we drive through increasingly flashier neighborhoods on the way to the address Marco gave her. But by the way Grace bites at her lip and her more rapid than usual speech and quick laugh, I'm sure she's nervous about this party. I should be trying to calm her down. But I'm matching her nerve for nerve as I tap out a beat on my thigh with my fingers.

He might not even be there. I might be letting the birds, butterflies, and bats out for a free flying session in my stomach for no good reason. I haven't messaged him to find out if he's going, because I'm worried that would read too desperate and stalkerish.

Grace finds a parking spot two hundred feet down the street from the location where trusty Google Maps has guided us.

We're a little late. Which is a useful party technique for when you're turning up to a party where you don't know the host.

"Wow, this is fancy," I comment as we walk up the long driveway and the large house comes into view. The house looks like it is having an identity crisis and can't decide if it's a house or mansion. Music is pumping out of the windows and open doors, and already people are stumbling around the front lawn. It's classic proof that money and intelligence don't always go hand in hand—assuming the owners actually agreed to host a back-to-school party. Whatever the case, hopefully they have a comprehensive insurance policy.

Marco is waiting for us on the front porch.

"Hey." The smile on Marco's face when he sees Grace is bigger than a billboard.

"Hey." Grace returns his smile, although hers has the usual Grace enigmatic twist. "You remember Ryan?"

"Yeah, Cody's stepbrother, right? How's it going?"

I'm not Cody's stepbrother. We just share two half-sisters. But as I follow Marco into the house, I decide now is not the right time for an in-depth discussion about Cody's and my family tree.

This house is like something out of some futuristic novel, all stainless steel and glass surfaces. I crane my head, scanning the room. But it's not the décor I'm checking out.

No Cody inside.

A double set of French doors are wide open, leading to a wooden deck, which in turn leads to a glistening pool that's lit up with solar lights around the edges.

I'm drawn to the pool like a magnet. I would claim it's because of my innate connection with water, but it might have more to do with all the people who are stripping down to their underwear to go swimming.

Leaving Marco fetching Grace a drink like the gallant gentleman he is, I wander out onto the deck and take up a position against the railing where I can observe the proceedings.

I do a quick inventory of the people getting ready to swim.

Still no Cody.

My stomach falls, and my shoulders deflate. I try to ignore the heavy feeling overtaking my body. I've had a long period of Cody withdrawal. I was really looking forward to a fix tonight.

People are plunging into the pool now, and the noise of

splashing and laughter echoes around the backyard. But for once I don't feel like joining in. I feel removed from all the wide smiles and shrieks and shouts, like it's a language I don't speak.

"I didn't know there would be rhinoceros here tonight," a voice says behind me.

I whirl around. Cody's standing there, a grin lighting up his face.

That grin causes something bright and bubbly to froth up in my chest.

He's wearing a short-sleeved button-down blue Hawaiian shirt and jeans. He's had a haircut since the beach, and it suits him, though I have a pang for his free-roaming curls.

"Yeah, this is a real zoo. I figured they needed something horny," I manage.

Cody's grin grows wider, and he arches his eyebrow. "If this is a zoo, what animal am I?"

"You're a meerkat," I say.

"Meerkat? Why a meerkat?"

Because they're smart and cute. I don't say this aloud though.

"Small and rodent-like."

Cody huffs out a laugh. "You really know how to compliment a guy."

"I try."

We amuse ourselves as we head to the kitchen to grab beers, deciding what zoo animals other partygoers would be. The tall girl in a bright pink dress that ends just before her underwear is definitely a flamingo. The guy chugging beer from a yard glass? He's a warthog, while the surrounding crowd are hyenas with their anticipatory faces and raucous laughter.

With every one of Cody's deep chuckles, the bubbles in my chest grow larger and larger.

I check out the room for Grace, but she's tucked away on a corner couch with Marco, pressed up against him in a way that makes me think she might not appreciate an interruption. Even from someone as awesome as me.

"Your guy Marco, he's solid, right?" I ask Cody.

Cody follows my gaze. "Yeah, he's a great guy."

"Good."

We amble back out to the deck.

Normally at a party I'm attracted to wherever the most noise and laughter is happening because that's natural Ryan habitat. Usually I'd be in the pool in a flash, introducing the Appleton crowd to the fun of shoulder wrestling instead of the game of Marco Polo they've got going on.

Tonight I'm happy enough to stay put, watching the action rather than joining in. It may have something to do with Cody beside me.

The deck becomes crowded as more people file out to watch what's going on in the pool.

Someone crashes into me, which sends me like a domino into Cody. He's trapped between the railing and me. He reaches out a hand to steady me, but my body presses up against his. Heat charges through me like it's leading the cavalry on an important quest. It's flanked by the armies of arousal and desire.

Shit. I quickly take a step back, putting space between us. It's like how you used to dance with someone at junior high, with two feet of a no-go zone between you.

I take a gulp of my beer, trying to calm my racing heart as a memory I've been trying to suppress rises to the surface.

That moment with the hose, I'd been so tempted to kiss him.

As I watch Cody out of the corner of my eye, I can't help replaying that moment. What would he have done if I'd leaned in and pressed my lips onto his? I have no idea if he's into guys at all. The way he stared back at me made me think he wasn't completely against the idea. But I've always had an epic imagination, so maybe my mind filtered stuff so I only saw what I wanted to see.

I drain my beer, setting the empty cup at my feet, but make no move to go inside and get another.

Cody's watching his classmates mess around in the pool with a ghost of a smile.

Maybe I should just casually bring up the topic in conversation? Like, point to the swimmers and politely ask Cody which type of bodies turns him on. I mean, he kissed Angie Baker, so it doesn't take many deductive powers to guess girls are on his list. But maybe guys are too?

Although, would it be too obvious why I'm asking?

Cody angles his body toward me. "So, not too long until Kate moves home now, right?"

It's like he's poured a whole dose of reality over me. Reminding me why this crush on him is a bad idea. Stuff is so messed up between our parents, and because of Mel and Kate, we will always be connected in some way. I can't exactly cut him out of my life if things become awkward. And I remember Harvey's reaction from the party. I can probably live without the judgement that would come if I hook up with my sisters' other brother.

"Yeah, not long now," I say. "Hopefully they figure out where they're living before then."

A crease appears on Cody's forehead. "I thought she was coming to stay with us until after the baby was born?"

Oh shit.

I stick my hands in my pockets. "Yeah, I don't think my mum's very happy about that idea."

Cody's eyebrows fly upwards. "Really?"

"Just more of the usual shit."

He shakes his head. "I feel so sorry for Kate and Mel sometimes. It must suck, always being caught in the middle of our parents."

"Yeah." He's right. It sucks for our sisters to spend their lives in a minefield created by their parents, knowing a single misstep will cause a bomb to go off. And it sucks for us too.

"Why do you think your mum and my dad hate each other so much?" Cody asks. "It's been like twenty years, right? You'd think they would have gotten over it by now."

"I know. I mean, my mum is actually a decent person most of the time. But she totally loses it with anything related to your dad."

"It's like that with my dad too." Cody frowns.

"Maybe some relationships are so toxic that when they end, it's like nuclear waste. It takes hundreds of years to decay," I suggest.

Cody grins. "A science metaphor. Impressive." The smile lighting up his face turns on a switch inside my chest.

I snort. "I'm nerding it up at the moment. I'm doing a full math and science course this year."

"Seriously?"

"Yep. I'm totally channeling Einstein."

Cody fixes me with his intense gaze. "What do you want that to lead to?"

I look down at the ground, scraping the toe of my Converse along the bottom of the railing. "I thought I might look at becoming a paramedic."

"That's cool."

"My mum is skeptical about the idea. I don't think she

thinks I'm serious enough. She's probably right. I'll be goofing around doing something stupid and will mess up."

"Are you kidding, Ryan? You were amazing when you saved that kid, so focused. You'll be an incredible paramedic." He says the words with such certainty, like they are the absolute truth.

I try to control the blood flooding my face. Forget about our parent's relationship being radioactive, it feels like my face has just been contaminated, judging by the amount of heat it's giving out.

"Yeah, the problem is the biology teacher was my year nine science teacher, and she hates me," I say.

"Why does she hate you?"

"Among other things, I may or may not have tried to set some personal gas alight with the Bunsen burner."

Cody grins. "Thanks for that mental image."

"No problem. I aim to please."

I finally raise my eyes to his, and we grin at each other.

"I'll tutor you, if you want?" His voice is casual, but there's a tremor of something underneath.

My heart skips. Cody tutoring me means a regular, scheduled time for us to hang out.

"Are you any good at biology?" I ask.

Cody just quirks an eyebrow.

"Oh right, you're a genius at biology, like you are at everything else. Why did I even bother asking?"

Cody swallows. "So, do you want a tutor? You can pay me in more surfing lessons."

"Yeah sure, sounds like a deal." I shrug my shoulders like it doesn't really matter. Like my heart hasn't just started skittering at the prospect of Cody tutoring me, more surfing lessons. More Cody.

"Awesome."

He grins at me, and I know I'm matching it, lip curve for lip curve.

I try to douse down the happiness that continues to bubble inside me with every Cody smile.

And now I've got a whole lot of tutoring to look forward to.

Chapter 14

Sunday afternoon I'm in the back seat of my parent's car on my way to exciting times unpacking boxes.

Kate and Chris ended up deciding to get their own apartment straight away rather than endure the gauntlet of bruised parents' egos by choosing one over the other. Which sucks for them, as I know they wanted to save up some money before the baby comes.

In the car I put up a mild level of complaint that I've got other things I'd prefer to be doing, but Mum makes it clear that if I want to keep borrowing her car, my presence is a mandatory thing.

Apparently, Frank and Heather are helping them unpack in the morning and we're rostered on the afternoon shift. I say a quick prayer to the moving gods that Frank and Heather have advanced unpacking skills, so the bulk of the work will be done by the time we get there.

There's only one problem— when we turn up Frank's car is in the driveway.

My shoulders lift. Chances are Cody's been roped into helping Kate unpack too.

The other weekend Cody and I spent the entire party hanging out together. And we've been continuing to message each other every day since. Just sending each other funny shit we know will make the other laugh. Every time I see a message from him on my phone, another bubble of happiness froths up inside my chest.

But that's okay. You're allowed to be happy when your friend contacts you.

Happiness isn't exactly the mood of the hour right now though.

Mum exhales a large breath when we pull into the space next to Frank, her jaw jutting out in a determined way.

"It'll be okay," Dad says.

I think he's mainly trying to reassure himself.

Kate greets us at the door with a grim but resigned look, the kind an undertaker might perfect. "Dad and Heather are still here."

"I thought they were helping you out in the morning and we were doing the afternoon?" Mum says.

"I can't exactly kick them out, can I?"

Mum sniffs as though that's exactly what she'd do if it was her.

We follow Kate down the narrow hallway to the open-plan living space. Frank and Heather are in the tiny kitchen, surrounded by half-unpacked boxes of kitchen utensils.

I spot Cody sitting on the floor next to a bookshelf, a half-empty box of books next to him.

"Good afternoon," Mum says stiffly, plastering a smile on her face.

"Hello," Heather replies, while Frank grunts out a sound that could be interpreted as a greeting.

The only smiles here that would pass a lie detector

test are the ones Cody and I are giving each other. He tilts an eyebrow up, and I match it, so we have our own non-verbal greeting that escapes the scrutiny of the parents.

I manage to tear my gaze away from Cody and check out the place. It's a small apartment. When you add in two sets of parents who can't stand each other, it becomes positively claustrophobic.

Kate's standing by the dining table with this look on her face like she wouldn't mind if the walls collapsed in on her.

Chris comes out from the hallway and greets Mum, Dad, and me with false cheer, running his hands through his dark hair.

"What can we do to help?" Mum's voice is tight.

"I'm just about to put together our bed. I'd appreciate some help," Chris says.

Getting Mum and Dad far away from Frank and Heather is a stroke of genius. I've questioned the guy's intelligence after the accidental pregnancy thing, but it appears he has some smarts.

I sidle over to where Cody is kneeling by the bookshelf. "Need a hand?"

"Sure. Although I didn't realize unpacking was part of your advanced skill set," Cody says with a smile.

"I've been dragged here kicking and screaming," I reply as I sit down on the floor next to him. "Let me guess, you volunteered enthusiastically like the dutiful brother you are?"

"Of course. I also brought a housewarming gift that Kate loves." He nods at a weird potted plant sitting on the table a few feet away.

"What is it?"

"It's a money tree. It's supposed to bring good luck."

I shake my head. "You are seriously the definition of a suck-ass."

He grins at me, scrunching up his nose, and my stomach does a matching scrunch before I can stop it.

Friends. I remind my body. *Cody and I are just friends.*

I work side by side with my friend, unloading boxes of books onto the bookshelf. It's natural for you to notice the way your friend's long slim hands grasp one of Chris's old biomechanics textbooks, right? And the fact that my skin heats up in the places where my arm brushes up against his, is simply due to laws of friction. And noticing his clean, fresh scent that's a mixture of soap and something uniquely Cody just means my nostrils are working correctly.

Unfortunately stacking books on a shelf doesn't take that long, and when we've finished, I hate the idea of moving away from Cody. I really don't want to sort pots and pans in the kitchen or something like that.

"Maybe we should put the books into categories?" I ask in an undertone.

"Great idea," Cody says.

Mum comes back out into the living room when Cody and I are halfway through our sorting.

"We've finished constructing the bed. What else needs to go into the bedroom?" she asks Kate.

"The boxes for the bedroom are stacked over here." Kate nods at a pile by the wall.

Mum walks over to inspect the boxes.

"I hope Kate and Chris don't have any stuff that they don't want the parental units seeing," I say in an undertone to Cody.

Cody quirks an eyebrow. "What kind of stuff?"

I shrug. "I don't know. I can just imagine my Mum discovering a prostate massager or something."

I'm expecting Cody to blush as he usually does when I say things like that, but he simply snickers. "Imagine her holding it up asking where she should put it."

Oh God. I crack up laughing at that. Cody joins in with his loud chuckle. Our laughter shatters the silence.

When I glance up, Frank, Heather, and Mum are all glaring in our direction. Mum grabs a box and retreats into the bedroom.

Kate's the only one amused. "Care to share the joke?"

"Nah, it's okay." Cody blushes while I continue to laugh.

Cody and I shuffle the books around for a while. After arranging them by category, we then decide we should have arranged them alphabetically instead, so we start again.

When Mum reemerges from the bedroom to grab another box, she stops and surveys the living space with a critical eye.

"I really think you should think about rearranging things in here. Put the bigger couch against that wall, so it faces the television."

"But that will make it hard to pull the curtains. And we'd have to move the bookshelf," Kate argues.

"But the bookshelf is blocking part of the window, and there's not much natural light in here to begin with."

"Let Kate and Chris decide where to put the furniture," Frank interjects.

Mum freezes. She slowly swivels her head toward Frank like she's one of those predator birds that has just spotted a likely victim. "Sorry, I didn't realize this conversation involved you."

Shit. If Mum uses that tone on me, the red siren alert starts in my head. *Abort. Abort. Abort.*

Unfortunately, Frank doesn't appear to have any

survival instincts. "They're the ones who have to live here, Julia, not you. Let them do it their way."

Mum huffs up. "I'm just offering the benefit of my experience."

Cody shoots me an exasperated look. I totally agree with his sentiment. Furniture? They're seriously turning furniture into a battleground?

Dad comes out of the bedroom to grab a box and stops short when he gauges the temperature of the room.

"Maybe you should let them make their own decisions," Frank says.

Mum snorts. "That's rich, coming from you."

Frank narrows his eyes. "What do you mean by that?"

"I mean, when have you ever let either Mel or Kate make a decision without trying to influence them?"

"I help guide them with the big decisions. It's what good parents do. I don't micromanage their lives."

Mum reacts like she's been stung. "Don't talk to me about being a good parent." Her voice is deathly low.

Kate suddenly puts both of her hands on her stomach, pressing in.

Dad is the only parental unit who notices. "Are you okay?" He nods at her stomach, and suddenly all attention is directed toward Kate.

"Yeah, the baby is just kicking," she says softly.

A prickly, awful silence fills the room.

Mum tries to plaster a smile overtop of her anger. "I remember the first time I felt you kick."

"Really, when was that?" Kate's voice is eager.

"I was just past twenty weeks pregnant. I was at the supermarket. I abandoned my grocery cart and rushed home…" she trails off. She flicks a glance at Frank, who stares back with a wooden expression.

"Right." Heather cuts through the tense silence. "I think we probably should get going."

"Yes, we need to go home," Frank says stiffly.

Cody has been sitting next to me, immobile. He suddenly comes to life, standing up, stretching.

Our eyes catch.

"Can I trust you to finish the job properly?" he asks quietly.

"I think I've got the alphabet mastered," I reply.

A grin tugs at the corners of his mouth.

"Thanks for all your help," Kate says to Frank and Heather as she walks them toward the front door.

Cody's the last to leave the room. He turns back to look at me. "See you Wednesday."

"Yeah, see you then."

Mum waits until the front door has banged shut before turning to me.

"Wednesday? Why are you seeing Cody on Wednesday?"

"He's tutoring me in biology," I reply as I pick up another book.

Mum's arms drop to her sides. "Oh… okay. Are you paying him?"

"What? Nah, it's okay, Mum. Don't worry about it. We're friends now."

Her forehead furrows. "I don't want to have Frank rant at me that my son is distracting his son from his studies or music."

"Don't worry about it," I repeat.

Chapter 15

When Wednesday arrives, somehow my stomach has tied itself into a complicated knot.

It's stupid to be nervous about Cody coming over. We've spent so much time together recently. But when the knock on the front door comes, I almost stumble on my way to answer it.

"Hey." Cody's biting at his bottom lip.

"Come in."

"Thanks."

As he follows me through the living room, I can't help seeing it through his eyes. I think Cody's been to my house once when we were kids for a birthday party for Mel, but not for ages.

Our place is definitely not as flashy as his house. Mum's been moaning about replacing the carpet but has decided since I'm the one to blame for most of the stains, they'll wait until I leave home to do it.

Cody steps around a stain in the middle of the lounge, which was the result of me attempting the baking powder, red food coloring, and vinegar homemade volcano experiment one day when I was ten. I don't blame him for his avoidance. It looks like there should be a body chalk outline somewhere in close proximity.

He stops when he passes the bookshelf and picks up a photo of Kate, Mel, and me, taken when I was eight.

"I'd forgotten about Kate's perm," he says.

"Lucky you. I try to block out the memory, but it returns to me in the dead of night sometimes."

Cody grins as he picks up another photo, this time of the three of us in front of the Christmas tree, dressed in the worst Christmas themed sweaters known to man. My jersey has a lopsided Rudolph on it with a demonic grin. Thank God Mum moved on quickly from her knitting phase.

It's weird to think Cody probably has his own versions of these photos, only where he is subbed in instead of me. Mel and Kate's interchangeable brothers.

"Great sweaters."

"Yep, it's fair to say that was the highlight of my fashion career."

"I'd forgotten how long your hair used to be." He's moved on to look at a school photo of me from my first year at high school.

"Yeah, it was halfway down my back at one point."

"Why did you cut it?"

I almost go with my standard "I got sick of it," but for some reason I decide to tell Cody the truth.

"Someone at school called me a Barbie doll."

He almost drops the frame. "Really?"

"Yeah, year nine. I wasn't as comfortable in my masculinity then as I am now." I say the words as a joke, but I'm fairly sure Cody hears the truth in them by the look he gives me. "So I cut it off to shoulder length."

"Then you shaved it all off, what, last June?"

"Yeah, that was to raise money for kid's cancer. I got sponsored nearly a grand."

"Wow. Do you miss having long hair?" He puts the frame back gently on the shelf.

I shrug. "Sometimes. I did rock the man-bun look."

He grins.

"Right. My biology textbook isn't going to teach itself." I nod toward the dining room. I've set up my biology stuff at the table there. The desk in my room is small, and also it somehow felt safer in my campaign to put Cody squarely in the friend's box, to not have him in my room.

Cody follows me and takes a seat, reaching for the textbook. "What are you doing at the moment?"

"Genetics. And it's really kicking my ass."

"Cool, let's start there then."

And so we dig deep into the wonderful world of alleles and chromosomes.

"Who do you think you're more like, your mum or your dad?" I ask him as I stretch back after I've done so many dihybrid crosses it feels like my eyes are crossing too.

"Well, I look more like my mum," he begins.

Yeah, I'm glad Cody looks like his mum. There's almost no resemblance between him and Mel and Kate, which makes the fact I find him attractive less weird.

"But obviously I got the musical stuff from my dad," he continues.

"Do you think your dad is living out his unfulfilled musical ambitions through you?" I ask.

Cody's eyebrow shoots up. "Woah, where did that question come from?"

I run my fingertips along the scratch in the dining room table, another casualty of my unsupervised after-school antics as a child.

"I don't know. He just seems to place a lot of pressure on you."

"Yeah, I know he does. Sometimes it's a bit much." Cody leans back in his chair. "But I love music. And if I'm going to succeed in playing professionally, I need to be disciplined and focused."

"You are already really disciplined and focused," I say. "Seriously, I admire the shit out of how you can practice for so many hours."

Cody plays with his pen, twirling it in his long fingers. "I can get too intense sometimes. Like, Mum was worried when I was a kid that I was spending too much time practicing, which is why she enrolled me in tennis lessons."

"And then you turned out to be incredible at that too."

"I wish I could be more like you."

I widen my eyes. "What, a complete screw-up?"

Cody shrugs. "You're not a screw-up. But I mean I wish I could go with the flow more like you do. Not get so caught up in making sure everything I do is perfect. Not be so concerned about what people think about me."

Wow. There's a lot to unpack there. That Cody wants to be more like me is a more bizarre concept than salted pork ice cream.

"Do you remember Mel's birthday party at the lake that time and how you jumped in and started wrestling with that fake crocodile," he asks.

"Yeah, I remember. I totally won that fight."

"Against a plastic crocodile?"

"Hey, you've got to take all the wins you can get."

He smiles a half-grin before he continues. "I was so jealous of you, because it was so hot and you were having so much fun, and all I wanted to do was dive in too, but I knew my parents would get angry if I did."

I snort. "Shit, I got told off so badly after that. My

mum always had an extra freak out if I misbehaved in front of your parents."

Cody huffs out a laugh. "I swear my parents would always try to get me to show off at any events where you guys were at."

"I did always think you were a bit of a show-off," I say.

He grins properly at me, that slow-moving grin that overtakes his face.

A bolt of attraction races through me. I have to use all of my WWF moves to wrestle it back under control.

Cody takes a deep breath, looking away. "Talking about showing off, my music teacher just confirmed I'm playing at this concert showcase at the Royal Theatre. Someone has pulled out, and they have invited me to take their place."

"Seriously? The Royal Theatre?" Even I know that's a big deal.

"Yeah, I'll only play three songs, but still, it's an incredible honor. Some of the other musicians playing are amazing."

I let out a low whistle. "Go, you. That's awesome. Are you going to play one of your own compositions?"

"Nah, I'll just stick to the tried and true."

"Did you ever finish that song you were writing at the beach?"

"I'm still fiddling around with it, but I recorded a version." Cody hesitates. "Do you want to listen to it?"

"Of course, I want to."

Cody pulls out his phone, his brow creased in concentration. He finds his app and presses play on an audio file.

The music seems to float out from his phone. I flick a glance at him, and a faint blush treks its way up his cheeks. The song starts off slowly with this kind of haunting sadness but builds to an incredible crescendo.

"Holy shit, that's amazing," I say when it's finished.

The flush on Cody's cheeks spreads down his neck, and he bites his lip.

"Seriously, Cody, I've got goose bumps." I show him my arms.

"You like it?"

"I love it. It's sad but happy too. A happy kind of sad. Does that make any sense?"

He just stares at me. One of those potent Cody stares that should come with a warning.

My cheeks heat under his scrutiny. "Sorry, my music interpretation skills aren't that advanced. You're about to tell me it's actually about when zombies take over the earth, aren't you?"

"No." He clears his throat. "It's about... uh... longing for something. And you just gave the perfect definition. It's a kind of happy sadness."

"It's very cool."

"I'm still playing around with it." Cody drops his eyes. "Anyway, we better get back to biology."

Oh yeah, biology, that's right. That's what we're supposed to be doing here.

I take a deep breath and try to clear from my mind all those pesky thoughts that want to dwell on other things besides biology. Like how Cody's quiet confidence is attractive, but when he lets me see the real him, somehow, it's even more attractive. Damn, I really should write Valentine's Day cards.

We're still studying when Mum comes home. She bustles through the dining room, carrying a bag of groceries, coming to an abrupt stop when she sees us.

"Oh, hi, Cody." She fixes a smile on her face that is a few notches below genuine.

"Hi, Julia," Cody replies.

"Cody's just been helping me with genetics," I say, leaning back and stretching.

"I should get going," Cody says as Mum retreats.

"Yeah, okay."

If he was anyone else, I'd ask him to stay for dinner. But having Cody around the dinner table with my parents would be awkward, multiplied by a factor of cringeworthy.

I follow him as he walks to the front door.

"Same time next week?" he says as he opens the door.

"Yup. You, me, and my biology textbook. It's a hot threesome."

Cody scratches the side of his face. "Um… yeah." His eyes meet mine, trapping me. There's something about Cody that makes him impossible to look away from.

"See you then," I say in an attempt to break the spell.

"See you." Despite saying the words, he doesn't leave. Instead, he stays in the weird moment between us.

I'm aware Mum's hovering in the hallway. She coughs, and Cody finally looks away from me, shuffling his feet.

He turns away and jogs down the front steps, raising a hand in farewell without looking back.

I walk away from the door with this unsatisfied feeling. I get it a lot with Cody. Especially when we're saying good-bye.

Mum raises her eyebrows when I join her in the kitchen. "Are you sure you shouldn't be paying him?"

"Nah, Mum, it's fine."

"So, he's just tutoring you out of the goodness of his heart?"

"Yeah, he's a good person."

Good.

That word doesn't come even close to describing Cody. But now isn't the time to contemplate the other words I should use in its place.

Chapter 16

The next few weeks fly by in a blur of school, tutoring sessions, and Cody.

Cody's busy getting ready for his concert, working so hard, practicing nearly every spare moment he gets. He's stressed about screwing up. On my urging he sends me audio files of some pieces he's preparing, and I send him back crazy interpretations of the music to amuse him. Like, I decide Mozart's piano sonatas were composed to be a treatment for constipation back in the day.

Wednesdays quickly become my favorite day. We spend most of the time studying—in fact; I got a B+ on my first quiz. I don't know who was more amazed, Mrs. Steinberg or me. But we also veer off on these random chats.

I tell Cody stuff I've never told anyone, not even Harvey and Oz. Things like how I'm sure Mum only had me so Dad could have his own biological child and how sometimes she gives out the vibe that we both owe her, and that's part of the reason I think Dad caves to her in arguments even when I know he agrees with me. And Cody talks to me too. About the pressure he feels to live up to his parents' and teachers' expectations. About how Appleton sometimes feels like this enclave of white privilege that churns out clones and he never feels like he fits, so he's always putting on an act.

Sunday is his big concert. I check the time all afternoon, imagining Cody getting ready to perform. I wonder if he has some kind of pre-performance ritual that he does, like top sports people before a big game.

I don't want to distract him, but I want him to know I'm thinking about him.

Eventually around eightish, I decide to message him.

good luck break a leg and all that

Even if he doesn't see it before he performs, he'll know I was thinking about him. For some reason, that's important to me.

Within a minute, my phone beeps with his response.

not worried about my limbs currently because think I just puked up my stomach lining

I stare at his words.

Shit. What can I do to help?

I know nothing about how to calm nerves down before a performance. The last time I was on stage was the year five play. And I was a tree, which meant the spotlight wasn't exactly focused on me.

Before I can talk myself out of it, I call him.

"Hey," he answers.

"Did you really just pray to the porcelain gods?" I ask.

"Yep, there was some serious worshipping going on." Cody's trying to make his voice light, but I can hear the vein of tension running through it.

"Is that normal for you before a performance?"

"Normally I feel a bit queasy, but I've never thrown up before. Now I'm shit scared I'll throw up on stage. Give the audience a different kind of performance than the one they're expecting."

"Oh shit. What can I do? Do you want me to come there?"

As soon as the words are out of my mouth, I feel like an idiot. How is me being there going to help him in any way?

Cody clears his throat. "Yeah, that would be great."

I look at my watch. "I'm not going to get there before you start though."

"It doesn't matter. I'd like you here. I'd like to look out at the audience and know you're there," he says softly.

"You want the one guy who's not going to care if you play chopsticks, right?"

There are a few beats of silence. "Right. I want that guy," Cody says finally.

"Okay, I'm on my way." I toe my feet into my Converse sneakers. I'm dressed in a hoodie and jeans, so I'll stand out at the theater like a nun in a nightclub, but I don't want to take the time to change. The most important thing is getting there fast.

"Thanks." I can still hear the tension in his voice.

I bolt down the hallway, putting my phone against my shoulder, when I spot Mum in the kitchen. "Can I take your car? It's kind of urgent."

"Sure." Mum gives me a puzzled look. "Everything okay?"

I grab the keys off the hook. "Yeah, it will be."

"You there?" I say into the phone as I jog out to the car.

"Yeah, I'm here."

"I'm getting in the car now. I'll be there soon. In the meantime, close your eyes, okay?"

"Close my eyes?"

"Trust me."

"I trust you. Okay, my eyes are closed. Now what am I doing?"

"Okay, I want you to imagine you're out on your board. It's early morning, the sun is just rising. There is no one there but you and the waves. You're just floating there, feeling the rise and fall of the waves beneath you. Just concentrate on breathing in and out, floating on the sea."

I can hear his breathing slow down, softening as my phone switches over to the car's Bluetooth. For a minute there's no other sound between us but Cody's breathing.

"Thank you," he whispers.

"No problem. Just keep doing it. If you start panicking again, just think of that."

"I will," he says. "Oh shit, I've got to go. I think they're looking for me."

"Where are you?"

"Hiding in a stall in a bathroom."

I huff out a laugh. "You go show everyone how incredible you are."

"I'll try," he says.

I'm expecting him to hang up, but he stays on the line.

"Ryan?" he says.

"Yeah?"

He doesn't speak for a few seconds.

"Thanks," he says eventually.

"No worries. I'll see you soon."

BY THE TIME I find a parking spot and get into the theater, Cody's already a few minutes into his performance.

I have to fork out over fifty bucks to get a ticket. And that's the student price. I try to argue with the person in the ticketing booth that I should get a discount considering the concert has already started and I only plan to listen to one performance, but she's one of those weird breed of humans who's immune to my charm.

I creep into the back of the theater. I don't even attempt to find my seat. I just prop myself up near an ornate wall light and watch him. There's a baby grand piano in the middle of the stage and a golden spotlight is on Cody wearing a tuxedo, his curls tamed with hair product. As he finishes the song and begins his next one, I inch along the side of the auditorium slowly, trying to get close enough to see his expression, to see that look of complete concentration on his face that Cody has trademarked.

Even I know that he's absolutely nailing it.

His fingers flutter over the keyboard in a blur of wizardry.

The place inside me where jealousy of Cody's achievements used to hang out is vacant now. Maybe it's because I now know what those achievements cost, how hard he works for it. Instead, I only feel pride.

He finishes up with Mozart's Fantasia in D minor.

He's talked to me so much about how hard it is to get the fingering in the piece correct, how much he's had to practice, but from how he plays it, you'd think he was born with the ability to move his hands and fingers in that order. It comes across so natural and effortless.

The audience has been silent during his performance, but as soon as he plays the last note, people rise to their feet as one, clapping. A standing ovation. He's getting a freaking standing ovation. And he deserves no less.

Cody gives a bow. A small grin plays across his lips, whereas I'm sure my grin is threatening to overtake my face. I almost wolf-whistle my approval then remember my surroundings and settle for clapping so hard I threaten to dislocate my wrists. If wrists can be dislocated.

Another thing I probably have to learn before I become a paramedic.

Cody walks offstage, and the concert ends. Around me, people are shuffling out of the rows, the buzz of conversation rising.

I hesitate. What do I do now?

I so want to track down Cody. I want to see his happiness. I want to tell him in person how amazing he was.

But his parents will be with him, and I know me being there will add a layer of awkwardness that Cody doesn't deserve. He deserves just to bask in everyone's admiration for his performance, not worry about whether his parents are being polite to me.

I take a quick selfie with the empty stage in the background and send it to him.

just watched best classical music performance ever

My phone beeps just as I'm climbing into the car.

where you now?

heading home

Despite my message, I don't put my keys into the ignition. Instead, I sit there and wait for his reply.

My phone rings.

When I answer, Cody's voice sounds breathless. There's lots of noise and chatter in the background.

"We're heading out for dessert somewhere to celebrate. You want to come?"

"Have you run that idea past your parents?" I ask.

"It's my big night. They won't argue. And Mel and Kate will be there, plus a few friends."

I hesitate. Because I really want to see Cody. But my reasons for not wanting to gate-crash his celebration still stand.

"Nah, I don't want to get in the way."

"Okay." There's disappointment in his tone.

"Congrats on the performance though." Have I ever said a sentence as unfulfilling as that one? That is such a pale imitation of what I really want to say.

"Thanks." He pauses, and there's a chatter of conversation in the background. I can make out Kate's voice moaning about the fact she's not allowed to have any of the champagne.

"Talk later?" he says.

"Yeah, later."

Chapter 17

The entire drive home, all I can think about is Cody. Cody, who's now at some fancy restaurant celebrating with his family and friends. I want to be there with him desperately. Instead, I'm skulking home like I'm the deranged uncle you stash in the attic when polite company arrives.

I stalk into the house and stuff the keys back on the hook with more force than necessary.

"Where did you have to go in such a hurry?" Mum asks as she pads into the kitchen. She's wearing tiger print pajamas, her reading glasses perched on her head.

I'm not in the mood to lie. I'm not in the mood to dance around the sharp eggshells that remain from Mum and Frank's marriage, trying not to shred my flesh. I want to stomp and stamp all over those frigging delicate eggshells.

"I went to Cody's concert."

"Cody's concert?" Mum repeats the words like they're some foreign language.

"Yeah, he was playing a concert at the Royal Theatre. He wanted me there."

Her forehead wrinkles. "Why did he want you there?"

"I've told you before. We're friends."

The word *friends* feels heavy tonight. It sinks to the floor the moment it falls off my tongue.

"Oh, okay." Her tone contradicts her words, a reminder that me hanging out with her ex-husband's son is actually not on her okay list.

I move past her, thumping up the stairs.

In my room I sit hunched over on my bed, my head in my hands. I want to message Cody so badly. Just to have him reply, have one of those Cody messages, a fraction of Cody's thoughts zooming back at me.

I grab my phone out of my pocket. I turn it over, staring at it like it contains the answer.

In the end I put my phone on my bedside table. I'm not going to interrupt his celebration. I want Cody to bask in the admiration for all his hard work and talent, not remember all the messed up factors that surround our friendship.

I strip off my pants and shirt and climb under the duvet. Staring at the ceiling, thoughts of Cody continue to circulate in my brain. How good he looked in a tuxedo. The way he smiled when he got the standing ovation. They're nice thoughts to drift off to sleep to.

I stir when my phone buzzes.

Because waking up isn't really my thing, I'm still fumbling for my phone when it lights up again with my second reminder. One hand closes around my phone. I rub my eyes with my other hand, clearing them enough to focus on the screen.

The message is from Cody.

you awake

Adrenaline surges through me, and I almost drop my phone in my haste to answer.

am now

shit sorry

no worries I'm pretty enough don't need beauty sleep. what's up?

parked outside. come for drive?

My heart starts a frantic whirling, like it's one of those windup toys you just need to pull the string to start.

be out in 3

I glance at my clock. It's after midnight.

Chucking on jeans and a sweater, I flick a glance in the mirror as I leave my bedroom. Shit, my hair looks like someone with a rampaging lawnmower has spent the evening getting creative with it.

I do a quick finger comb as I head down the stairs, keeping my steps light and avoiding the squeaky step so I don't wake Mum and Dad. I really don't need a parental inquisition right now.

Cody's car is waiting for me on the street.

"Didn't realize you're such a night owl," I say as I open the car door. I'm trying to hide my happiness that's rising inside me, but I'm sure my grin needs its own zip code as I jump in and clip my seatbelt.

"I'm not usually. But I find it hard to relax after a concert."

Cody's dressed formally, wearing a buttoned-up blue shirt with black pants. It must be what he changed into after the tux, his post-concert outfit. His curls are springing loose from their hair gel prison.

"It's nice of you to share your insomnia with me. Sharing is caring and all that," I say.

He slides me a smile as he starts the car. "You're right, sharing is caring."

Silence settles between us. On the radio, Adam Levine croons about the toll that love is taking on him.

I stare at Cody's profile as we drive.

He's got that slight crease between his forehead like he often does when he's concentrating. His fingers tap out the rhythm of the song on the steering wheel. When he pauses at the lights, he glances at me and seems surprised to find me watching him.

His lips curve into a hesitant smile.

Mine move automatically to match his.

Cody drives us to the lookout. On Friday and Saturday nights so many cars park here it turns into a pop-up party. At this time on a Sunday night though, it's deserted.

"You want to get out?" he suggests.

"Sure."

We jump onto the hood of his car. The city is laid out like a sparkly picnic blanket in front of us. It's chilly, but the warmth of the engine soaks through my jeans. The streetlight nearby provides a dull orange glow.

"How was the restaurant?" I ask.

"It was good." He glances at me. "I wish you'd come."

"Yeah," I manage. I play with the edge of his wind-shield wipers, running my fingers carefully along the smooth blades.

Cody huffs out a deep breath. "I'm so glad you called me. I don't think anyone else could have talked me back from the ledge like that."

I swallow, keeping my eyes on the wipers. "Just doing my usual thing. You know, being a superhero, channeling Peter Parker."

"Don't joke about it. Seriously, Ryan, I think that was one of the nicest things anyone has ever done for me."

I meet his gaze. "Anytime."

The silence hangs between us.

Cody continues to stare at me, those blue eyes burning with the intensity of a thousand suns.

I can't wrench my eyes away from him. I'm fairly sure

civilizations rise and fall in the time that Cody and I stay wrapped in each other's gaze.

He leans toward me. My breath hitches. Surely, he can't be about to—

He kisses me.

I'm so stunned at the feeling of his lips against mine that I forget to kiss him back.

Cody draws back after a few seconds. "Sorry…" he starts to stammer.

I finally manage to react. "No."

He cuts off his words abruptly. "No what?" he whispers.

"No. Don't apologize."

This time, I'm the one who closes the distance between us. I'm the one who reaches up to cup the side of his face, who presses my lips to his. It starts out soft but quickly turns heated.

Our mouths open, and as soon as my tongue touches his, an electric current flashes through my body. Kissing Cody makes so much sense. It makes sense in the way that strawberries and ice cream make sense. The way lightning and thunder are always paired.

He moans, and the sound sends me into another level of turned on. My hand slides into his hair, tugging him to me, and he comes willingly. My senses are consumed with him. The smell of his aftershave, the lingering taste of something sweet, the feel of his soft curls under my fingers.

All the feelings I've tried so hard to bury come rushing to the surface, like I've just hit an oil well. A gushing, bubbling, boiling stream of feelings for the guy I'm now kissing.

When we finally pull apart, we're both panting. Cody's pupils are dilated, black swallowing the blue, as he stares at me.

Damn.

Cody continues to breathe heavily, like he's just run a marathon. But the smile creeping onto his face makes me realize that if this was a race, then we're both sharing the winner's podium right now.

"Holy shit," he says.

I couldn't have put it any better myself.

"Um… yeah." I rake my hand through my hair, not wanting to look him straight in the eyes. Because I get the feeling that my kiss has just revealed a lot of stuff I wasn't planning on admitting. Even to myself. "That was unexpected," I find myself adding.

"What? You're telling me you haven't ever thought about doing that?" This is the thing about Cody—he calls me on my shit.

"Maybe the thought had entered my head." I lean back on my elbows, and Cody mirrors me. I take deep breaths of the night air, trying to calm myself. The warmth from the hood is fading, but that's okay. We've just proven we can generate our own heat.

Questions swirl in my mind until I can't help but ask one of them. "So, are you bi or just experimenting or…"

Cody swivels his head toward me. "Are you asking me for a label?"

"Um… I guess."

He sits up, folding his arms across his chest. "I thought you didn't like labels."

"I don't. It's just that I heard you hooked up with Angie Baker at Jamie's party, so I'm just trying to get it straight in my head. Or not so straight, as the case may be."

"I think when it comes to me, not straight is your answer," he says softly.

"Seriously? So how not straight are we talking? A slight bend or more than that?"

"We're talking about a ninety-degree angle. Totally perpendicular."

"But Angie…"

"Angie was my attempt to… straighten myself. It didn't work. Which is why I tried to drink myself into oblivion."

"So, that's the shit you were dealing with."

"Yeah."

"But it's not like we live in the dark ages anymore."

"My mum…" He swallows, uncrossing his arms. "She'll have a problem with it, I'm fairly sure. You know, because of her church and everything."

"So was that… your first time? I mean, have you ever… um… like… kissed a guy before?" I mangle my question so badly it's like it's been through the garbage disposal.

"No, I haven't," he says quietly.

I'm the first guy he's ever kissed. Potentially his first kiss that has ever meant something. Yeah, I don't want to dwell on that because I'm worried about what might come spewing out of my mouth. I need to reset this mood, fast.

I roll my eyes. "So typical, Cody."

"What?" He's got a defensive look on his face.

"That you're amazing at something on your first try."

The smile that lights up his face takes my breath away. Not really helping the not-spilling-my-guts cause, though.

"Well, the logistics aren't actually different from kissing a girl," he points out.

"Nah, except for the stubble burn you sometimes get."

He flushes and looks down at his lap. "So… you've kissed a few guys before, then."

"Yeah, a few." I cough, suddenly awkward. I sit up a bit straighter. "Not like this, though."

"What do you mean, not like this?"

Oh shit. My face heats. Damn the still night. I need a breeze to cool my face.

"Not anyone I'm friends with," I say quickly.

"What about that guy Nico?" His voice is tight. "You know, the guy who came to the beach?"

"Nah, we became friends after we hooked up, actually. He was just experimenting. He's got a girlfriend now."

"Oh," Cody traces a pattern on the hood with his foot before raising his eyes to me. "You're not seeing anyone at the moment, right?"

"No."

He clears his throat. "Do you want this, I mean… do you want us—" He gestures between us. "—to be a thing?"

My heart thumps like it's battering its way out of my body. "If you're asking if I want more make out sessions like that one, then my answer is hell to the yeah."

A tentative smile spreads across his face. I feel a matching one on mine.

"We can't tell anyone though," he says.

"What do you mean? You don't think our parents will crack open the bottles of champagne and toast to our happiness?"

Cody grimaces. "Yeah, I'm sure if I go home and announce I'm gay and I'm dating his ex-wife's son, my dad's first reaction will not be to celebrate."

"At least the fact it's me might distract them from the gay part," I say.

"You have a point." He leans back, looking up at the stars.

I follow his lead, tilting my head back to examine the night sky. The light pollution of the city means we only can see the brighter stars. It's weird to think there are a lot more stars out there shining away that we never get to see.

"Do you think your parents will care?" he asks. His tone is casual, but I sense something larger and darker lurks underneath.

"They already know I'm into guys. But if they knew you and I were a thing, they probably wouldn't be that happy," I admit. "In case you haven't noticed, my mum isn't exactly your dad's biggest fan. But then, I'm used to disappointing my parents. You could even say I've made it my life mission."

Cody's gaze is fixed on me. "So, you're okay keeping this a secret from them?"

"Yeah, it's fine. I get for you, it's a bigger deal. Disappointing your parents is probably something you haven't done much."

"Not really," Cody says.

"From my experience, it's like riding a bike. It gets easier the more you practice."

A grin overtakes his face. "I'll keep that in mind."

"My mum has this cushion that says *I'd rather be someone's shot of whiskey than everyone's cup of tea*." I give a casual shrug, although I feel the tips of my ears heat after sharing this. It's dumb, but for someone who definitely isn't everyone's cup of tea, being one person's whisky has always appealed to me. "Although personally I'm probably more like a shot of tequila, because that's way cooler than whiskey."

Cody dips his head for a second before meeting my gaze and holding it for a heartbeat or two. "You're definitely tequila," he says finally.

"You think?"

"Yeah, tequila is an acquired taste. Just like you."

I snort.

"And we don't need Mel and Kate poking their noses into our business," I continue.

"Nah, definitely not."

"So, I'm happy to keep this on the down low," I say.

"Cool. But you know, I think we need something to seal the deal," he says, shuffling closer to me.

I raise an eyebrow. "Oh yeah? What kind of something?"

"This."

And Cody's lips are on mine. And we're kissing again.

Cody. Holy hell. It's all about Cody.

When we finally pull away from each other, he's looking dazed, his lips red and puffy.

I'm fairly sure I look the same.

Forget running marathons. My pulse is racing like we've just galloped around the galaxy a few times.

Chapter 18

I wake up the next morning, and there's this moment when I think I'm just living my usual mundane Ryan existence, before the memories slam into me. Then everything comes back in a flash, and my grin feels so bright I'm surprised it doesn't light up the room.

Because nothing is mundane anymore.

Cody. Cody kissing me. Cody and I agreeing to keep kissing each other.

I gather up all the reasons why it isn't a good idea if Cody and I hook up and throw open a drawer in my mind, sweep them all in there, and close it with a bang. Because I don't have enough self-control not to explore this thing with Cody. He's my favorite person on the planet at the moment. The fact I now get to kiss him too is like added bonus levels, which changes a game from being freaking amazing to out-of-this-world incredible.

I'm grinning as I go downstairs for breakfast.

I'm grinning when I head off to school.

My grin takes a slight dip in biology—because we're

studying cellular respiration now, and that particular life system reinforces the whack-job theory that aliens populated the earth.

But when I get a message from Cody at lunchtime, my mood is back in the life-is-awesome category.

have been getting congrats about concert today. But it's not only reason I'm smiling.

I tap out a quick reply.

i've been described as mood adjuster before but don't think it's ever meant positively

My phone pings almost immediately.

definitely positive this time

"You're looking pleased with yourself," Oz comments as I put my phone in my pocket. We're sitting outside in the sun on a picnic table in the small courtyard next to the cafeteria.

"It's a particularly awesome day," I reply, stretching back and letting the rays warm my face.

"Care to share what's particularly awesome?"

"Mrs. Steinberg's outfit. She has such great taste in cable sweaters."

Oz rolls his eyes.

"We were thinking of having a PlayStation marathon after school, like we used to back in middle school. Kind of feel I need to blow off some steam. You in?" Harvey asks. With his baseball cap on backwards, he looks like he's starring in some nineties sitcom revival. Or channeling some gangsta rapper.

"Sure, I'm in."

"Then you should spend the afternoon getting prepared to *lose*." Harvey draws out the last word like it's a piece of chewing gum.

"Seriously, you're starting the smack talk now?" I say.

"Don't forget I've seen your game. It's weaker than a geriatric arm wrestle."

"Hey, it's all pun and games," Harvey says.

Oz and I groan.

My phone vibrates in my pocket, and I'm sure my heart gives a corresponding twitch.

Sure enough, it's another message from Cody.

piano lesson cancelled. want to surf after school?

I message him back immediately.

sure

My heart speeds up at the thought of seeing Cody this afternoon. Will things feel different between us now? Awkward? Last night was like a dream. Is it going to be different under the harsh sunlight?

I glance up from my phone to find Harvey and Oz watching me.

"Sorry. Might have to take a rain check on the PlayStation battle," I say as I stash my phone back away.

Harvey raises an eyebrow. "You got a better offer?"

My cheeks heat. "Something like that."

AS ARRANGED, Cody's car is parked next to the curb outside school. Appleton gets off earlier than our school does. One of the many advantages of paying for an education rather than just taking what the government offers for free.

"Hey," I say, opening the door.

"Hey," Cody replies.

Somehow, those two simple words seem loaded with more meaning than a dictionary.

I jump into the front seat.

Cody's in his Appleton uniform, his red and white

striped tie askew where he must have tugged at it, his white shirtsleeves bunched up.

I didn't realize the disheveled preppy look did it for me, but apparently it does, judging by the warm flush spreading through my body. I pull my gaze away from him and stare through the windshield where my classmates are all flowing from the school with the usual look of escaped prisoners on their face.

I spot some familiar faces in the crowd.

Shit. Harvey's seen me. He scowls and says something to Oz, who looks in my direction.

I don't have time to worry about that now as Cody's pulling out into the traffic.

Some R&B track is playing on the speakers. I bend forward and fiddle with the volume, turning it up so it's thumping through the car.

Cody immediately reaches over and turns it down a few notches.

"The only way you should listen to that R&B shit is at full volume," I tell Cody.

"I want to be a musician, remember? Not damaging my hearing is quite important to me."

I roll my eyes. "It's all about Cody."

"Don't you forget that," he says as he switches lanes so he can get to the off-ramp.

Memories of last night float back. Then, it was all about Cody for me.

But Cody says nothing even vaguely personal as we drive toward my house.

Should I say anything? I mean, we agreed to keep kissing last night. Does that make us boyfriends now? I assume it's official. But you know what they say about the word assume.

I open my mouth, then hesitate. I'm not sure I have the

right words to hammer out the details with him. The fine print will have to wait.

By the time we've gone by my house and his house to collect our surfboards and get changed then driven to the beach, most of the afternoon has drained away. It's a weird time of year, still hot like summer, but the days are getting shorter, reminding me that summer doesn't last forever.

When we finally make it onto the sand, Cody unveils his new surfboard from its bag.

I stare down at it, jealousy rising in me.

"You bought a JV?"

"Well, you said they were the best brand," he says.

"Yeah, but they're expensive."

"I had some money left over from my last birthday."

Cody's birthday must be coming up soon. I know that because it's two months before mine. It's so typical Cody, that he'd still have money stashed away from eleven months ago. A wave of affection crashes over my jealousy, washing all traces away.

"Ready to test it out?" I ask.

"Sure."

We grab our boards and wade out until we can jump on and start paddling. The waves are small today, but it doesn't matter. Although we're at a different beach, it feels so familiar. There's the same peacefulness that comes from being out in the water with Cody catching waves beside me.

Cody mucks around getting used to his new board. He offers me a turn, but I decide to stick with my own. Sometimes it's best not to know what you're missing out on.

"I needed that," I say when we finally head to shore. I shake my hair, trying to get rid of the excess water. There's a reason dogs use this strategy. It's effective.

"Yeah, it was great," Cody says.

"You want to grab some dinner?" he asks as we carry our surfboards up the path to the parking lot.

"Sure."

We stash our surfboards on the roof rack and then open one of the back doors to shield us from the street while we change out of our wetsuits.

I've trained myself to avert my gaze when Cody is stripping off, so I do it automatically now. But as I'm tugging my T-shirt on over my head, it suddenly occurs to me that I don't have to avoid looking at him anymore. I glance across the car.

Not surprisingly, he's caught on faster than me, as his eyes are fixed somewhere around my abs.

"Enjoying the view?" I ask.

He raises his gaze guiltily to meet mine. "Definitely."

We stare at each other for a few heated seconds.

I break eye contact, huffing out a laugh as I finish pulling my T-shirt on. Cody's only in his towel, so I unashamedly lean back against the car, the metal warm even through my T-shirt, and watch as he finishes getting dressed.

The corner of his mouth quirks up as he pulls on boxers and shorts under his towel then grabs a hoody to throw over his T-shirt.

We walk side by side to one of the cafés that overlooks the beach and snag a table outside.

The advantage of my short hair is it's almost dry already.

Cody's hair is still damp, his curls coming back to life as it dries. One curl is drying at a weird angle, and without thinking, I reach over and brush it off his forehead.

Cody's blue eyes widen.

Shit.

I bury my nose in my menu to avoid his gaze.

As I scan the menu, it occurs to me that to other diners we're just two guys hanging out together. Some might work out we're on a date. The homophobes of the world would have a problem with it, although I care more about what ants think than anyone who judges someone based on who they're attracted to. But to everyone else, we're simply two guys hanging out.

If only things could be that straightforward.

But then, why the hell can't they be? We're not related. We're not even stepbrothers.

And okay, part of the reason we know each other so well is because we know each other's families. However, it's not like we've spent tons of time together growing up in a blended family utopia. And I know Cody's experience of being Kate and Mel's brother has been very different to mine.

In this messed up world, finding something like what Cody and I have is rare. Even I know that. After all, I've never been shy about hooking up with people, so I've got lots of other experiences to sift through. And I've never had anything that comes close to this.

"You're looking serious over there," Cody comments.

"I'm trying to decide between the hamburger and the nachos," I say. "It's a big decision."

"A life changing one," Cody deadpans back.

"Momentous," I agree.

We catch each other's eyes, and Cody gives a half-smile then looks away.

I reach across the table. His hand is lying flat on the table, and I lay my palm on top of the back of his hand.

"I'm glad we're doing this," I say.

A small grin creeps up Cody's face. "Me too."

The waiter comes over to take our order, and I retract my hand.

When he leaves, I lean back, looking out over the ocean where the sun is setting.

"Summer's almost over," I say.

"It was my favorite summer ever," Cody says.

"Yeah, it was epic," I agree.

Cody fiddles with the candle that's flickering away in the middle of the table, dipping his fingertips into the pool of hot wax that's forming at the base of the flame. "That's such a Ryan word," he says.

"What? Epic?"

"Yeah, you use it a lot."

"What other words do I use?"

"Awesome is up there in Ryan usage as well."

"Epic. Awesome. All words I could use to describe myself," I say.

Cody laughs. "You also use seriously a lot too."

"Yeah, well, I am such a serious guy," I take a sip of my drink. "I didn't realize you were doing such a complete study of my vocab."

"You're saying you didn't learn things about me this summer?" he asks.

"Oh, my level of Cody knowledge has expanded beyond belief."

"What things did you learn?" He's looking at me seriously now.

I shrug. "You work really, really hard. And you worry too much about what other people think about you, but partly it's because you consider other people's feelings more than most people. So it's not actually a bad thing."

Cody withdraws his hand from the candle and studies me for a moment.

"You're so much more than you pretend to be, you know?" he says, eventually.

So are you. I don't say this aloud though. Instead, I go for humor.

"Yeah, I'm much more than the handsome, man-stud package that everyone wants a piece of. I have hidden depths."

Cody rolls his eyes.

The waiter delivers our meals then, and thankfully our conversation moves on to other stuff. That's the thing about Cody and me. We can shoot the shit with each other forever. We never run out of things to say.

We split the bill when it comes, and I can't help wondering what comes next.

"You ready to head off?" Cody asks.

"Yeah."

I follow him out of the restaurant, my mind racing. We've agreed to keep making out. But so far, apart from checking each other out when we were changing and a few lingering, heated stares, nothing seems different between us.

It all changes when we get back to the car.

The air between us thickens with intensity and antic- ipation.

Cody fiddles with his keys. "Do you want to go straight home?"

"Nope."

The silence is pulses with an expectant beat.

I clear my throat. "Why don't we head down to Lagoon Bay? There's a lookout parking spot that's nearly always empty."

"It's getting dark."

"Yeah, I'm not actually that concerned about the view outside the car."

Blotches creep up Cody's neck, but he sticks the keys in the ignition and follows my directions to Lagoon Bay.

Sure enough, when we pull up, we're the only car in the parking lot.

"Shit, it's so clichéd, parking up like this," he says, undoing his seatbelt.

"There's a reason clichés become clichés," I say, unclicking my own. "It's because they were awesome ideas to begin with."

He smiles.

I lean across and kiss his smile. He goes still under my lips, then he opens his mouth, his tongue colliding with mine, and it's on.

We make out hungrily, desperately. His hands tug my hair, and one of mine is caught up in his curls. I trail my other hand lightly down the back of his neck.

Eventually, I pull away. I know Cody doesn't have much experience with this kind of stuff. And I don't want to rush things, no matter how much some parts of my body are screaming a different message right now.

"We should probably head home," I say reluctantly.

Cody's face is flushed. "Yeah, okay."

But instead of starting the car, he leans over and gives me a soft kiss, and I melt like the wax in a candle. Our make out session starts out slower this time. But it soon becomes even more heated than our previous kisses combined. A nuclear explosion kind of heat.

He moves his hands under my T-shirt, leaving a trail of fire on my skin.

"Damn." I wrestle myself away and shuffle on my seat so I'm as far from Cody as I can physically get. I gulp down a breath. "You need to start the car now," I instruct.

"Yeah, okay." His hands are shaking as he puts the key in the ignition.

We're silent on the way home. But it's a good silence.

I don't dare kiss him when we're parked outside my

house. But I grab his hand, give it a squeeze, stroking my thumb across the top of his thumb.

He looks down and a blush treks up his cheeks.

It takes all my self-control to open the door.

"We should do that again sometime. Because that was pretty epic," I say as I leave.

Chapter 19

Unfortunately, my life doesn't give me lengthy periods of time for awesome replays. You know, like replaying some things that happen when you're parked in a deserted parking lot at Lagoon Bay.

School the next day and the memory of Cody sliding his hand under my shirt doesn't go well with my home-room teacher's lecture on trash in the cafeteria.

Plus, I've got to put in some serious work to dig myself out of the hole I'm in with my friends. I know it was bad to blow off Harvey and Oz for hanging out with Cody. The good thing is Harvey's not very good at giving someone the cold shoulder. He likes to talk too much. And Oz is so laid back that nothing ruffles his feathers for long.

So, after a concentrated effort of charm and humor from me, halfway through homeroom things are back to normal.

And I think it's over.

Until lunch.

I'm sitting with Harvey, Oz, Grace, and Mia at the picnic table, because summer this year has definitely decided it wants to stick around at the party past its usual curfew. Harvey's carving into the picnic table with the end of a Bic pen. Like everything at our school, the picnic table is ancient. It's littered with graffiti, layer upon layer, generation upon generation. It probably goes back to Noah's ark. I'm sure if I looked hard enough, I'd find a heart inscribed with *Sheep One loves Sheep Two*.

"Shit." I throw my phone on the table in frustration.

"What's wrong?" Mia asks.

"My phone is just taking ages to upgrade."

"Don't worry. You're the king of the upgraders," Harvey sneers.

My shoulders stiffen. "What the hell do you mean by that?"

"You know." He doesn't look up from his carving.

"Actually, I don't. Are you going to explain your cryptic words or just give me a crossword to solve?"

"You've ditched us to hang out with the private school crowd. All those Appleton idiots." He finally looks up, his lips curling over his words.

Shit. I glance over at Oz and Grace, who are both following our conversation like it's the next Marvel installment.

I can't tell my friends that Cody and I are together. It would kind of defeat the whole "secret" part of secret relationship. But it sucks not to be honest with Oz and Harvey and have them think I'm ditching them to hang out with another group of friends.

"Why don't we do the PlayStation thing this afternoon instead?" I suggest.

"Too late. Oz and I did it without you."

"I'm hanging out with 'those Appleton idiots' at the moment too." Grace arches an eyebrow. "Do you have a problem with that, Harvey?"

Shit. Grace normally never engages in this kind of thing. She must really like Marco if she's prepared to defend him.

"That's different. You're going out with one of them," Harvey backpedals.

I scratch at my knee, not making eye contact with anyone.

When the conversation has finally moved on, I look up to find Grace watching me from across the table. She gives me one of her enigmatic smiles, and paranoia shoots through me.

Does she suspect about me and Cody? Does Marco? Are people at Appleton gossiping behind Cody's back? Will it get back to his parents?

I know I'm doing some flying leaps in the logic world, but it's hard to tame my imagination. Keeping this whole thing a secret might be harder than I've realized.

THAT NIGHT, I'm reminded about the main reason Cody and I need to be on the down low. Mel and Kate are around for dinner, and it demonstrates how our family is messed up enough without throwing the dynamite stick that I'm hooking up with their other brother into the inferno.

"This is so nice to have everyone together," Mum says with a smile as she dishes up lasagna to Mel and Kate that night. Mum's not that great of a cook overall, but her lasagna is a cheesy, meaty, crispy-topped slice of perfection.

I shovel the first forkful into my mouth.

"It's so great to be back," Kate says.

"How's Chris finding the new job?" Dad asks.

Chris is working support for a tech company, which is why he's not here tonight, as he's on the night shift.

"It's going well so far," Kate says. "He really likes the team he's working with."

"Have you put out any feelers for jobs?" Mum asks Kate. "I know you'll want to take some time off with the baby, but it can't hurt to let firms know you're around."

"I don't know if I'll go back to being an accountant." Kate's trying for a casual tone, not making eye contact as she helps herself to the beans.

"But you just got registered." Mum's brow pinches.

"I know. But I've spent enough time working as an accountant to realize I don't really like it."

Mum huffs. "In this economy you can't afford to be picky. Your resume already will look choppy, like you can't stick to anything."

"Do you have another area you think you're interested in?" Dad asks. He must have been a tightrope walker in a previous life the way he balances being a good stepdad and not pissing off Mum.

"Not really. I was going to take my time on maternity leave to think about it," Kate says.

"Hmm," Mum says.

"Anyway, how's school going for you, Ryan?" Kate turns to me. She knows the easiest way to get parental scrutiny off her is to redirect it to my average scholastic career.

It's a proven fact that Mum can talk for hours about how I'm not living up to my potential. I've been meaning to investigate whether Mum will qualify for *The Guinness Book of World Records* for the longest parental lecture, but I've never gotten around to it.

"School's good. I got an *A* on my biology test." I grin at her. "Is science something you've ever considered as a career option?"

Ha. I just returned her shot with a clean backhand slice. Even Cody the tennis player would be impressed.

"Ryan's done a great job of getting his grades up so far this semester," Mum says proudly.

"And have you decided what you want to do when you graduate, besides go surfing all the time?" Kate asks.

"I'm thinking about being a paramedic," I say calmly.

"A paramedic? Really?" It's amazing how Kate can inject so much skepticism into three words. It's a talent.

"Yeah, a paramedic." I meet her gaze straight on. "I've actually contacted the local precinct to see if I can watch them in action, make sure it's something I'd like to do. After all, I don't want to spend all the time, effort, and money training for a job then change my mind after only a few months."

Kate gives me a horrid look. It's game, set, and match to me.

"Hasn't Cody been helping you study?" Mel asks. I've forgotten about how my sisters do this, tag team their attacks on me. But this time, her attempt to help Kate out causes my heart rate to speed up for an unanticipated reason.

I turn to her. "How do you know that?"

"Dad and Heather were talking about it."

My heart thuds harder. "What did they say?"

Mel gives me a weird look. "Just that he's been tutoring you."

Kate frowns. "I didn't realize you and Cody were friends." Now both of my sisters are looking at me like I'm a puzzle they need to solve.

My mouth dries out. Will they work out Cody and I are more than friends?

Yep, paranoia is definitely taking over the building.

I take a huge gulp of my water.

"You know we hung out at the beach together this summer. He's kind of cool," I manage.

"It's nice of him to tutor you. I hope you're not taking advantage of him," Kate says.

I cough as an image of last night floats into my mind. Was I taking advantage of Cody? If so, he was definitely taking advantage of me in return.

A flush sweeps through my body at the memory. Yeah, top of the list of things not to think about at the dinner table.

"Now, I was thinking I'll schedule some vacation time around when the baby comes." Thankfully, Mum changes the subject. Unfortunately, it takes the conversation from one minefield straight into another.

Kate fiddles with her fork, poking at the lasagna noodles. Sometimes they can be slippery suckers. "Well, Chris is taking some time off. And we were thinking we'd like some time to spend together as a family, just the three of us."

Mum makes a ha-harrumphing sound. "If that's what you want."

She reaches over to grab some more garlic bread, while Mel, Kate, and I exchange looks. Mum backing down so quickly is out of character. Like on the ghostly-spirit-invading-her-brain scale.

"Although I don't think you appreciate how difficult the first few weeks with a newborn can be. God knows, I would have loved the support when you were a baby. But I didn't have family close by, and it's not like your father was much help."

And there it is. The Mum rant we were expecting. At least we don't need to call the exorcist.

Kate takes a deep breath, releasing it shakily. "I appreciate your offer, really. But I'm just saying I don't want you to use up your vacation leave unnecessarily."

Mum doesn't reply for a moment. The silence is filled by the scraping of knives and forks across plates.

I increase my fork speed, shoveling food into my mouth as fast as I can. I don't need psychic abilities to know the direction this conversation is heading.

Finally, Mum speaks. "Have you thought about how you will structure it when the baby arrives so everyone gets a fair turn at visiting?"

Kate puts down her fork with more force than necessary. "I'd actually like not to have to schedule when everyone can visit. I'd like it if everyone can act like grown-ups and just get along."

The lasagna has turned into glue inside me, sticking my internal organs into one garbling mess. Because this is what Cody and I are up against.

Mum looks like she's just taken a sip of vinegar rather than wine. "I've got to get ready for my book club," she says abruptly, scraping her chair as she stands. Pausing at the doorway, she looks back at Kate, her voice low. "You have no idea what that man did to me, so I'd appreciate it if you didn't judge."

With that, she sweeps out of the room.

Kate stares at her plate, and shit, I'm sure waterworks are under production in her eyes. Mel reaches over and gives her shoulder a squeeze.

"So, have you set up the nursery yet?" Dad asks in a bright voice.

AFTER I'VE DONE the dishes, I head through the living room to find Kate on her knees next to one of the bookshelves.

"What are you doing?"

"Looking for photo albums."

"Why?"

"Chris's mum gave me this book to put together for the baby." Kate stretches, her hands on her lower back. "It's got a whole section on parents and grandparents, and I'm struggling to put it together because there is so much stuff I don't know."

"What do you mean, stuff you don't know?" I ask.

Kate shrugs. "That's one of the crappy things about having divorced parents. Part of the story about how you came about goes missing. I mean, Mum and Dad never want to tell the story about how they first met and fell in love. But it's part of me and Mel."

"Yeah, I guess."

"I mean, you've heard dozens of times how Mum met Max, right? Mum loves telling about how we were at the barbecue and Mel fell in the fountain and Max fished her out."

"Yeah." I shove my hands in my pockets.

Kate's right. I've heard the rest of the story many, many times. How Dad had seen Mum as soon as she'd arrived at the barbecue, but he'd been too nervous to approach her. But then Mel had toppled into the fountain, and Dad rushed over and scooped her out, and he went with Mum to the Emergency Room afterwards even though Mel was completely fine (Mum has always been overly paranoid when it comes to the health of her children. If doctors gave out frequent flier miles, we'd all have gold status).

If Mel hadn't fallen in the fountain, Dad might never have worked up the courage to approach Mum, and I would probably not be here.

It's crazy to think the part chance plays in everything. It screws with your mind.

Especially when now I want to take the "what ifs" in a different direction.

What would have happened if Mum and Frank had never been married? If somehow Mum had met Dad earlier instead and Frank had met Heather and Cody and I had simply met at some party with none of the family crap between us.

Things would be so much easier.

But then, would Cody and I have gotten together if we hadn't hung out at the beach together? Would we be the same people if we hadn't grown up without our sisters, without our families like they are now? It is all so complicated.

Kate's giving me a weird look. I realize I've just zoned out.

"It's strange what Mum said earlier about what Dad did to her," Kate says. "I was thinking about that the other day, how Mum or Dad never talk about why they split up."

"It's fairly obvious they don't get along so well," I say.

"Yeah, but they obviously did at one stage."

"Do you remember them breaking up?"

"I was like three and a half when they separated. I have vague memories of Mum crying lots." Kate pulls a face as she grabs an album from the bookshelf and flicks through it. "She might have had postnatal depression. They didn't diagnose it very well back then. I hope that is something I don't have to worry about." She flicks through another few pages of photos, then pushes the album away. "All these photo albums are from when we're older."

"I think there're some boxes in the attic with old photos and stuff," I say.

Sorting the attic was one of my punishments last year for being a bit too free with my invites to friends on a weekend when Mum and Dad were away. I'm not sure the punishment fit the crime, but I do now have an in-depth knowledge of all the old crap Mum refuses to throw away. And I remember one box in particular where I'd opened the top then closed it again when I saw it contained lots of old photos.

"Cool. I'll go have a look now." Kate stands up.

From memory, the boxes were heavy, so I follow Kate up to the attic and show her where the box is stacked behind the old rocking horse.

Kate opens it, disturbing a layer of dust.

"Oh, this is perfect," she breathes, holding up a picture of Mum. Mum's got a blonde toddler on her hip, and her stomach is in the same state as Kate's is now.

"Is that you or Mel?" I ask. I can never tell. Kate and Mel were pretty much indistinguishable blonde blobs for the first few years of their lives.

Kate squints closer. "It looks like Mel, but it must have been me, 'cause Mel would've been older when Mum was pregnant with you." She rummages around to find another similar photo that's obviously been taken on the same day.

"Do you think Mum would mind if I take the boxes? I'll just scan everything and bring them back."

"I'm sure she won't care."

Kate continues to study the first photo, her forehead twisted.

"I'll carry the boxes down for you," I offer.

Her eyebrows shoot up.

"What? I can be considerate, you know," I say.

"I guess there's always a first time for everything,"

Chapter 20

On Friday after school, I'm chilling at home when I get a message.

parents going away for the weekend. want to come over??

I reply immediately.

hell yeah

stay the night?

I swallow as I look at those three words. There's a subtext lurking in there, I'm pretty sure.

sure

awesome

My heart's beating faster as I stash my phone away.

I've never been a prude when it comes to sex. My motto has always been *if it feels good, why not do it?* So my belt is sufficiently notched.

But my stomach is churning as I have a quick shower. Why am I so freaked out about taking things further with Cody? Maybe because he means more to me than all my previous hook-ups combined. I don't want to screw things up.

"Where are you off to?" Mum asks as I head out.

"I'm hanging out at Oz's place. I might crash there tonight," I try to keep my voice nonchalant. There are some things parental units don't need to know. And what I'm planning to do with her ex-husband's son is definitely on that list.

"Okay," Mum says.

When I pull up outside Cody's house, I take a minute to compose myself. But no amount of deep breaths calms me down. My palms are acting like they've just invented sweat and need to get into high-level production straight away. I wipe them on my jeans as I walk up the steps of the porch.

Cody opens the front door before I have a chance to knock.

"Hey." He's dressed in jeans and a blue T-shirt. He tugs at the bottom of his T-shirt as he stands back and lets me in.

"Hey."

We stand there in the hallway, looking at each other.

"Um, I'll give you the grand tour if you want."

I gesture with my hand. "Tour away."

Cody takes me through the living room, dining room, and through to the kitchen.

"Do you want something to drink?" He hovers next to the pristine kitchen bench.

"Nah, I'm fine."

He bites on the bottom of his lip as he leads me through another door and down the hallway into his room.

It's much the same as the last time I was here. The bed is made, everything neat and tidy, i.e. the polar opposite of my room. Posters of musicians I don't recognize are plastered on his wall. There's also a large photo of a sunset over a beach on the wall opposite his bed. I don't remember noticing it last time I was here, but then I wasn't really in inventory mode.

"And this is my room," he says redundantly.

"I've been here before, remember?" I say. "The night you were drunk."

"Oh yeah, that's right. I mean, I don't remember much of that night because I was out of it. But it was so good of you to get me home—"

I cut off his babbling by kissing him. Cody responds enthusiastically, our tongues sliding together in a way that's becoming familiar. Familiar and oh so good.

We stumble back to his bed.

Last time I was here, I hesitated before taking off Cody's shoes. This time, it's all about clothes removal. Hurried, frantic removal of clothes so we can be skin to skin in record time.

Our kisses are messy and frantic.

I pull away from him, panting. "We don't have to do anything," I say.

Something close to hurt flashes across Cody's face. "Are you kidding me? You don't want this?"

"Oh, trust me, I want this. But I don't want you to, you know, feel any pressure… to feel you have to take things further just because you invited me here…"

His eyes soften. "I appreciate your concern for my virtue."

I huff out a laugh. "Yeah, it's a war between my concern for your virtue and what I want to do with you. It's an epic battle."

He leans forward and ghosts his lips over mine. "I'm totally onboard with us doing what you want," he whispers.

My breath hitches.

His touch is tentative as he runs his fingers down my side, leaving my skin tingling.

Yeah, I'm supposed to be the experienced one in this situation. But somehow the fact it's Cody touching me wipes my mind blank.

He wraps his hand around me.

Holy shit.

"Is this okay?" he asks.

"It's definitely okay," I manage to gasp. "One would even say it's bordering on the territory of epic."

He huffs out a laugh, and I feel the puff of breath on my skin.

"I guess I have to work hard to make sure it reaches epic," he says.

And then we're kissing again and Cody's touching me and how is it possible that something can feel this incredible?

Eventually I manage to get with the program and work out the reciprocal thing, so I'm stroking him at the same time he's touching me.

His eyes flutter shut.

And I watch his face carefully, looking for the signs I'm getting the rhythm and pressure right.

His mouth is slightly open, and I sense by his rapid rise and fall of his chest that he's getting close.

He opens his eyes, and his dark pupil has eclipsed the blue.

"Ryan," he says.

And my mouth is back on his, and we're kissing as Cody shudders. And feeling him go triggers me, and I'm adding to the sticky mess between us. Cody slowly pulls his mouth away from mine.

"Oh wow," he says.

I flop back on the pillow. "That's a good wow, right?"

"Oh hell yes."

My heart is thumping so hard it's surprising it's staying in my chest. And I don't think it's purely due to the athletic portion of what we just did.

I've gotten off with other people before, but it has never, ever been like this.

Cody reaches for his discarded T-shirt and wipes at the mess between us. Then he lies down next to me.

"I'm so glad…" he begins, then stops

"What are you glad about?" Because I really, really want to know what Cody is thinking right now.

"That this, you know… my first…" He scratches his nose, and his neck flushes. But then his eyes find mine. "I'm glad it's with you."

Oh holy hell. My insides don't know what to do with that. So I just kiss him again instead.

THE NEXT MORNING, when my brain processes where I am, the first thing I do is turn toward Cody. The things we did last night… I want to make sure he doesn't regret stuff this morning.

Cody's already awake. He's lying there staring at the ceiling with a huge grin on his face.

The tightness in my chest loosens. Okay, so I'm guessing he's not regretting anything.

"You okay over there?" My voice is still husky with sleep.

"Just replaying some key highlights from last night."

I shuffle closer to him and reach out to touch his chest.

"You want to keep doing replays in your head, or do you want a reenactment?" My tone is casual as I trail my fingers down towards the fun zone.

"I vote for reenactment," he gasps.

"Good decision."

But it doesn't turn into a reenactment. Instead, it turns to a whole new episode where I'm kissing Cody in different places, trying to catalog all the different sounds I can coax out of him. It's like the best game ever invented.

Eventually I reach the part of him that's straining to be touched and proceed to show him exactly what other talents my mouth has besides telling awesome jokes.

When I finish, his eyes are glassy and he's breathing like he's just run a race.

And I can't help my self-satisfied smirk as I flop down on the pillow next to him.

"Did I suck out your brain too?" I ask.

"It feels like it," he murmurs.

"Then my job here is done."

But Cody has a determined look on his face as he moves over to hover over me. "My turn," he says.

"Well, they do say that payback is the best thing ever," I reply.

"I'm pretty sure that's not the exact saying."

"It is in my world," I say as he starts kissing my chest.

IT'S MID-MORNING, and we're still in bed.

Cody's using me as a pillow, and I'm running my hand up and down his arm, trying to contain whatever this is that's swelling inside me.

Cody lifts his head, shifting off me onto the pillow. He turns to face me, and unconsciously I mirror him so we're both curled up, staring into each other's eyes.

"Hey, you," he says.

"Hey."

He's got that Cody look of concentration as he reaches

out and traces a finger down my cheek bone and across my jaw. Like he's a blind man reading braille for the first time.

My skin tingles under his fingers, and I close my eyes because I don't want my expression to betray me. I don't want these oversized feelings to escape in a way I can't control.

My eyes fly open when someone pounds on the door.

"Cody."

Shit. It's Mel's voice.

She hammers on the door again. "Are you in there?"

Cody's eyes are wide, startled.

"Uh… yeah, I'm here," he croaks.

I hear the door handle turning, and adrenaline pumps through me.

"Why is your door locked?" Mel demands, rattling the door handle.

I'm expecting Cody to freak out. But instead of worry, amusement spreads across his face.

I blink.

"Use your imagination, Mel," he calls back.

There's a pause. I can only imagine Mel's face as she stands in the hallway, trying to process what that means.

"Do you have a visitor?" she asks finally.

"That would be an affirmative."

"Well, tell your visitor they're welcome to stay for breakfast." I can hear the smile in her voice. Her footsteps thud away.

I'm expecting Cody to lose his shit any second now. But his expression stays strangely nonchalant.

"You want me to jump out the window?" I ask.

He looks at me for a long time. "Do you think Mel will freak out if she finds out about us?" he asks finally.

"Uh… yeah. Probably. Definitely."

He rolls over onto his back and talks to the ceiling. "I guess the more important question is, do you care?"

"What?"

"Do you care if Mel knows?" he asks.

My pulse races. "No."

He shrugs. "Then I don't think you need to jump out the window."

"You're seriously okay with Mel knowing about us?" I clarify.

"She's going to find out sometime," he says. "I'm sure she'll keep it to herself if we ask her to."

Okaaay. I so didn't predict this reaction. "Are you sure? Like completely sure?"

He gives a careless shrug. "After last night and this morning, I'm feeling a bit reckless."

He leans over and kisses me. It's a good persuasion tool.

As he pulls away, I feel a grin overtake my face. It may have a touch of evil in it.

"Let's just mess with her a little," I suggest.

A FEW MINUTES LATER, I saunter out into the kitchen.

Mel glances up with a grin that fades rapidly when she sees me and is replaced with a look of confusion.

"What are you doing here?" I ask.

Mel blinks. "Isn't that my line?"

"I don't know. Is it?" I open the fridge and help myself to some orange juice.

I'm pouring it at the counter when Cody comes in, stretching and yawning. He's pulled on a T-shirt, but he's still in his boxers.

"Want some orange juice?" I'm already pouring a second glass.

He gives me a co-conspirators grin. "Great. Thanks." He takes the glass and drains it in three gulps.

"You're thirsty," I comment.

"I've been doing thirsty work." He gives me another grin then heads to the pantry. "You want cereal or toast?"

"What cereal do you have?"

"Nothing with raisins."

"Of course. Fine. I'll survive on raisin-free cereal just this once."

I slip around to sit at the breakfast bar.

Cody grabs two bowls of cereal and spoons, sliding them across the counter.

Mel stays stationed by the sink, her eyebrows threatening to rocket off her forehead.

"What is happening here?" she asks, looking between us.

"We're having breakfast," I state.

Cody comes and sits on the stool next to me, sitting slightly closer than normal.

Mel's eyes dart between us as Cody and I eat our breakfast and have an intense debate whether Rice Krispies are better than Corn Flakes.

"Anyone want coffee?" she finally asks.

"Nah, I'm okay thanks," Cody says.

"Not for me either."

Mel's shoulders relax as she uses the fancy pod machine to brew herself a cup. I can see she's doubting herself, thinking that I've just crashed here for the night.

While personally I think coffee tastes like ground up dirt, Mel looks like she's having an epiphany of biblical proportions as she takes a first sip.

Cody finishes his cereal and stacks his bowl in the dishwasher.

"I think I'll have a shower," he announces.

I snort. "Good idea. You do kind of smell."

Cody cuffs my shoulder as he goes past. He pauses at the door to throw a pointed look at me.

Right. Time to trigger the freak out.

"Do you want some company?" I ask innocently.

Mel splutters on her mouthful, spraying coffee all over the table.

"Yeah, that would be epic," Cody replies with a small grin.

"I'll be there in a minute," I say, leaning back on my stool. "You get it warmed up."

Mel's still coughing, her eyes wide.

"Sure, I'll warm it up." Cody slides me a blazing hot look as he leaves that I'm fairly sure isn't just for Mel's benefit.

I'm going to get lucky again. I can't suppress my smile. Life is awesome.

"What the hell?" Mel says when she recovers.

"What?"

"Is this for real?"

I force a look of confusion on my face. "Is what for real?"

"Don't play with me, numb nuts. You and Cody?"

"If you're asking if I'm actually going to join Cody in the shower, then the answer is yes, it is for real."

"Oh my God."

"Funny, that's exactly what I hope to get Cody saying in a few minutes." I give her a wink.

Mel just gapes at me. She appears to have lost the power of speech.

"Remember when you and Kate always used to say to me why can't you be more like Cody? And you'd always tell me how sweet and amazing he is," I say.

"Yes…" Mel says slowly.

I shrug. "I figured if you can't beat 'em, join 'em. I'm now a Cody convert too." I stand up and flick her a grin. "And on that note, I think I'll head to the shower."

For the record, I get an almost constant stream of Oh my Gods from Cody. But I decide not to share that information with Mel.

There are some things sisters definitely don't need to know.

Chapter 21

Once we're out of the shower, Cody and I collapse onto the couch and mindlessly watch some reruns of *The Walking Dead*. After one episode, Cody gets up and raids the fridge, coming back with an assortment of snacks.

We're sitting shoulder to shoulder, but we don't engage in any type of PDA. Mainly because Mel is perched on a chair on the other side of the room and is watching us with intense curiosity. Like she can't quite believe what her eyes are showing her.

A car pulls up in the driveway.

I seize up and inch away from Cody.

Through the front window, I see Kate climbing out of her car. Shit. It's like she's grown even larger in the few days since I last saw her. You'd think she was brewing multiple babies inside her stomach. But I'm not letting my sister's womb capacity distract me from what's happening here.

"You rang Kate?" I challenge Mel.

She ignores me, opening the door as soon as Kate arrives on the doorstep.

"What's this major news you couldn't tell me over the phone?" Kate asks as she steps inside.

"It's that." Mel points toward Cody and me on the couch.

Kate gives her a funny look.

"Yeah, it's Cody and Ryan. We talked about how they're hanging out together the other night. It's kind of cool." She spots the remains of our feast. "Hey, do you have any more cookies? I'm famished."

She heads in the direction of the kitchen.

"No, Kate, you've missed the point," Mel calls impatiently after her.

Yeah, I'm not hanging around so my sisters can watch Cody and me like we're giant pandas in the zoo.

I stand up. "You want to head off?" I ask him. "Go surfing or something?"

"I vote for the 'or something,'" he says, grinning.

I offer him my hand, and he grabs it. But he doesn't let go once I've pulled him to his feet. Instead, he laces his fingers through mine.

Kate comes back into the lounge and freezes, a cookie halfway to her mouth. Her gaze zooms in on where Cody and I are holding hands. "What the hell?"

"I told you," Mel says triumphantly.

"Are you two together?" Her eyes dart to Mel for confirmation. "Like together, together?"

Cody clears his throat. "Ah… yeah. We are."

"You're gay?" Kate clarifies.

Cody's eyes fix on a spot on the carpet. "Yeah. I am."

"Isn't that kind of obvious by the fact that we're together?" I say.

"Okay, I mean, that's… well, it's absolutely fine, of course, but this…" She waves her hand in our direction. "Mum and Dad are going to completely freak." There's something approaching awe in her voice. Kate's done her fair share of freaking Mum and Frank out over the years, so it should be flattering that we've done something that impresses her.

"They don't need to know," Cody says. He drops my hand and stuffs his own hands in his pockets.

"We need to record Dad's face when he finds out. It'll be a YouTube sensation," Mel says.

"This is something none of the parents need to know about," Cody says. His voice is no nonsense. I've never heard him use that tone before. From the looks on their faces, Kate and Mel haven't either.

"Okay, okay," Mel says.

"Promise?"

"I promise," Mel says.

Cody shoots a look at Kate.

She puts her hands up in surrender. "They're definitely not going to hear it from me. I don't want to be responsible for Dad having a heart attack."

This is where Cody's lifetime of being a wonderful brother helps me for once. Because I'm fairly certain they would have tortured me for a while before agreeing to anything.

"Good." Cody looks at me. "We off?"

"Well, you might be. But I'm perfectly fresh."

Cody elbows me in the ribs in response to my joke, and I grab at his hands in response. We jostle for a second, both grinning, Cody twisting to get away from me, but I'm not letting go. I pin his hands together and snake my free hand around to tickle him under his rib cage where I know he's sensitive, and he laughs his deep chuckle. I laugh as well, as Cody has the type of laugh that should never be lonely.

I glance at our sisters. Forget pandas in a zoo. They're

staring at us like we're purple and pink alien-unicorn hybrids who've just started hula-hooping.

I remove my hands from Cody. He runs his hands through his hair as I grab my keys and phone from the coffee table.

"Let's hit the road," I suggest.

"Yeah, okay." Cody says. He nods toward Kate and Mel. "See you guys later."

"Yeah, later," Mel says weakly as we make our exit.

I catch a snatch of Kate's voice just as the door shuts behind me. "Okay, so I didn't see that one coming."

Chapter 22

Cody and I spend the rest of the day together. He's remarkably unconcerned about the whole telling-our-sisters thing. I'm not quite as relaxed as him, although I hide my discomfort. I just get the feeling it's not the last I've heard on the issue.

On Monday Mrs. Steinberg welcomes us to the week by springing a pop quiz. But thanks to Cody's tutoring, I'm staying up-to-date with the work, so I'm pretty sure I manage to pass.

As I'm leaving class with Grace and Mia, the star chart my mum had when I was a kid as an incentive to do well in tests flashes into my mind. Can I talk Cody into setting up a rewards system for my biology results? Although I'll suggest different prizes than the Star Wars figurines my mum used to offer.

"What are you plotting?" Grace asks.

"Plotting, me?" I ask with an air of innocence.

"That's definitely your Ryan-is-plotting something face," she says.

"I have no idea what you're talking about."

We reach the picnic tables where everyone is hanging out, and the usual clowning around begins. But something is off with Oz. He's sitting at the end of the table, not saying much.

When I try to engage him in a friendly arm wrestle, he shrugs me off.

After the bell rings, I hang back to talk to Harvey.

"What's up with Oz? He's not pissed about the PlayStation thing, is he?" I don't get it. Oz isn't the type of person to hold grudges.

Harvey looks at me silently for a few seconds before answering. "His grandmother's really sick. They don't know if she will make it."

"Oh." I pull up. "Why didn't he tell me?"

Harvey shrugs. "No idea."

The second bell rings. I've got to go or there's a late detention slip with my name on it in the immediate future.

LAST PERIOD I HAVE ENGLISH. I slip into a seat next to Oz.

"Hey, sorry about your grandmother," I say in an undertone.

He stiffens. "Did Harvey tell you?"

"Yeah. Why didn't you say something to me?"

Oz shrugs. "What would have you said?"

I don't know how to answer that question. I fiddle with my pen.

"That's the thing," Oz continues. "You're always good for a laugh, but you're not exactly the go-to person when shit gets serious, are you?"

His words cut at me. I drop my pen through the small gap between our desks and use the time leaning down to pick it up to wipe my face clean.

"I guess not," I say finally.

OZ'S WORDS swirl around my head when I get home. How I'm not the person anyone turns to for important stuff.

I know I joke around a lot. But the idea that no one can trust me with anything serious doesn't sit well inside me. I mean, I want to be a paramedic. That's the definition of shit turning serious, isn't it?

I'm in the kitchen making myself a sandwich when I hear a car pulling up. I'm vaguely hoping it's Cody, even though I know he's got a piano lesson this afternoon. I walk out into the hallway, stuffing the sandwich into my mouth.

But it's not Cody. It's Mel. She's barely out of her car before another car pulls into the driveway next to her. Kate's car.

Something coils deep in my gut.

I open the door just as Mel arrives on the doorstep.

"What are you two doing here?" I ask.

"We want to talk to you."

Oh God. It's a sisterly intervention. It's been a while since I've had the delight of one of these. And I have a sneaking suspicion I know the theme of this one.

"Shit, you're getting huge!" I say to Kate as she arrives inside, trying to distract.

"I am growing another human inside of me," Kate says stiffly.

"If you lay on the beach right now, I'm pretty sure volunteers would turn up to save the stranded whale."

"Thanks, Ryan, that's exactly what I needed to hear."

"No problem. I live to please."

"You know, when I saw Cody the other day, he offered

to give me a foot massage. You call me a whale. And you wonder why he's our favorite."

She's saying it to rile me up, but I smirk in reply. "I hope you took him up on that offer. Cody gives amazing massages."

Kate flicks a glance to Mel. "About that."

"About what?"

"About you and Cody."

My shoulders stiffen, but I keep my voice light. "Let me guess. You're here to tell me we're both your brothers, you love us lots, and hope we make each other really happy. That's so nice of you."

Kate snorts. "Yeah, that wasn't exactly what we were planning to lead with."

"How long has it been going on?" Mel asks.

"Is that any of your business?"

"Actually, I think who our brother dates qualifies as our business under the big sister laws," Kate says.

The big sister laws. God. They had me convinced they were real for the first ten years of my life.

"And when our brothers are dating each other, it doubly qualifies as our business," Mel adds.

"I know technically you're not related. It's just... weird," Kate says.

I fold my arms across my chest. "As you said, we're not related. We barely knew each other before this summer. I don't get how it's weird."

"Um... because of us?" Kate points at Mel then at herself. "Kind of a major thing you have in common that most boyfriends don't?"

"I always knew the existence of you two would come back to bite me somehow," I mutter.

"Seriously, Ryan, some people will have a problem with

you and Cody together. And I'm not just talking about Mum and Dad."

"Who cares what close-minded people think?" I say.

Kate rolls her eyes. "Hey, I'm all for star-crossed lovers. But you need to think this through."

"I have thought it through."

Mel huffs to show me how much she believes in that theory.

"Cody does nothing by halves, Ryan," Kate continues. "He'll be taking this seriously. And if you're just messing around with him…"

I see red. My vision is swarming with angry red jellyfish with paintbrushes coloring the whole ocean a violent scarlet.

"Oh my God, I'm taking this seriously too!" The words burst out of me.

"I find that hard to believe," Kate says calmly.

My breath comes in shallow pants. I turn away so my sisters can't see my face as I try to compose myself. What the hell can I say to convince them I'm not fooling around with Cody? They're always going to believe the worst of me. And why should I turn myself inside out, expose my guts, just to persuade them? It's none of their business how I feel about Cody.

I go for my standard default. When in doubt, joke.

"This is between me and Cody. And last time I checked, Cody was *very* happy with how things stood between us." I layer so much innuendo into my voice that even frat house boys would blush.

Kate pulls a face, while Mel rolls her eyes.

"Are you trying to gross us out?" Mel asks.

"Yup. Is it working?"

"Yes. What you and Cody get up to is so far past my need-to-know line."

"Great. My work here is done."

"This can't come out before my baby shower." Kate juts out her chin. "It's difficult enough dealing with Mum and Dad in the same room for two hours. We're not dropping this into the mix."

"Trust me, they're not hearing anything from us," I reply.

Chapter 23

I'm mildly grumpy with Cody next time I see him. Which is not fair, I know. It's not his fault our sisters are biased toward him.

But when the perfect guy picks me up in his perfect car looking every inch his perfect self, I have to bat away my old feelings of resentment.

"Did you get the pleasure of a visit from our sisters?" I ask as we hit traffic. I've been stewing on it but didn't want to ask him over text.

He looks startled. "How did you know?"

"Um… because they came to see me too."

Cody flicks his indicator to turn right. Is it my imagination, or does he look guilty?

"Yeah, they turned up the other day to talk to me."

"I'm willing to bet you didn't get the same lecture I got." I cross my arms across my chest.

He shrugs. "We mainly discussed how I should come out to Mum and Dad."

I flick a quick glance at him. We haven't really discussed how he feels about his sexuality and the idea of coming out. I, of course, think it's epic that Cody is gay because I reap a lot of the benefits. I go for the blunt question. "Do they think your parents will have a problem with you being gay?"

Cody's forehead furrows. "Dad, no. He's pretty liberal about stuff, and he's worked with lots of gay people, so none of us think he'll care once he gets over the surprise." He shifts in his seat. "I'm not so sure about Mum because of the religious thing. She's never discussed her view with any of us, although Kate pointed out that she was always nice to her friend Daisy who was openly gay, so there's hope."

"Of course there's hope." I give him a brief smile before I get to the million-dollar question. "So, did Mel and Kate say anything about me?"

He hesitates. "Kate suggested Mum and Dad might find it easier to handle if I had a different boyfriend."

I slump back in my seat. I knew it.

"She also asked me what we have in common," he continues.

My breath hitches. "What did you say?"

He slides a look at me. "Our sense of humor."

"You're almost as funny as me," I agree absent-mindedly.

I can guess the subtext of Kate and Mel's conversation with him. *Hey Cody, it's okay if you're gay, but you shouldn't just hook up with the first guy you find who also likes boys. You can do better than our other brother.*

Hurt rises inside me. Even my own sisters don't think I'm good enough for Cody.

We pull up in the driveway of Cody's perfect house.

"You okay?" He's watching me closely.

I swallow and plaster on an easygoing smile. "Yeah, I'm fine."

He checks his watch. "Mum's not going to be home from work for a few hours. You want to hang out here for a bit?"

"Sure."

I follow him inside. We head to the kitchen.

"You want something to eat?"

"How do I always answer that question?"

He grins and grabs bread and butter to make a sandwich.

I watch him, our sisters' comments swirling around in my head.

Cody puts the knife down. "Are you sure you're okay? What did Mel and Kate say to you?"

"Nothing much. Just what you'd expect." I think Cody can tell from my voice that I don't want to talk about it.

He slides a sandwich over to me. It's baloney and cheese, my favorite.

I chew on my sandwich as I stare out the window where the swimming pool glistens invitingly. Cody's swimming pool is twice the size of ours. No wonder Mel and Kate always wanted to hang out here rather than at our house. It's too cold to swim though. Autumn is definitely running the show.

I glance back to where Cody's still watching me, a crease on his forehead.

"You want a jam session?" I ask.

His expression immediately brightens. "Definitely."

I load my plate into the dishwasher and follow him to his room. He grabs his spare guitar out of his closet. We play *Shotgun* and *Imagine* together, and he teaches me the chords to *Hotel California*. It's tricky, but when I finally get it right, the look of pride in his eyes makes me squirm.

The next time through, he sings along, and I'm glad I have to look down at my fingers so he can't see my expression. I could listen to Cody sing forever and never get bored.

"So, it's my birthday next week," he says when he finishes, setting his guitar aside.

"Yeah, I know. Don't worry. I'm saving for your present." I prop my guitar on the floor so it's leaning up against the bed.

Cody rolls his eyes. "Actually, I was thinking about my birthday party. Dad likes to make big deals about our eighteenths."

That's right. I can vaguely remember the fight Frank and Mum had when Kate turned eighteen. Mum thought it was ridiculous to spend so much money on a party. I think she refused to pay half and Kate got upset. All I can remember from her party is everyone's tense faces and being told off for double dipping in the chocolate fountain.

"So, do you want to come?" Cody asks.

"It's probably best if I don't," I say.

Cody frowns. He puffs out such a long sigh that it causes a temporary disruption of the curls on his forehead. "It's so screwed up. I want you there."

"I want to be there," I say honestly.

"So, come."

"Seriously?"

"Yeah, who cares what anyone thinks. Mum and Dad will have to cope with the fact that we're friends."

"Is that what we are? Because I'm pretty sure I don't do to all my friends, the things I do with you," I say as I shuffle closer to him. I'm meaning it as a joke, but I can see from his face that my words fall flatter than roadkill.

"I really hope you don't do what we do with any of your friends," he says slowly. "It's just us, right? I mean, you're not with anyone else?"

"Are you kidding me?" I draw back from him. "You seriously need to ask me that question?"

"Sometimes it's tough to work out where I stand." He bites his lip.

I swallow. Hard.

"You're standing front and center at the moment," I say cautiously.

Cody gives me that intense stare of his. The type that feels like an interrogation. And I really don't want to start babbling out truths now. So I go for my preferred method of distraction, which involves my lips on his lips.

And it totally works.

———

CODY IS RIGHT. It's screwed up. It's screwed up to be at my boyfriend's birthday party and not to spend any time with him. It's screwed up that I have to avoid talking to him too much, touching him, doing anything that will make people suspect we're more than friends.

Frank and Heather have reserved the private room in The Topiary for his birthday. It's this restaurant with a large garden featuring a number of plants shaped into exotic animals placed throughout. Of course because it's night, no one is out in the garden enjoying the weird-shaped shrubs. Instead, there's about a hundred people jammed into a room that still smells vaguely plant-like.

I stuff a handful of savory cheese pastry sticks into my mouth as I watch Cody on the other side of the room. The pastry flakes in my mouth like a desiccation agent.

He's dressed in a navy blue shirt that perfectly matches the edge of his eyes. I know this, because I know all the shades of Cody's eyes now. That's the kind of thing you learn when you spend so much time staring at something.

"Ryan! I thought you might be here." Grace grabs my arm and pulls me into a half-hug.

"Oh, hey." I smile at her, sending an eyebrow raise in Marco's direction. "Hey, man, how's it going?"

"Good," Marco looks around. "This is a fancy party. For my eighteenth, I just had a few people over to play pool in the basement."

"Yeah, Cody's parents don't do things by halves."

Including grudges against ex-wives. Not that my mother isn't equally responsible in the whole thing.

I grab some puffy pastry thing from another tray sliding by.

"Ohh… they have those little quiche things. I'm going to grab some," Grace says.

I shake my head at her. "We can't take you anywhere." But Grace is already gone, chasing after the waiter with the tray, leaving Marco and me standing there together.

"You and Cody are hanging out lots at the moment, right?" Marco scratches at his nose.

My shoulders stiffen. "Yeah, we've been hanging out a bit," I say cautiously.

"Don't look so worried." He puffs out a laugh. "I was just going to say Cody seems way happier at the moment. More relaxed, you know? Like he's not taking stuff as seriously anymore."

"He definitely has caught that from me," I say.

"Well, it's good for him, whatever's going on." He slaps my shoulder.

Luckily Grace reappears with a handful of miniature quiches, sparing me from coming up with a reply. We stand and chat about epic finger foods from kids' parties for a while.

Marco seems like a good guy, and he makes Grace

laugh, which is the main thing. He says nothing more about Cody.

I try to avoid watching Cody too closely, being too obvious, but it's difficult. Cody draws my attention even on the other side of the room.

Besides, I've got a reason to keep my eye on him—I've got his present burning a hole in my pocket. I don't want it to mingle on the large table of presents just inside the door. I want to give it to him personally.

But for that, I need to get him alone.

Finally, I notice him slipping out the doors to the balcony.

Knowing Cody, he just wants a break from the crowd. But I'm hoping he won't mind my presence. Or my present, for that matter.

When I get outside, Cody stands against the railing, looking out at all the animal shapes. They're lit up at night, a whole zoo in front of us. No rhinoceros, though.

He turns when he hears me, his mouth already curving into an automatic smile. When he recognizes me, his whole face rearranges itself into a genuine grin, the type where his eyes crinkle around the edges.

"Fancy seeing you here," I say.

"Such a coincidence," he agrees.

Basking under his grin, for the first time all evening, I feel like I can breathe properly. "I've got something for you," I say as I take his present out and hand it over.

It's wrapped messily, as my experience trying to wrap it this afternoon confirmed that wrapping things neatly is not in my skill set. Cody wrestles with the mass of tape.

"There is something inside this, right? This isn't just your idea of a joke?"

"There's definitely something inside," I promise.

He eventually tears through the tape with his teeth and then has to wade through the layers of wrapping.

"It's nothing much," I say, nerves pinching my stomach.

Cody unwraps the last bit of paper to reveal his present.

A guitar pick.

I rake my hands through my hair. "I kind of wanted to get you something related to how we got to know each other. And you've already bought yourself a surfboard."

Cody turns the pick over in his hands. It's not just an ordinary guitar pick. Instead, it's personalized, with a picture of a sunrise over a beach printed on the surface.

"Is that Orakahau beach?"

"Yeah, I found this place online that prints whatever you want on guitar picks. I used one of the photos I took over summer." I shrug.

He raises his gaze to mine. "It's epic," he whispers.

We stare at each other, and I so badly want to kiss him. I take a step back so I don't give in to the impulse.

"Can I have your attention, please?" Frank's voice booms from inside.

"Shit. I've got to get in there." Cody slips the pick and wrapping paper into his pocket and heads back through the doors.

I trail after him, leaving a few feet between us.

Frank stands with Heather, Mel, and Kate on a small, raised stage. An ornate cake stands on a table off to one side.

Cody joins them on the stage, giving his father a quick smile.

The crowd settles down into a whispery quiet as Frank lifts the microphone again.

"Heather and I would like to thank you all for coming

to celebrate Cody's birthday. Cody has made Heather and I so proud over the years. Not just his achievements, but also his attitude, his kindness, the way he approaches everything and everyone with an open heart."

Cody ducks his head, blushing at his father's words.

Something stirs inside me. Okay, so I don't exactly like Frank. In fact, I'm fairly sure hatred of Frank came through the placenta when I was in my mother's womb, along with all the other vital nutrients. But I can't help my dislike melting a bit as he continues to speak, so obviously bristling with pride for Cody. And the stuff he says shows that he values who Cody is deep down.

"So, congratulations, Cody, on reaching this milestone. We know that the future holds bright things for you."

There's a polite round of applause, and then Heather steps forward, taking the microphone from Frank, fumbling with it for a second before finally starting to speak.

"I'm not much of a public speaker, but I would like to add a few words." She turns to look at Cody. "Cody, you have made me proud to be your mother every day of your life. I couldn't have wished for a better son. You deserve all the happiness in the world."

Cody chokes up as he gives his mother a hug, and people clap again.

She hands him the microphone. "Thanks, Mum and Dad. And thanks everyone for coming. Enjoy the party."

He goes to leave the stage, but Frank pulls him back.

"Don't go too fast. There's a cake to cut," Frank says. "And a song to sing."

Everyone laughs as Cody rolls his eyes.

The cake is revealed in the shape of piano keys, with eighteen candles, one on each key. Kate lights the candles, and everyone sings "Happy Birthday" to Cody. I keep my voice low as an extra gift to him. I'm sure it must be agonizing for someone as musically talented as him to witness a hundred people butchering a song.

Cody has his concentrating look on as he leans forward to blow out the candles. Everyone claps again, and he raises his eyes to the crowd, scanning. His gaze stops when he finds me.

Kate nudges him, and he obligingly takes the knife from her and makes the first slice.

Formalities over, he steps off the stage where he's immediately engulfed by well-wishers.

I drift over in Mel's direction, giving Cody a wide berth.

"Why didn't you do a speech?" I ask her.

"Dad wanted to keep it simple this time. You know, after the debacle of my twenty-first."

Shit. Mel's twenty-first. When Mum and Frank tried to outdo each other in who could be the most doting parent. They also roped Heather and Dad into doing speeches, and then of course, Kate, Cody, and I each had to mumble a few words. It went for over an hour, and my great aunt Anna almost fainted from having to stand up for so long.

"Good call," I say.

A woman approaches us then. She's tall and elegant-looking and randomly wearing a light blue sari, although she looks to be as Indian as I am.

"Hey, Aunt Jill," Mel says.

I look at her. It must be Frank's sister who lives in Australia. Cody's mentioned she's visiting, and I don't think I've ever seen her before.

"Lovely to see you, Melanie." She gives Mel a quick kiss on the check before turning her attention to me. "And who's this?" Anticipation is layered through her voice. It's obvious that she thinks I'm Mel's boyfriend or something.

I'm fairly sure the freaked-out look on Mel's face is matched by my own.

"This is Ryan, my other half-brother."

"Oh." She blinks. "You're Julia's son?" Her voice is flat.

"Yeah, I am."

She raises her eyebrow and looks around. "Is Julia here? I thought Frank and Julia still couldn't stand each other."

"They can't. I'm… um… friends with Cody."

Her eyebrows retreat even further into her hairline. "I can't imagine your friendship is encouraged by either of your parents."

"Yeah, well, not really. But it's not that big of a deal. I mean, they split before we were even born." I can hear the defensiveness in my voice.

She just gives me a long look. "There are some things you can never recover from," she says finally.

I furrow my brow at that. She glances over at Mel, who's also looking confused.

"Anyway, it was nice to meet you. Give Julia my best."

"Okay."

She leaves in a swirl of perfume.

"You're such a shit liar," Mel says after Jill is out of earshot.

"Actually, last time I did a tally, you'd fallen for my lies approximately eighty-nine percent of the time."

Mel narrows her eyes at me. "What lies?"

"Like the time I told you that outfit suited you."

"You're such an ass."

Waiters are going past with platters of cake, so I scoop a piece off a tray and stuff half of it in my mouth. Yum. Chocolate. Good choice.

Mel's looking at me evaluatively. "Have you and Cody actually thought this through?"

My pulse races as I finish chewing the cake and swallow. "Thought what through?"

"Where this… thing between you is leading?"

"Yeah, we've thought about it. We've already written the words for our fiftieth wedding anniversary speech. Is that what you mean?"

Mel rolls her eyes. "I mean, it can't exactly end well, can it?"

Her words cause the cake to turn cartwheels in my stomach. It's not actually what she's saying, but the matter-of-fact way she says the words. Like even a dumbass would have figured it out.

Cody and I will not end well.

I haven't given much thought about where my relationship with Cody is heading. I've been too caught up in the moment, too happy to bask in the sunshine of being with Cody, to think much about the storm clouds that lurk overhead.

Unease settles inside me.

Romeo and Juliet probably thought it would all work out too.

Chapter 24

The next morning, I get a message from Harvey.

hey, just to let you know, Oz's grandmother passed away yesterday

I think about what Oz said. About how I'm good for laughs but not more serious stuff.

I flick a quick message back.

when's the funeral?

tomorrow

Shit. I've arranged to spend tomorrow with Cody. Surfing if the weather is good enough. After his party and the torture of being near him but not actually getting to spend time together, I'm itching to hang out with him.

I send Harvey a message.

you going?

don't know

I think about how I'd feel if one of my family members died. Whether I'd want my friends there. Yeah, I probably would.

think we should go. support him

Harvey's reply comes back quickly.

ok. do you want me to pick you up?

sure

HARVEY PICKS me up the next morning. We're both looking uncharacteristically flash for a Sunday morning. Like we're going to church, although the funeral is being held at the local community center because Oz's family isn't religious.

"Oz probably won't even recognize us," Harvey says as he tugs at his necktie.

"Yeah, probably not." My neck is already itching under the stiff collar of my best shirt.

Over a hundred people sit inside the community center when we arrive. Harvey and I grab seats near the back. I spot Oz up the front with his mum, dad, and brother.

Funerals for old people are way different from funerals for younger people. The only other funeral I've ever been to was when I was twelve and our next-door neighbor's son died in a motorcycle accident.

There was all this anger and grief at that funeral about how robbed Adam had been. But Oz's nan was eighty-nine, and people share dozens of fond stories about her life with soft smiles and quiet tears.

Afterwards, we find Oz milling around the table with the food.

"Hey, man," Harvey says quietly.

"Hey," Oz shoves his hands in his pockets, looking between us. "Thanks for coming."

"No problem," I say.

"It was a really nice service," Harvey offers.

"Yeah, thanks." We all stare at each other. I fidget with my cuff as the silence grows. Now doesn't seem the time for our usual messing around.

Luckily, someone else comes up to talk to Oz then.

"You want to head off soon?" Harvey asks me in an undertone.

"Actually, I don't need a ride home. Someone's picking me up."

Harvey raises his eyebrows. "Who?"

"Cody."

"Oh. Right."

I glance at my watch. He should be here any minute. I grab a club sandwich and a slice of pie. The club sandwiches are egg and ham, which is almost as epic a combination as baloney and cheese.

Oz finishes talking to whatever long-lost relative and joins me in sampling the food.

"Your stepbrother is here to pick you up," Harvey says. He's looking out the big bay window to where Cody's car is idling in the parking lot. Right on cue, my phone vibrates in my pocket.

"He's not my stepbrother," I say. My voice comes out as a growl.

Harvey's eyes widen. "Right, okay then. That's me told."

Oz is standing next to Harvey, looking at me with an identical level of skepticism.

Shit. They're my friends. I probably should be straight with them.

I take a deep breath then plunge on. "I'm fairly sure Cody and I do stuff together that most stepbrothers don't," I say. "But it's okay, because we are not and have never been stepbrothers."

Harvey jerks his head back. "It's like that then, is it?"

"Yeah, it's like that. But it's on the down low, okay? Because things are weird between our parents."

"Yeah, okay," Oz says.

I flick a glance at Harvey. He's staring out the window at where Cody is parked.

"I hope you know what you're doing," he says finally.

Chapter 25

The next Sunday, it's Kate's baby shower.

Before we leave, I send Mum into gales of hysterical laughter when I ask if I need to take my bathing suit.

"So, there's no water involved at all?" I try to clarify between her fits of hysterics.

"No." Mum's wheezing so hard from her laughter that Dad offers her a glass of water. He's grinning too. Yay. I love providing accidental amusement to my parents.

"Why is it called a baby shower then?" I ask.

"I guess it's because we're showering Kate in love and gifts."

"Why not call it a baby bath? We could bathe Kate in love and gifts. Full immersion rather than just dripping water."

Mum tousles my hair as she goes past to put her glass in the dishwasher. "Never change, Ryan. Promise me you'll never change."

"I'm fairly sure that theme goes against nearly all of your other parenting messages," I comment.

Mum's good mood fades in the car. She's sitting in the

front seat while Dad's driving. Kate's present is in her lap, and she's tearing the end of the ribbon into little fraying strips.

I'm anxious too. It was hard enough at Cody's birthday party to pretend nothing is going on between us. Now we've just scaled down the size of the event, and upped the number of parental units who might figure things out.

Kate's chosen to have her baby shower at this cutesy restaurant that serves what looks like regular afternoon tea but puts it on tiered plates and calls it high tea. But after the baby shower ridiculing, I'm not asking any questions.

We're separated out in a back room to give us privacy. Personally, I think this is a bad thing. Mum and Frank would probably behave themselves better if there was public scrutiny.

Kate's invited a few of her old school friends, but as soon as we arrive, it's plainly obvious there aren't enough other people to provide a buffer zone between the two enemy camps.

Mel gives me a strained smile. Cody's there too, already sitting at one of the tables.

I edge my way around to Cody under the guise of greeting him.

"Hey," I say.

"Hey," he replies. His face is strained, and he flicks his gaze away from me.

Cement forms in my stomach. "What's wrong?"

"I think my dad suspects us," he says in a low voice.

"Why?"

"The official photos from the photographer for my birthday came back."

Cody fiddles with his phone, then flashes it under my nose.

On screen is a picture of us. It must have been taken

near the end of the night, long after the cake cutting, when I let myself drift back over toward him. We're standing about a foot apart with absolutely no physical contact between us, but we're laughing together, and there's so much affection in our expressions I can barely stand to look at it.

I can imagine Frank and Heather felt the same way.

"I feel shit that I'm keeping stuff from them," he mutters, stuffing his phone back into his pocket.

I tense. Because this is what I fear deep down. That Cody's desire to be the perfect son will eclipse what we have together. That he'll decide there are lots of other fish in the sea, fish that don't come already tangled up in nets and lines with sharp hooks in them.

He'll realize that Mel and Kate are right. He can do a whole lot better than me.

"Yeah, I get it," is all I manage.

Despite Cody's warning, when it comes time to find somewhere to sit, I make sure I'm next to him. From the way he shuffles over and brushes his leg against mine under the table, he's not complaining.

Kate opens her presents and exclaims over all the tiny outfits. It's hard to believe a real human will fit into the clothes. Actually, it's even harder to believe that a real human is growing inside my sister right now.

Cody has brought his own present, one of those miniature piano things.

"You got to start the baby on the right instrument young," he says.

Kate gives a belly laugh.

For once the perfect brother hasn't completely outdone me, because I've got my own present for Kate and Chris.

Kate's face screws up in confusion as she unwraps a bag of raisins.

"Raisins?" she asks. "You realize the baby won't be eating anything but milk for the first six months, right?"

"Yeah, they're for you. I read somewhere that babies like the taste of whatever their mother eats during pregnancy. So you've got to eat loads of raisins to make sure your child doesn't have any weird phobias. Really, I'm giving your child a lifetime of enjoying raisins."

"Oh right. Um… thanks, Ryan."

I can feel Cody's body silently shaking next to me as he tries to control his laughter. I sneak a look at him and scrunch my nose.

He scrunches his nose in return.

Someone kicks me in the shins under the table. Ouch.

I look across, and Mel's raising her eyebrows, throwing us a pointed look.

Oh, right.

I try to control myself; I really do. But Cody's right there! And my body is now used to expecting that when Cody's in close proximity, epic things happen.

Besides, all the parents are focused on Kate and Chris. They're not paying attention to us.

I deliberately drop my napkin. When I reach down to grab it, I use the opportunity to trail my fingers along Cody's calf.

When I straighten back up, Cody's neck is flushed.

"Stop it," he says between clenched teeth.

"Stop what?" I ask innocently. I move my leg, pressing my thigh into his.

The flush creeps further up his neck. "Bathroom," he breathes.

I give a small nod.

A minute later, Cody stands up, his blush still evident. Avoiding my eyes, he pushes his chair back and weaves his way through the tables in the direction of the bathroom.

He's not paying enough attention to where he's going and whacks into a chair, reaching out to stop it from tipping over.

I wait for a few minutes before following him, ignoring Mel's gaze that's boring holes in my back.

When I make it to the bathroom, he's leaning against the sink.

"Nice play. CIA agents should come to you for training," I say.

He quirks an eyebrow. "Do you want to spend time talking about my levels of subterfuge, or do you want to do other stuff?"

"Definitely other stuff," I say.

Cody grabs my hand and pulls me into a stall, locking it behind us. As soon as he turns back, I'm up in his personal space, my mouth finding his automatically. Our kisses are hot, hard, and furious.

The sound of the door opening bursts my Cody-kissing bubble. I wrench my lips away from him, staring into his dark, panicked gaze.

A guy hums to himself as he uses the urinal.

"Shit," Cody mouths.

I put the toilet seat down and kneel on it, so if anyone looks under the stalls, they'll only see one pair of legs.

We wait until the guy finishes his business, and we hear the click of the door shutting. Climbing off the toilet, I lean up against the wall. Cody's hair is disheveled, and I can't help reaching over to rearrange his curls back into place.

The fear fades from his face into something softer. "This is stupid," he says.

"Yeah." Even though my brain is only functioning on half its normal supply of blood right now, I know he's right. It's way too risky.

Giving him one last kiss, I unlock the stall, sneaking out of the bathroom.

And bump straight into Frank.

Shit. I try very hard to pull my I-wasn't-just-making-out-with-your-son face.

It does nothing to dilute his suspicious look. "Have you seen Cody?"

"Um… yeah. I think he… ah… went to use the bathroom after me."

Mel's right. I'm a shit liar. I can feel my face heating up, and Frank gives me a skeptical look.

Crap. Crap. Crap.

I stumble back to the table.

Cody reemerges a few minutes later, walking back to the table with his dad. I feel Frank's gaze land on us as Cody retakes his seat.

Luckily, people are standing up to play games now, so it's a chance to separate myself from Cody and escape Frank's scrutiny.

As we play the games, I try not to interact with Cody so I don't increase Frank's suspicion. But then I start to worry that it's going to make it worse if I avoid Cody, like we're trying to hide something. Shit. How much interaction is normal between guys who get on well but aren't sticking their tongues down each other's throats?

There's a chance I'm overthinking this.

The last game we play is one where we have to use a piece of string to guess the size of Kate's bump, which she then measures against the real thing to judge the winner.

I ridiculously overestimate how large she is, which Kate takes offense to.

After the game has wrapped up, Cody and I dangle our strings next to each other. He went in the other direction and underestimated the size of her bump, which I mock him about.

"It's way better to be too big than too little," I state. "That's my theory, anyway."

Cody grins at me. "I'm aware that's your theory."

The air between us sizzles.

I rip my gaze away to find Frank standing a few feet from us, watching. Shit.

"Cody says you're doing well in biology now," Frank says abruptly.

"Um… yeah." I wind the string around my hand.

"Maybe you've reached the point where you don't need a tutor anymore?"

Mum's at a nearby table putting tinfoil over the left-overs. But it turns out she's not too busy to defend me. Or maybe she's looking for any excuse to argue against Frank.

"The boys are allowed to be friends, Frank."

Frank's gaze narrows, his eyes going tight. "I've tried to explain to Cody that some friendships are healthier than others," he mutters.

Mum's spine stiffens. "What the hell do you mean by that? Ryan is a great kid."

Frank snorts.

"May I remind you that it was your son who was so drunk at a party that my son had to rescue him?" Mum says. Her grip on the tinfoil tube has tightened. There's a chance she's about to turn it into a weapon.

Beside me, Cody shuffles from one foot to the other. Shit. Our parents are like this when they think we're friends. Imagine what they'd be like if they discovered the truth.

"Cody doesn't need distractions. He's at an age where a few wrong moves can screw up his whole life," Frank says. "I don't want that for him."

Mum bristles, putting the tinfoil down with a bang. "Are you ever going to forgive me for getting pregnant? You realize I screwed up my life as well? It wasn't just your magical music career that had to be sacrificed. I had to give up my dreams too."

Well, that escalated quickly. It's a supreme talent they have.

Kate steps forward. "As I'm the product of your unplanned pregnancy, I don't want to hear about how much I screwed up your lives, okay?" Her voice is defiant, but tears glisten in her eyes.

Chris leans over and squeezes her hand.

Luckily, her words deflate both Mum and Frank. Mum picks up the tinfoil again and continues to wrap up leftover sandwiches with venom, snapping the foil violently. I don't think tinfoil has ever been so abused.

Cody meets my eyes, and I can see my own distress reflected in them.

We've just given our parents another arena to battle in. Fantastic.

HALF AN HOUR after I get home, I get a message from Cody.

that was shit what happened between your mum and my dad

I twist my phone in my hands as I decide how to reply. Do I want to start a conversation about the crap we're going to have to deal with at some point? Instead, I go for a different angle.

good news is we can't repeat our parents' history

what do you mean?

you can't impregnate me so you won't have to give up your music career to support me and our child

Cody's reply comes back almost immediately.

knew there was an upside to liking boys
yeah don't forget it

Chapter 26

On Wednesday, Cody turns up at my house for our usual tutoring session. He doesn't say anything regarding his dad's comments about tutoring me, and I don't mention it either.

I can feel the combined weight of our parents' disapproval hanging over both of us though.

Our tutoring sessions have now moved into my bedroom because they've become a combination of tutoring and making out. I guess I'm getting a biology lesson either way. I definitely prefer the practical lessons where I have my hands on Cody's body.

We don't fool around the entire time though, because Cody's even more committed to me doing well in biology than I am.

"So, you just have to decide whether the mutation means that particular triplet will now code for a different amino acid," he says, pointing to a table in the textbook.

"Yeah, I see." I lean over and nudge my nose at the spot just behind his ear, which I know drives him crazy.

"And if it codes for a different amino acid, then it's likely the mutation will affect the organism."

"Right." I continue with my nudging.

He throws his pen down. "Are you paying attention to what I'm saying?"

"I'm multitasking," I say.

"Multitasking, huh?"

"Yeah, I'm a great multi-tasker." I press my lips softly to that same spot.

He sucks in a deep breath then spins around to capture my mouth in a lazy kiss.

But things between Cody and I never stay in lazy mode. They make the quantum leap to hot and heavy incredibly quickly.

I'm so caught up in kissing him, I don't hear footsteps on the stairs or that creaky floorboard outside my room that usually gives warning that someone is approaching.

Suddenly the door is edging open.

Cody and I jump apart.

But from the expression on Mum's face as she stands in my doorway, I don't think our reflexes were quick enough.

Shit.

It's like a game of freeze tag where we're all frozen in position, staring at each other.

I don't want to berate my mother for coming into my room without knocking. Because it would confirm the suspicion that's currently running rampant all over her face.

I recover first. "You're home early."

"I finished early today." Mum's eyes dart between Cody and me.

"Did you want something?" I ask.

Mum clears her throat. "I was just checking to see if

you had any dirty clothes. I'm about to throw in a load of laundry."

"Um… I should have some."

I hunt out my dirty socks that have somehow found their way under my bed.

"These should probably come with a health hazard label," Mum jokes as I hand them over. But her smile doesn't reach her eyes, and she continues to stand there watching us before retreating. She leaves the door wide open and I don't hear her footsteps, which means she's hovering in the hallway.

Cody's got his freaked-out face on. "I better get going."

"I'll walk you out, make sure you don't steal anything," I say.

When we emerge from my room, Mum makes like she's just heading down the stairs now.

We follow her down. Cody makes a beeline for the front door.

"Bye," he says to Mum's back.

"Bye, Cody," her voice is polite.

On the doorstep Cody turns to me, biting his lower lip. Which sucks, because all I can think of now is how I want to be nibbling on it. But I'm sure Mum will be watching out the window right now.

"Do you think she saw?"

I don't want to lie to him. But I don't want to add to his freak out.

"Maybe," I say.

"Shit."

"Don't stress. There's nothing we can do about it now."

"It just seems dangerous for your parents to know. What if they say something to my parents?"

"Yeah, because our parents confide everything in each other. They're besties like that."

Cody's eyebrows draw together. "Message me and let me know if she says anything, okay?"

"Okay."

I watch him climb into his car and drive away.

When I head back inside, Mum comes out of the laundry carrying an empty basket.

"You survived the fumes then," I say.

"Yeah." She sets the basket down on the table then fixes me with a look.

I stand there, waiting.

"You and Cody…" Mum says hesitantly.

Oh shit. Here it comes.

"Yeah?"

"You're just friends… right?"

Here's where I could lie, give Mum the answer I know she desperately wants. But I don't. Because denying this thing with Cody doesn't feel like a little lie. It feels like trying to deny the existence of my right foot.

"Um… we're a bit more than friends, actually."

Her face falls. "How much more?"

"Do you seriously want details?" I raise an eyebrow.

"I'm taking it his parents don't know?"

"No. Of course not."

She looks down, running her finger absentmindedly across the edge of the basket. "Is it… something you see continuing for a while?"

I clear my throat. "Yeah. I mean, possibly."

"I see."

"Look on the bright side. At least you know the future in-laws already."

Mum jerks her head up. "Do you think that's funny?"

"What? No. I don't think it's funny at all."

Mum's nostrils flare. "Is that why you're doing this, Ryan? Because you think it's amusing to see how Frank and I will react?"

Oh, for God's sake. So typical that she thinks it's all about her and Frank. Some of my anger comes out in my voice.

"No. I actually don't think it's at all funny. It's not funny that the guy I—" I swallow. "—the guy I care about has parents who you hate."

"I don't hate Frank and Heather."

I snort. "Sure, Mum. You keep telling yourself that."

AFTER DINNER, I'm in my room trying to make sense of the biology Cody was attempting to explain to me this afternoon, when there's a knock on the door.

"Come in."

Dad pokes his head around. At least one of my parents understands the concept of knocking.

"Can we have a chat?" he asks.

My muscle fibers feel twitchy, like my body is preparing to go into fight-or-flight mode.

I lean back in my chair and level him with a look. "Seriously? She sent you in here?"

Dad rubs at the back of his neck. "Your mum just thought I should have a talk with you."

"If this is another birds and the bees talk, I think we can both agree the first one provided a lifetime supply of awkwardness. We don't need a repeat."

Ha. I was thirteen, and I swear my father had scripted out ahead of time every word he would say. However, he was definitely not prepared for my question, "Okay, so that covers everything with girls. But what about when you have sex with a guy?"

"This is not a birds and the bees talk," he says. "Though I hope you remember the key points of that, about staying safe in all situations."

"Trust me, the words 'always use a condom' are forever imprinted on my brain," I mutter.

"That's good to hear." Dad moves across my room to perch on the end of my bed, facing me.

I stare at him expectantly. I'm not about to make this easy for him.

"Cody seems like a great guy," he begins hesitantly.

"He is." I glance over at the photo I've pinned on the wall beside my bed. The one I had printed on Cody's guitar pick. Orakahau beach at sunrise. The optimistic, life-is-awesome feeling that the photo normally inspires in me fails to launch right now.

"And if he was anyone else, your mum and I would be happy to see you settling down and having a proper relationship," Dad continues.

"But he's not anyone else," I prompt.

Dad sighs, pushing his glasses back up his nose. "No, he's not. Relationships are complicated things, Ryan. And like it or not, families play a part in any relationship. And you and Cody, you share sisters, don't forget. What happens if things end badly between you? How do you think it will affect your relationship with Mel and Kate?"

I shrug. "Mel and Kate have always liked Cody more than me. They'll be on his side for sure."

"Mel and Kate are your sisters, and deep down I know they care for you and you care for them."

"Maybe Cody and I will go live on some island in the Caribbean, far, far away from all of you," I say.

Dad gives me a look. "How does that fit in with Cody's plans to become a musician?"

I give another shrug, looking down at my desk. I pretend my textbook is a fascinating read.

"You're young. You don't want something like this distracting you from your future."

I snap my head up. "He's not distracting me. If anything, Cody is helping me. And I'm helping him too."

"Just think about what I've said, okay?"

"You don't get it, Dad." The words tumble out without permission.

"What don't I get?"

I'm silent for a few seconds. I don't know how to put into words, what I want to say.

"It's not like a tap. You can't just turn it off because it's not convenient," I say finally.

"We just want to make sure you're going into this with your eyes open."

My eyes are taped open, into a wide-eyed stare. I can't blink, even if I wanted to.

Chapter 27

The good thing about my parents knowing is not having to hide it anymore. Which means Cody doesn't have to be here only under the guise of tutoring.

On Saturday afternoon he comes over just as Mum is going out. She doesn't even bother to hide her grimace when she sees him. I'm sure she's adopted the same attitude to my relationship with Cody as she did to my short-lived death metal obsession—hoping it's a phase I'll grow out of quickly.

As soon as we get to my room, I dive on my bed then pat the spot beside me.

Cody obligingly plops down next to me, but his forehead is creased.

"Your mum really isn't happy about us, is she?"

"Not really," I admit.

He runs his hands through his hair and puffs out a breath. "That sucks."

I shrug. "We're like Romeo and Juliet with the messed-up families."

Cody props himself up on his arm. "Who's Romeo and who's Juliet?"

"Well, you are a lot prettier than me," I say.

"I'll take that as a compliment." He leans forward and kisses me.

Sometimes when Cody and I are apart, doubt creeps into my head because so many things seem stacked against us. But as soon as we're back together, the doubt dissolves. I think the solution is to not spend much time away from him.

I kiss him back hard, and Cody moans into my mouth. The sounds Cody makes when we're fooling around is my personal favorite playlist.

Unfortunately, just as we're settling into the kiss, Cody's phone intrudes, buzzing in his pocket.

Cody pulls away from me to check it. "It's my dad."

Frank. If ever there was a libido killer, he's it.

I lean backwards, breathing hard. "Are you going to answer it?"

"Nah, he'll call back if it's important. Besides, I'm busy." Cody chucks his phone on the bed. He has a gleam in his eye as he tugs my T-shirt, pulling it over my head. His fingers map a path down my chest. It's beginning to be a well-travelled path.

Cody's phone buzzes again where it's facedown on my duvet, like an angry wasp about to sting.

He picks it up. "Shit. It's Dad again."

"You better answer it," I say.

"Okay. Hold that thought."

"Oh, I'll definitely hold it."

But Cody misses my hilarious innuendo because he's too busy answering the phone.

"Hey, Dad, what's up?"

I immediately know something's wrong. Cody's entire body folds in on itself, like an air mattress deflating.

"When did it happen?" His face is ashen.

"Yeah, I'll be there as soon as I can."

Cody hangs up. He's blinking rapidly, but I get the feeling he's not seeing much at the moment.

"What's wrong?"

"It's my mum," he says. "I need to get to the hospital."

WE ARRIVE at the hospital before Frank. On the phone, Frank told Cody that Heather collapsed at the gym and was rushed to hospital by ambulance, and the unfriendly receptionist won't tell us anything more.

They won't let Cody in to see her because they're still evaluating her, whatever that means. So we sit on the cold, hard plastic chairs in a small waiting room the receptionist pointed us to. A pile of what once were magazines but are now torn, tatty corpses stacked on a chair by the door. An attempt to make the room cheery with a large picture of flowers on one wall is immediately undone by the over-whelming smell of disinfectant.

Frank arrives looking flustered. He takes an automatic step towards us before his gaze slides to me and his shoulders slump.

I have a stab of regret that at one of the worst moments in his life, I'm making it worse for him. But as long as I'm providing some comfort to Cody, I'm staying.

"What's he doing here?" Frank asks. I seize up.

"We were together when you called me," Cody says.

Frank looks between us, his eyebrows bunching together in a scowl.

"The receptionist won't tell me anything," Cody says.

"I'll try to find a doctor." Frank moves briskly away.

"Do you want me to go?" I ask Cody when Frank has disappeared.

"No. Stay. Please."

Cody leans his head back against the wall, closing his eyes. He seems to be offering up a silent prayer.

All the words I want to offer—*It'll be okay. I'm sure it's nothing serious. Your mum will be fine*—they dry up on my tongue when I see the look on Cody's face. Because I can't offer him any guarantees. And I know that's all he wants right now.

Frank comes back into the waiting room.

Cody snaps his eyes open. "Did they tell you anything?"

"No. They're still evaluating her."

Frank sits down on one of the plastic seats, then jumps up almost immediately and starts pacing. He glances a few times at us, but not for long. It's like he can't bear to keep his eyes on us.

Mel arrives in a fluster of tears and questions. She gives her dad a hug then Cody before turning to me.

"Hey, Ry." She gives my shoulder a squeeze.

Somehow Mel's arrival makes me feel even more out of place. Which is weird because Mel is part of my family. But it just highlights the fact that I'm not part of this particular family.

Who should I be offering comfort to?

My boyfriend, whose mother is sick? Definitely.

My half-sister, whose stepmother is sick? Probably.

My mother's ex-husband, whose wife is sick? Maybe. But I'm the last person in the world he wants comfort from.

And I can't think of any words that will help anyone. So I stay mute.

Mel takes a seat against the other wall. Her eyes dart

between Frank and me.

Frank's eyes narrow.

Is he wondering why Mel hasn't asked why I'm here? Is Mel's acceptance of my presence with Cody automatically making Frank suspicious about the true nature of our relationship?

Damn, there are so many layers of complications between us all.

A doctor comes into the waiting room, and Frank strides over to her. Cody jumps up too, and Mel follows with an anxious look on her face.

I stay on the cold, hard seats.

"Heather Abbot's family?" The doctor is in her mid-twenties yet wears a tired expression of someone a lot older.

Frank's face is a combination of anticipation and fear. "Yes, I'm her husband. This is my son and daughter."

Even if I was standing right there, I don't think he'd acknowledge me. Because I'm no one in this scenario.

"Your wife had a stroke," she says.

"A stroke?" Frank reels back.

Cody raises his hands to his mouth.

"It looks like a minor one, but it's lucky she was brought to the hospital so quickly."

The doctor continues to talk, but I'm distracted from my eavesdropping by Cody's phone. He's left it on the seat next to me, and now it starts to buzz. Kate's name flashes on the screen.

Should I answer it? I know they haven't been able to get hold of Kate yet. She hasn't replied to anyone's messages.

I glance at Frank, Cody, and Mel, but they're still talking to the doctor. Cody's running his hands through his hair, biting his lip.

I pick up his phone and answer it.

"Hey, it's me," I say in a hushed voice.

"Ryan? Why are you answering Cody's phone? What's going on?"

"I'm at the hospital with Cody. Heather collapsed. The doctor is just talking to your dad now. She's saying they think it's a stroke."

"Oh, my God. I'll be right there."

"Yeah, okay."

Kate hangs up, and I put the phone gently back down on the seat.

The doctor leaves, and Cody stumbles back over to me. His hair is so rumpled, and my fingers twitch to smooth it out, but I resist the urge.

"Um… Kate called. I told her to come here," I tell him in a low voice.

"Oh… okay." Cody rubs his forehead. "Mum's had a stroke."

"Yeah, I heard the doctor say that."

"She's only fifty-two," he whispers. "How could she have a stroke?"

"They got her to the hospital fast. Apparently that's really positive," Mel says.

The conversation swirls around this topic for a while, recycling the little the doctor said, wringing out every ounce of meaning.

Frank doesn't say anything. He's sitting down a few empty chairs away, his head in his hands.

"I'll go grab us some coffee or something," Mel says. "I think we're in for a long wait."

Damn. I should have offered to grab coffee. Anything to get me away from Frank.

But then, I don't want to leave Cody.

When Mel leaves, Cody's face crumbles in on itself.

I can't stand to see him like this.

A tear slides down his face, and without thinking, I reach up and wipe it away with my thumb. His skin is smooth, and he leans into my hand so my palm is cupping the side of his face.

"No," Frank says.

I snap my head up, jerking my hand from Cody's face like I've been scorched.

Frank's shaking his head violently, staring at the two of us. "No," he repeats.

"Dad…" Cody begins. He swallows, glancing at me.

Frank's glare is unrelenting as he pins Cody and me with it. "Whatever this is, it ends now. Your mum will need all the support she can get. You cannot do this to her."

Cody flinches. "But Dad…"

"You are not doing this to your mum," he says, standing up. "She needs us. She does not need this." He gestures at me. "It ends now."

He gives me a filthy glare as he stalks away, following where Mel disappeared down the hallway.

"Shit," Cody says. He slumps down, looking so miserable.

I grab his hand and squeeze it. "Yeah," I say. Because he's pretty much summed up the situation.

Cody's breathing hard, his chin trembling. He slowly withdraws his hand from mine. "You should probably go."

I try to push down the hurt swelling inside me. "Yeah, okay."

"I'll walk you out," he says.

"No, you stay here."

"No, I'm coming."

Our footsteps make solemn sounds on the linoleum as we walk down the hallway.

The front entranceway of the hospital is busy. People in

different colored scrubs bustle past. One guy comes in the electronic doors holding a bunch of bright yellow helium balloons. I follow the progress of the balloons bobbing down the hallway before I finally turn to Cody.

"I'm sorry," he says. His voice cracks, splintering.

"I get it," I say. I try to ignore the tightness in my chest as I continue. "I guess we always knew this thing had an expiration date. I was just hoping it was something with a long-life expiry."

Cody doesn't even attempt a smile. He stares at me, his blue eyes pools of misery.

I have to look away.

Taking a deep breath, I force the next words out. "I just want to do whatever I can to help," I say. "If that means staying away, I can do that."

Emotions wrestle on his face. "Please," he says finally.

And so I turn and walk away.

Chapter 28

I send Cody a message that night.

hope your mum is doing ok. thinking of you all. let me know if there is anything I can do to help.

As the hours turn into a day, I give up checking my phone every few minutes for a reply.

Over the next week, I discover the one good thing about Cody and I sharing sisters—I can keep tabs on what's happening with Heather via Mel and Kate.

Luckily, Heather's stroke wasn't too bad. Mel reports that her speech is slurred, and the left side of her face is droopy, and she's struggling to walk properly. But because she was taken to the hospital so quickly, her chances of making a full recovery are high. She's discharged from hospital after three days.

Apparently, Frank has employed home help to be with her during the day and drive her to appointments. Cody's pulled out of his school's next musical concert so he can be with her as much as possible.

My mum is in that awkward position of what to do

when something bad happens to someone you don't like very much. Her solution is to bake a casserole.

"Can you deliver this to Frank and Heather?" she asks me as I wander into the kitchen and she's just finished making a tuna noodle casserole.

I shake my head. "No. I'm not going there anymore."

"Oh," she pulls up. "Have things... changed between you?"

"Yeah. With his mum and stuff..." I trail off.

"It's probably for the best," Mum says.

I turn away so she can't see my face. How can the way I'm feeling right now be for the best? How?

Mum gets Kate to deliver the casserole instead.

OVER THE NEXT FEW WEEKS, I respect what Cody wants. I don't contact him.

There's this giant void in my life that nothing can fill. I try my hardest. I hang out with my friends. I study. I go surfing as much as I can, even though the weather has definitely turned to autumn and both the water and the air have a chill I can't escape from.

"So, this thing with you and Cody. It's over now?" Mel asks one night when she's over for dinner and we're doing the dishes together.

I shrug as I scrub at some baked cheese on a dish. I have no idea if Cody and I are completely over or if this is just a break. It's up to him. It has nothing to do with me.

All I know is that I feel like my insides have been ground up and pummeled.

I get that he can't handle his father's disapproval at the moment. I get that he needs to focus on his mum, that he doesn't want to do anything to upset her. I get all that.

When I think about Cody—which is first thing every morning, last thing every night, and multiple times during the day—it feels like I'm out surfing in waves that are far too big for me and I've tumbled off my board. I'm trying to claw my way to the surface, but I only manage to get small mouthfuls of air before I'm sucked underwater again.

KATE GOES into labor one Saturday morning, which sends Mum into a frenzy. Although it turns out that babies don't come that fast. We hang out at home all afternoon and evening, waiting.

Chris provides hourly updates. Things are progressing, but slowly.

Mum calls him around ten, but I catch a few snatches of words like cervix and dilation and decide I don't need to know exact details.

When I wake up the next morning, there's still no baby.

My phone finally beeps with a message from Chris around Sunday lunchtime.

It's a boy!

I run down the stairs, but for once Mum has been monitoring her phone because she's standing in the living room, already crying.

Dad comes in from the garden, holding his phone.

"Congrats, Grandma." He wraps her in a hug.

"So, are we going to go meet this kid or what?" I ask after the hugging extends way too long.

Mum takes a deep breath. "Let's go."

On the way to the hospital, the idea that I might be about to see Cody for the first time in two weeks sinks in. Anticipation and dread start a battle for control of my throat. The mixture is boiling up inside me when we reach Kate's room.

Is he inside? Am I about to come face to face with Cody? How will he react? How will Frank react when he sees me?

But when we go in, the room is empty besides Kate and Chris.

Oh yeah, and a baby.

I don't know if I'm relieved or disappointed. I don't appear to be capable of straightforward emotions anymore.

Mum makes a beeline for Kate lying propped up on the hospital bed. Kate looks tired but beams, holding a bundle of blankets. It doesn't take much brainpower to work out my nephew is inside.

Mum gives her a kiss on the top of her head and peers down at the baby, her face going all soft.

"Congratulations." Dad shakes Chris's hand.

"Oh, yeah, congrats," I say.

Chris gives me a hug too, then hugs Mum. Basically, it's a whole hugging festival happening in room 22.

I go to give Kate a hug and look at the newest member of the family.

Jesus.

It takes Herculean control to stop myself recoiling back. The baby has got a weird-shaped cone head, and his features are all scrunched up in the middle of his face, and his skin has a weird blueish-purplish tinge.

The kid is not winning any beauty awards at the moment, that's for sure. The closest thing I can come to describing him is a mutant Smurf.

Luckily, I have a survival instinct, so I keep that observation to myself.

"Do you want to hold your grandson?" Kate asks Mum.

Tears well in Mum's eyes as she nods. Kate carefully lowers the baby into Mum's arms. I'm peering over her shoulder, trying to scrounge a single feature I can compliment, when there's a noise at the door.

It's Frank.

My breath slams out of me.

Because, behind Frank comes Heather in a wheelchair with Cody pushing her. He scans the room, stopping when his gaze locks on me.

For a second we just stare at each other before he looks down and fiddles with the wheelchair brake.

I stumble backwards, collapsing into one of the visitor's chairs in the corner.

I can do this. I can do this.

"Hello," Frank says stiffly. He goes around to Kate's other side, giving her a quick hug, glancing over to his grandson in Mum's arms.

"It's a little boy," Mum says softly, lifting her gaze to Frank.

Frank's staring at her, and there's something in his eyes that's not the usual animosity they have when they look at each other.

Sadness.

I recognize it because it's an emotion that I'm overly familiar with at the moment.

Why are they so sad? Have they finally realized that this is what happens when you mess up your family? That it continues to mess up the next generations too?

I flick a glance at Cody, and he's standing with one hand holding Heather's wheelchair, his gaze fixed on the floor. But I can't miss the look of despair on his face.

Oh God.

Although, am I just projecting what I'm feeling onto him? Is he just awkward because seeing your ex is always some degree of awkward?

"Have you decided on a name yet?" Dad asks.

Kate smiles. "Yes. Ethan."

"Oh, that's lovely," Mum says.

Frank manages an upturn of his lips. "Ethan what?"

Kate's eyes dart to Chris. "We haven't decided on a middle name yet."

"Ethan Ryan has a nice ring to it," I say. "Just putting it out there."

Kate rolls her eyes. "Thanks, Ryan. I'll keep that in mind."

Mum reluctantly hands Ethan over to Frank, and Cody approaches, staring down at Ethan with his brow furrowed, with that Cody look of concentration.

The pain stabs at me unexpectedly, and my eyes sting.

"I'm going to grab something from the vending machine," I mutter, avoiding eye contact as I leave.

On the way to the vending machine, I spot a bathroom, so I duck inside.

Gripping the sides of the basin, I stare at myself in the mirror. I look haunted, like I've just seen all the *Chucky* movies back-to-back.

I really need to get my shit together.

I'm splashing some water on my face when the bathroom door opens.

Cody.

Shit.

We stare at each other.

Did he follow me in here? Or is it a total coincidence?

Hope surges inside me that he wanted to talk to me, but Cody looks seriously freaked.

The hope dies a dismal death. Coincidence then.

"Hey," he says.

"Hey," I reply, my voice thick.

The last bathroom we were in together was at Kate's baby shower. Was that really only a few weeks ago? I wonder if Cody is remembering that now.

He hesitates, then comes over to stand at the sink next to me. His hand trembles as he turns on the tap.

"Your mum seems better," I say as I grab some paper towels. My eyes meet his in the mirror.

Unspoken words lie trapped on my tongue. *Will you ever want me again? Will you ever get past your dad's disapproval? Do you feel anything near the same way about me as I feel for you?*

"Yeah," he says.

I finish drying my hands.

My hand is on the doorknob when Cody speaks. "Ryan." His voice is coated in so much anguish and desperation that I whirl around.

He closes the distance between us in a few steps, and he's kissing me.

Actually, it goes past the definition of kissing. Cody is consuming my mouth. I can taste his desperation, feel it in the way his tongue tangles with mine, the way his lips are unyieldingly hard. I kiss him back with the same ferocity. Like I'm an addict getting my first hit in weeks.

We stumble back against the door. Cody crowding me so I can feel his whole body pressed against mine.

It feels incredible. Amazing.

It feels… right.

"Shit." He abruptly pulls away and retreats a few steps, raking his hands through his hair. Regret is in every line of his body. It gashes me. He can't look me in the eyes.

My thudding heart is now playing the beat of a sad, sad song.

"I'm sorry. I didn't mean for that to happen," he mutters, still not looking at me.

My throat is clogged, but somehow I force out a light-hearted tone. "It's okay. I want to be a paramedic, you know. Emergency mouth-to-mouth is kind of our thing."

Cody doesn't even lift a corner of his mouth in response. "Sorry," he repeats. He pushes past me, leaving me standing there alone.

"It's okay," I say again to the empty bathroom.

WHEN I SLIP BACK into Kate's room, Cody's sitting on the windowsill. The sun behind him highlights his curls, so he looks like one of those avenging angels from the movies. One of those characters where you're not sure whether they're coming to earth to reap destruction or salvation.

I lean against the opposite wall and force myself to smile. I make myself laugh. I tell jokes and make comparisons about the baby and bald movie stars.

Basically, I do everything I can possibly do to paper over the cracks forming deep inside me. Because I get the feeling that once I fall into the blackness, I'm not finding my way out anytime soon.

The few times my eyes dart to Cody, he's studying the floor with his intense concentration face on. As if the linoleum contains the answers to all the secrets of the universe.

Is he trying as hard as I am not to fall apart? Or is he simply avoiding looking at me because he's embarrassed?

When it all boils down, he can walk away from me.

But I could never walk away from him.

The knowledge sits in my throat, providing a choking sensation every time I swallow.

Because that's what it comes down to, right? Cody can

walk away, find someone who his parents will approve of. I'm sure his mum will get over the gay thing if he brings home someone like him. Another musician, maybe. Someone who is smart, focused, someone who suits him better than me.

He can replace me. But there is no way I can ever replace him.

Chapter 29

It doesn't take long for Ethan to become another rope in Mum and Frank's endless tug-of-war game.

He's a tiny baby who, from what I've seen, currently can't do anything more than poop, sleep, cry, and eat. Yet somehow his existence has triggered another level of carnage. Mum and Frank are turning grandparenting into a competitive sport. Next thing you know, they'll be registering it for the Olympics.

Mum gets all offended that Kate decided to use some crib that came from Frank's aunt instead of the one she brought her.

"She said it offers more support for his back or something ridiculous like that," I hear her complaining to Dad one night, her voice tight. "I know it's really because she doesn't want to upset her father. She's always been a Daddy's girl. Always worried more about what he thinks than about my feelings."

Dad murmurs something in reply.

"And she didn't even want to hear my advice on the best way to wrap him. Apparently, Heather has this technique that works perfectly, so she doesn't want to try another way."

I quickly discover that the best strategy is to avoid any mention of babies or else it triggers a Mum rant. On the plus side, I now know a lot more about why babies should sleep on their backs rather than their sides.

Saturday night, I wander into the kitchen to find Mum baking peanut brownies. As they're Kate's favorite, I assume they're for her.

"Are you taking those to Kate?" I ask innocently.

Mum's back stiffens. "No. Kate's made it perfectly clear she doesn't need anything from me," she snaps.

Oh shit. More crap has obviously gone down.

"Whatever," I say, backing out of the room.

I'm heading out to a party with my friends. I should be studying for my upcoming biology exam, but I want to forget about my messed up family for a while. I want to forget about Cody's messed up family and the places where our messed up families overlap. I want to forget about missing him, forget about his eyes and smile and laugh and talking to him and listening to his songs and the way it feels to kiss him.

I just want to forget.

AT THE PARTY, I throw myself into Operation Forget. Which starts off by pouring a cup of beer down my throat.

"You pacing yourself?" Oz asks.

"Yup. I'm going exactly the right pace I want to go tonight," I say as I pour myself another drink from the keg and swing half of it back in one gulp.

"Hey, man," Oz says, concern in his voice.

But I turn away from him and wander through the living room. Already the remains of crushed potato chips litter the carpet. Someone's going to have fun cleaning it up tomorrow. Not my problem, though.

Although, I can relate to the chips—I know what it's like to be ground up into pieces.

Shit, I really need to get out of my head tonight.

"Hey, Ryan." In the hallway, Jasmine from my chemistry class gazes at me with her large eyes. Randomly, she's sucking on a lollipop.

"You want one?" She offers me a wrapped green lollipop from the pocket of her jean jacket.

"Nah, it's okay. I'm sweet enough," I say. My brain already feels fuzzy from the beer. I lean against the wall and take another swing from my cup, draining it.

"I bet you are." Jasmine flicks me a wink that's about as subtle as a Miley Cyrus dance move.

I just stare at her, my brain pulling a blank about how to reply.

Shit. It's like I've forgotten how to flirt. It used to be one of my superpowers.

"Ryan!" Someone calls my name, saving me from the awkward silence that's building up between Jasmine and me.

"See you around," I mutter, turning and heading toward the sound like it's a life preserver.

Until I realize who it is.

Grace.

And because he's pretty much attached to her hip, Marco is here as well.

My steps slow.

Just what I need. Because I'm sure I'm not going to get through this conversation without Cody's name being mentioned.

"Cody's a mess. What the hell happened between you guys?" Marco blurts at first sight.

My stomach drops. I knew it. My newly developed psychic powers reign supreme.

"Just what was always going to happen." I look away from his gaze, shrugging. "The shit between our families got in the way."

"Well, why don't you try to unclog some of the shit? Because he's f-king miserable."

Without realizing it, I've crushed my empty plastic cup in my hand.

I'm miserable. And I don't want to hear about Cody being miserable. I don't want to feel sorry for him, because ultimately, this is his decision.

"Yeah, this is the kind of shit that's not able to be cleaned away, you know?" I say.

Grace is looking at me with sympathy stamped on her face, which I really can't handle right now.

I need another beer.

As I head back to the kitchen, I realize anger has set up a permanent home in my stomach, sloshing bitterly.

Part of me is actually pissed at Cody. Pissed that he didn't care enough about us to stand up to his dad. I get that he was placed in an impossible situation. I get that. But now it's been weeks, and he still hasn't changed his mind. He kissed me at the hospital then regretted it.

I arrive in the crowded kitchen, snagging myself another cup as I make a beeline for the keg.

Oz intercepts me before I reach the keg. "Hey, slow down, okay?"

I reach past him. "What are you, my keeper?"

Oz grabs at my arm, stopping me. "Is this about Cody?"

I meet his gaze, and his brown eyes are watching me, concerned. I still my hand and swallow. "Yeah. Pretty much."

"Come on." He indicates his head toward the living room.

I reluctantly follow him, pushing past people laughing and talking loudly, avoiding eye contact with anyone.

Oz finds a recently vacated couch and sits down.

I park myself next to him. "You want a heart-to-heart?" I mock.

Oz doesn't let my tone deter him, giving me a cut-the-bullshit stare. "I'm checking you're okay. Because I've never seen you like this."

I look away from his gaze. "Yeah, well, it's never been like this for me before."

"Did you tell Cody that?"

I shrug. "What's the point?"

Oz goes to say something, but we're interrupted by Harvey perching on the side of the couch and leaning down.

"Gee, this conversation looks more serious than an Ebola convention. You guys need to channel a bulb and lighten the hell up." Harvey cackles at his own joke.

Neither Oz nor I laugh.

His face goes serious, and he looks between us. "What's going on?"

"Just talking about Ryan and Cody's breakup," Oz says reluctantly.

"It was always going to be a shit storm," Harvey says.

"Yeah," I say, standing up. "Yeah, it was."

I quit my quest to get another beer because I know Oz is still watching me and it's not worth arguing with him. Instead, I go watch the game of beer pong that has started on the dining room table.

"You in, Ryan?" Eddie asks me, offering me up an orange ping pong ball.

"Nah." I'm not in the playing mood tonight.

"Where did you run away to before?" It's Jasmine again, sidling up to me.

"Just needed a refreshment break," I say.

"I thought we could get to know each other better."

She's hot, with long hair and pouty lips. She's lost the lollipop, but her lips shine with its syrupy sweetness.

"You want to see if our chemistry extends outside the classroom?" I say.

I know she's into me by how hard she laughs at my joke. It wasn't that funny.

She presses up against me, making sure I feel her generous curves.

Previously, I would have been all over her, trying to lose myself in someone new. She's right there in front of me, an invitation in her eyes. A mouth offering potential ruin. But I can't.

Because it would be the wrong lips kissing me, the wrong hands sliding on my skin.

"Sorry," I say abruptly, pulling away.

"What's wrong?" she asks.

"I can't. I'm… I'm still hung up on someone."

Jasmine studies me, her head tilted to the side. "Have you told this girl how you feel?"

"It's not a her. It's a him. And yeah, he knows."

Jasmine shrugs. "Then you've done all you can, right?"

"Yeah, I guess." I stuff my hands in my pocket.

"Get back to me when you're in a different headspace," she says, sauntering away.

Fuck, I'd cut off my own head and transplant it onto someone else if it meant I'd get in a different headspace.

I walk outside. There's no one out here, partly because it's turn-your-chest-hair-into-icicles freezing tonight.

I'm sobering up now, big time. The cold night air slaps me back to reality.

I trudge over to the pool that glints darkly in the moonlight. It's cold, but I'm in a masochistic mood, so I strip off my shoes and socks, rolling up my jeans so I can sit on the edge of the swimming pool and dangle my feet in the water. The cold water finishes the job of sobering me up. Which is good, because my brain is churning over a new concept, and I need all of my brainpower to think this through.

Both Oz and Jasmine asked me something tonight that I can't stop thinking about.

Cody knows how I feel about him, doesn't he?

But I never really laid it out, did I? I walked away because of the amount I cared, not the opposite. He knows that, surely?

I think of how he asked if we were exclusive, how he said he didn't know where he stood with me. How our sisters accused me of just messing around with him.

That's the problem with joking around all the time. No one gets it when you're actually serious about something. I've been so worried about protecting myself, about not being good enough for him, I haven't been straight up with him about how I feel.

I need to tell him.

I take a long time, my feet dangling in the freezing water, to compose the few lines of my message. *hey, just want to say I'm still here. these last few months haven't just been messing around for me. you're my shot of tequila. i'll wait.*

My stomach is sloshing as I press the send button. Nerves and beer do not play nice together.

Ten minutes later, my phone lights up with his reply.

Don't wait for me.

Chapter 30

Don't wait for me.

The words are like vicious vultures, circulating in my head. Ready to peck me to death.

I'm in a deep, dark place. A hole at the bottom of the ocean. I can look up and see past the miles and miles of blackness to the a hint of light at the top, but there's no way I'm breaking the surface anytime soon.

I'm curled up in my bed. It's midmorning, and Mum and Dad have gone to work. Mum's left her car for me because I'm supposed to have my biology exam this morning. But I watch the time tick down on my clock on the wall with mild indifference.

Does it really matter if I don't show up?

Nothing matters much at the moment.

There's a creak on the stairs, and my pulse picks up. No one else is supposed to be in the house.

Then my muscles relax. If it's an axe murderer, then they can have me. Might be an easy way to go. End the pain.

"Hey, don't you have an exam today?" Mel's standing

in my doorway. Her expression is probably similar to an axe murderer as she sees me lying in bed.

"What are you doing here?" I manage.

"I wanted to study somewhere quiet, and Mum said I could do it here. She said you had your biology exam today." Mel raised an eyebrow pointedly.

"What's the point?" I mutter as I roll over.

But it appears my sister isn't done with me because I hear footsteps approaching my bed.

"What the hell is going on?" she asks.

"What do you mean, what's going on?" I stare resolutely at the wall. I've ripped down the photo of the sunrise at Orakahau, but a piece of squished Blu Tack is embedded in the wallpaper.

"I mean, why aren't you going to your exam?"

I reach out to squash the Blu Tack further into the wallpaper. "Why bother? I'm probably not going to get a good mark, anyway. What's the point of trying?"

"But you've been working hard."

Tears threaten, and I put a hand to my eye socket, trying to force them back. I'd punch them into submission if I could. Because it doesn't matter how hard I work on things, it turns to shit. Not caring is a much better option. Only it's fucking too late for that now, isn't it?

"This is not just about your exam, is it?" Mel says slowly.

"What do you mean?" I turn over to look at her.

"This retreat to your bed, shut out the world mode. This isn't just you freaking out about your exam."

I don't say anything.

Mel sits down tentatively on the edge of my bed.

"I told you this thing with Cody would end badly," she says.

"Yeah, 'I told you so' is really what I need right now." I scrub my face with my hand.

Shit. The tears that have been hanging out in my tear ducts decide now is a good time to make an exit. I rub my eyes angrily.

Mel's staring at me like I've grown another head. "Shit. You really care about him, don't you?"

I don't say anything. But I'm fairly sure my face is a fucking essay in misery.

Mel continues to stare at me. "I'm sorry, Ryan," she says finally.

"What for?" My voice is rough, raw.

She hesitates. "You've always been the happy-go-lucky one. Everything has always been a joke to you. I guess I forget that underneath it all, you feel things intensely too."

I snort. "It's the newsflash of the day. Surprise! Ryan has feelings."

"Have you told Cody about how you feel?"

I roll over to face the ceiling. "Yeah, I told him. It's not enough."

"Are you sure?"

"What do you mean?"

Mel shrugs. "I've seen you two together. And he looks at you like you're the best thing since Netflix."

"It's not enough for him." I kick at my sheets angrily. "I'm not enough for him."

"I don't think that's what is happening here," Mel says slowly.

I laugh the world's most bitter laugh. "You and Kate already told him that, remember? Told him he could do better than me. My whole life, all I've heard is how I'm not as good as Cody. I'm not good enough for him. That's what it boils down to, isn't it?"

Mel bites her lip, releasing it so there is an indent. "It's more complicated than that."

"Yeah, I get he can't get over your dad's disapproval, and with Heather being sick and all, he doesn't want to rock the boat. I get that… but…"

"But what?"

"I wouldn't just rock the boat. I'd sink a fucking battleship for him." My voice starts off fierce, but it drains away so the only thing left is a choking sadness.

Mel just stares at me. "Sometimes loving someone means giving them space to figure out their shit," she says softly.

I shoot a look at her. But I don't argue with her about the assumptions in that sentence.

We sit there in silence for a few minutes. Before suddenly she reaches forward and whips the duvet off me.

"Come on, sleeping beauty. You need to get going, or you're going to be late."

"Bite me," I say. But I shuffle up and swing my legs around so my feet make contact with the floor.

She hauls open my top drawer and rummages around, emerging with a T-shirt.

"You stink. Change your T-shirt," she instructs, shoving one at me.

"Someone drank their bossy juice this morning," I grumble.

"That's what big sisters are for."

Chapter 31

I make it to my exam on time.

The questions are hard. And it turns out wallowing in bed isn't the best exam prep. But Cody's tutoring pays off, and I manage to complete the whole exam, doing a decent enough job on most questions.

As I walk out, I have an insane moment when I want to send Cody a message about the exam and say thanks for all his help. But I don't.

That's what sucks the most. Losing our friendship. The other stuff was great, don't get me wrong, but I've also lost my best friend.

And I miss him.

As I get in the car, I head over to Kate's place. With things weird between her and Mum, I haven't seen much of my new nephew. But I realize I don't need Mum with me to visit Kate.

I knock on the door of her apartment. While I'm waiting, I can hear Ethan crying.

Kate finally answers the door. She's wearing an oversized sweater and hasn't combed her hair. And are those her pajama bottoms? It's almost 2 pm.

I've never seen her so frazzled.

"Here." She shoves Ethan at me.

I hold him gingerly. "What am I supposed to do with it?"

"Just walk around with him on your shoulder. Support his head with your hand. I need to have a shower."

I walk down the hallway toward the living room, following Kate's instructions, cradling his head carefully. Ethan's hair is soft under my palm.

I can already hear the shower starting.

Ethan continues to cry loudly in my ear. For something so little, he sure can make a lot of noise. I look sideways at him. His little face is scrunched up as he howls.

"Come on, come on," I say to him. "That's enough."

I sing the first line of "The Lion Sleeps Tonight," but if anything, his cries only increase. Yeah, my singing has that effect on people.

Shit. What the hell do you do with babies to stop them crying?

I jiggle up and down in a dance move that's worse than any *One Direction* routine.

Suddenly Ethan emits a burp so big, he'd impress a football team.

I'm impressed too, until I see that his burp has left a nasty reminder on my T-shirt.

"What the hell?" I say. "That's not good nephew etiquette."

Kate comes out of the bathroom. She looks a little more human, dressed in jeans and a T-shirt, her damp hair scraped back into a ponytail.

"Your baby just threw up on me," I inform her.

"Welcome to the club." She takes him from me and

puts him in the baby swing, which automatically rocks him backward and forward when she switches it on.

She grabs her phone, and suddenly the sound of piano music fills the air.

I think I recognize the song.

"Is this Cody playing?" I ask through a lump in my throat.

"Oh yeah, Cody made Ethan a soundtrack of his music. It seems to soothe him."

Funny how I'm the one who currently has baby vomit on my T-shirt and I'm still being outclassed by Cody. But I'm not even jealous or angry. Hearing his music just makes me miss Cody even more. Appropriately, the song that's playing now is the one he wrote himself, the one he said was about longing for something. 'Cause I might know a thing or two about that feeling right now.

Kate settles back on her haunches and blows out a deep breath.

"Are you okay?" I kind of feel obliged to ask, even though it is clear that she and okay parted company a while ago.

"It's just so hard." Kate's voice wobbles. "I'm so tired, and he cries all the time and wakes up so many times every night."

Well yeah, he's a baby. That's what he's supposed to do.

I don't say the words though.

What would Cody do? Although I'm trying to keep Cody out of my brain, it strikes me he would be so much better in this situation. He's the type of brother that would know what to say.

But he's not here. It's up to me.

Before I second guess myself, I put an arm around her. "I don't think it's supposed to be easy," I say. "There's a reason everyone moans about being a parent."

She leans into me and starts to sob. Full, horrible sobs that seem to come from a deep part of her.

"Hey, hey. It will be all right." I pat her back awkwardly.

"It's just so hard. I didn't realize how hard it would be."

I let her cry while making appropriate soothing sounds. Well, at least I hope they're appropriate.

She finally pulls back after giving my T-shirt a good soaking. Tears and baby vomit. There's an excess of body fluids being shared in this apartment today.

"You're going to be an awesome mum," I say.

Pulling a tissue out from her pocket, she blows her nose. "Thanks," she says finally.

"I mean it. You'll be like in the hall of fame for mothers, the mum that all other mother's come to for advice."

She manages half a grin. Then it fades, and she squints suspiciously at me. "Who are you?"

"What do you mean?"

"I mean, it's someone else's brain in Ryan's body, right?"

"This is my supportive brother act."

She sniffs. "I'm not familiar with it."

"Hey." I pretend to be mock offended, but really I'm so happy she seems to have stopped crying

She wipes her eyes on her sleeve. "God, I'm such a mess."

"Yeah, you pretty much are," I agree.

She punches me on the arm, and I shoulder nudge her back. We sit there for a while, shoulder to shoulder as Cody's music continues to swirl around us.

. . .

I HANG out at Kate's place, helping her out as much as I can until Chris gets home.

As I drive home, I think about what else I can do to help Kate.

Maybe I should message Mel and tell her about my visit? Get her to talk to Frank and Heather, see how they can provide more support to Kate.

But I know it's not Mel or Frank or Heather who Kate needs right now.

When I get home, Mum's in the kitchen cutting up potatoes.

"Where have you been?" Mum asks. "How did the exam go?"

"The exam was fine. And I've been at Kate's."

Mum stiffens. "Oh."

"Kate's having a hard time. The baby is crying all the time, and she's not sleeping much," I say carefully.

"Yes, well, Kate has made it very clear she can manage without me," Mum says.

I see the determined jut to her chin, and it's so similar to how Kate gets, it's almost funny.

Usually this is the point where I bow out. When I adopt my minimize conflict, why-bother-when-you-can't-change-anything attitude and keep my mouth shut.

Not this time, though.

"Mum, you need to let go of that shit and go help your daughter." Anger pulses in my voice.

Mum turns to me, her eyes widening in surprise.

"I might drop by there tomorrow," she says noncommittally.

Something insides me snaps. I'm so, so sick of all this shit.

I grab the keys from where I've just hung them up and thrust them at her. "No, Mum. Right now. We're going right now. We're going there, and you will help Kate. You need to put all that other crap aside."

Mum doesn't reply, just stares at me, her lips pinching together.

Dad wanders in, stopping still when he sees Mum and I in a standoff. "What's going on?"

"We're going to Kate's." I don't break eye contact with my mother. "Because Kate really needs her mum right now."

"I think that's a good idea, Julia," Dad says in a low voice.

"Fine. Let's go." Mum jerks her gaze away from mine.

Mum doesn't speak on the ride over to Kate's apartment. But that's okay, because I'm freaking out.

Shit. What if they have another fight? Will this make everything worse? Maybe I shouldn't have forced Mum to go.

She follows me wordlessly up the stairs, and I knock on the door.

Kate answers. She takes one look at Mum and bursts into tears.

Which causes Mum to burst into tears too.

Mum wraps Kate up in an enormous hug, rocking her slightly. It reminds me of the way Kate swayed when she was trying to settle Ethan this afternoon.

I try to keep up my supportive brother act, I really do. But when we get inside, Chris greets us with a wide smile and immediately retreats to the kitchen to make cups of coffee, leaving me to the mercy of Mum and Kate's conversation. They talk about the consistency of baby poop and cracked nipples, and I realize I've reached the limits of the good brother thing.

"I've got homework I've got to do," I say, standing up and edging toward the door.

"But we came together," Mum says.

"I can drop you home if you want," Chris says to me.

"I'll get an Uber." I'm sure ride sharing was invented so you could escape these types of conversations. I grab my phone out of my pocket to order my ride.

"Are you sure?" Mum asks.

"Yeah." I hit confirm.

"Are we grossing you out?" Kate asks with a glint in her eye that screams *payback time*. "Surely you, who introduced our family to the surprise apple burp, can handle a brief discussion on baby poop."

I scoff. "Like you could ever gross me out."

Kate turns to Mum. "Anyway, so can you remember how long it took for the post-partum bleeding to stop for you?"

"I'll wait on the sidewalk," I choke out as I make a mad dash down the hallway to the front door, ignoring the sound of Kate's laughter floating after me.

I'M WATCHING TV with Dad when Mum comes home. I've managed to get him addicted to *Ragnarok*. He seems to feel that somehow binge watching a Norwegian teenager trying to thwart the end of the world provides good father-son bonding.

I seize up at the noise of the front door opening. Hopefully, things ended up okay between them. Hopefully I'm not going to get a parental lecture about interfering.

Mum puts the keys back on the hook in the kitchen. Then she comes and stands in the doorway of the living room.

"How did it go?" Dad asks tentatively.

"It was good," she says quietly. She walks over and sinks into a chair, looking at me.

Oh shit. Tears glisten in her eyes. My heart thuds.

Mum wipes the corner of her eye. "You were right, Ryan. I can't believe I needed you to remind me of what's important." She takes a shaky breath. "It's so easy to get caught up in the petty stuff and forget what matters."

"Yeah, I know," I say.

When I go up to my room, I have a message on my phone from Kate.

Thanks for bringing Mum xx

I stick my phone on my bedside table and rub my forehead. Maybe that's the good thing to come out of this whole Cody thing. By thinking about what he would do in a situation, I've become a better brother.

It's the only positive I can find right now.

Chapter 32

The weeks trudge by. And I survive.

Sure, it sucks big-time being rejected. I can't see how I will ever move past feeling like something is missing without Cody.

But I put myself out there. I let Cody know how serious I was about us. It sucks so much to have tried at something and failed. However, it's much better than not having tried at all. Now at least no questions remain unanswered. Even if I don't like the answers, at least I know.

Unfortunately, all my rational thinking about Cody and me melts into a puddle of nothingness as I get ready for Ethan's christening. My hand shakes as I try to straighten my tie.

This is why I never should have had a relationship with my sisters' half-brother. Everyone tried to warn us. I can't escape from him like you can normally escape your ex. I'll see him at Kate and Mel events for the rest of our lives.

At some point he'll turn up with a new boyfriend. The thought hollows me. Having to see Cody with someone else, see him smile with someone else, laugh with someone else—it will be all kinds of awful.

Yet as I try to make myself regret Cody, I can't. Getting to know him changed me. In a good way.

Mum's wearing her usual I'm-bracing-myself-for-dealing-with-Frank face as we drive to the church. I'm sure I have a similar expression, although mine isn't tinged with hate like hers.

Ha. We're both about to face our exes. A great mother-son bonding moment. Are Frank and Cody having a similar father-son bonding moment?

It's so messed up.

I've never been in St John's Cathedral before, despite having grown up only ten minutes away.

Inside the church, there's a musty smell of empty space.

"Was I ever christened?" I ask Mum as we walk down the aisle of wooden pews. At the end of the church is a huge stained-glass window depicting the nativity scene with baby Jesus looking all holy in a manger.

"No, we didn't christen you. Your father and I decided not to. We felt it should be your choice."

"But Kate and Mel were christened?"

"Yes. Frank wanted it. They were christened here, actually."

"You used to come to church here?" My voice rings with disbelief. My mother is not the church-going type. I can't believe she's had a complete personality transplant since she divorced Frank.

"We didn't attend the congregation, but Frank's parents were Anglican, so this is where we christened the girls."

Kate's holding Ethan in one of the front pews, looking flustered. She's dressed in a yellow outfit. I wonder if she

chose the outfit so that if Ethan makes any generous dona-
tions of his stomach contents, it will blend in with the
fabric.

Mel's next to her in a bright blue dress that might be a
tad too short for church, but what do I know?

Mel meets my eye and gives me a how-are-you-doing?
eyebrow raise. Awesome, it appears I'm now going to
receive pity from my sisters rather than scorn.

Potential comments I could make to annoy her flash
through my head. I could try to reset things back to
normal. In the end, I don't attempt anything more than a
halfhearted shrug in response. I'm over faking it with my
sisters.

"Where's Chris?" Mum asks after she's cooed over
Ethan for an extended period.

"He's collecting his parents from the hotel because they
were worried about driving here." Kate delivers the words
in rapid fire. "But the minister wants to talk through the
ceremony with everyone who is participating. But Dad and
Cody aren't here yet… oh, here they come now."

We all crank our heads to get a view of Frank, Heather,
and Cody coming down the aisle.

Heather is walking slowly, leaning heavily on a walking
stick. But I barely notice her because I'm too busy looking
past her to Cody.

It's ridiculous how even though I've been bracing
myself for this moment, my gut still grinds and my heart
pounds like it's trying to escape from my body. I don't
blame it. I'd escape from this situation too if I could.

Cody's dressed in a white shirt paired with tan pants
with a light blue tie. It's funny, I've seen him in jeans and
T-shirts, in his school uniform, in a tuxedo, in a wetsuit.
I've also seen him with nothing on at all. Yet the sight of
him dressed up now makes my mouth go dry.

Don't wait for me.

The words ravage my brain. Reminding me that he didn't choose us. He chose the approval of his parents instead.

I look down, studying the wood grain of the pews like I'm going to be tested on it later.

A lady in black robes approaches us. She's in her mid-fifties, with closely cropped grey hair. "Abbot and Ramsey family?"

"Actually, it's Abbot, Ramsey, and Dayton families," Mum says. "But the Ramsey's aren't here yet."

"I'll take whoever I can get." Her smile is warm. "I'm Judy, the minister here. I just wanted to talk to anyone who is taking part in the ceremony."

"Chris and I went through the proceedings the other day," Kate says. "And I need to change Ethan's diaper. Why don't you guys go with Judy now? I'll send Chris's parents when they arrive."

"Okay," Mum agrees.

Because the universe likes screwing with me, Kate has asked both Cody and me to be Ethan's godfathers. Mel is godmother. Mum and Frank as grandparents are also part of the ceremony. So it's this awkward little group that follows the minister into a room off the side of the church.

As I walk in, I notice a sign on the opposite wall proclaiming, *God is love.* Yup, Judy will need all the love God can provide to handle this group.

Judy waits patiently until we've all shuffled in and taken a seat on an assortment of plastic chairs. Cody sits as far away from me as possible. It's probably deliberate. I have to swallow down the hurt that's clogging my throat.

"Kate and Chris have asked for a nontraditional christening service, so I just wanted to talk through what will happen," Judy says.

Yeah, 'cause I'm so familiar with the traditional christening services. I manage not to say this though.

She explains what each of us has to say and when. It doesn't sound too hard. Except the part where Cody and I have to stand next to each other and reply at the same time. Like we are one unit. I tighten my fist, and my nails dig into the flesh of my palm.

Everyone is well behaved as Judy talks. Mum and Frank smile and nod, acting like typical doting grandparents.

I sneak a glance at Cody. His hair is longer now, the same length as it was over summer at the beach. I try not to think about how soft his curls are, how many times I've run my hands through them. While I'm looking at him, I catch Cody side eying me. I quickly glance away.

"I'll just see if the other set of grandparents are here yet," Judy says, heading for the door.

Leaving Frank, Mum, Mel, Cody, and me there.

Mel bites her lip. I pretend to have developed an intense interest in the swirly pattern on the carpet to avoid looking at Cody.

"What christening gown are they using?" Frank asks abruptly in the silence. In the chair next to me, I can feel Mel stiffen.

"I think Kate decided to go with the Hill family one," Mum says.

"Did she now?" Derision is threaded through Frank's voice. I tense.

"She's using your aunt's crib, so she can use my family christening gown," Mum says.

"Because you've pressured her into it."

Hot anger surges up inside me. Suddenly, I'm furious at Cody. I'm furious at Frank, at Mum, at this whole shitty situation.

"Can't you two just stop?" My voice is deathly low, so low it doesn't sound like me.

Mum swivels her head to me, narrowing her eyes. "Stop what?"

Retreat. Retreat. A lifetime of experience has taught me that when I'm on the receiving end of that look, backing down is the only safe option. But my anger overrides any alarm system right now.

"Just stop your usual crap and see the bigger picture. You're grandparents now. Ethan doesn't deserve to go through the same shit you've put Kate and Mel through."

There's a stunned silence.

"Ryan's right." Cody rubs his forehead, not looking at me.

"Ryan doesn't know what he's talking about," Frank says.

"No," Cody says, his tone sharp. His hand drops away from his face, and he glares at his father. "Don't speak to Ryan like that. Don't you dare."

My breath slams out of me as Cody continues. "You know Ryan's right. You both know it. You use Mel and Kate as weapons against each other. Do you have any idea what it does to them? What it does to all of us?" His voice cracks at the end.

There's a shocked silence when he finishes.

"I don't think that's fair," Frank says finally.

"It's totally fair." Mel leans back in her chair, crossing her arms. "We're always having to walk such a fine line between you two, trying to make both parents happy. It's shitty and exhausting, to be honest."

"Don't swear," Frank says.

"She's just expressing herself," Mum says.

"She can express herself without being vulgar," Frank retorts.

"*For God's Sake, Just Stop!*" Cody roars so loudly that I flinch. "Can you hear yourselves? You can't stop sniping even now."

"We'll talk about this later," Frank whispers tersely as Judy comes back into the room, followed by Chris's parents. Their wide eyes and fixed smiles show that they've at least heard some raised voices.

Everyone plasters on their polite smile. My mouth feels like the corners have been tugged up by a puppeteer, and I try to concentrate on Judy's words. But it's difficult to hear much over the thrumming of my heart in my ears.

"So, as I was saying to Kate's family, there are a few changes to the usual christening procedures that I wanted to talk through…" Judy's professional tone is like a soothing balm on the room.

My heart is still racing as we head back into the church. As we find our seats in the pew, I stare at Cody. I can't help it.

He meets my eyes briefly then looks away, running a hand through his curls.

He stood up to his father for me. Does that mean anything? I'm an idiot if I start to hope, right?

I don't actually think I can handle hope. Because the crush of the inevitable disappointment is more than I can bear.

There are two other babies getting christened first. Which is a good thing, as I get to see what the other godfathers do. I get the feeling that a legendary Ryan mistake, even if it's on the amusing spectrum, will not be appreciated today. The other christenings also give me enough time to wrestle my heart back under control.

Which is fine, until I have to get up and go stand next to Cody.

Cody's shoulders are stiff, his hands clenched. It's like

an invisible current runs from his body to the surface of my skin, and I'm covered in receptors. I have such a craving to touch him. Just to move my hand a few inches, brush up against his skin. I crave touching him more than I think I've ever craved any food or drink in my life.

I glance at the congregation to find Heather's eyes on us. I fold my hands in front of me to stop the temptation.

Judy begins the ceremony, welcoming us all and explaining the purpose of a christening. I let her words wash over me, trying to keep my breathing under control.

I pull my attention back when Judy turns to Kate and Chris. "Kate and Chris, what name have you given to your child?"

Kate darts a look at Chris. She's got this weird grimace on her face.

"Ethan Joshua Abbot Ramsey." They both respond at the same time.

On my left, Mum hisses out a breath.

I flick a glance at her, and she's gone white.

Is she upset because Kate isn't using Dayton? But Kate has been Kate Abbot her entire life. Dayton is Dad's last name. Maybe Mum was expecting Kate to include her maiden name, Hill. Which seems like a cruel and unnecessary punishment to inflict that many names on a kid.

Something has offended her anyway, that much is obvious. Great. That's going to make the after-christening thing fun. Although let's face it, it wasn't ever going to be the highlight of my social calendar.

I look past Mum to see if Frank is gloating, but he's looking equally stricken.

What the hell?

THE REST of the Christening goes quickly.

Cody and I manage to do our bit without messing up, promising to support Ethan in his journey through life. I continue to feel Cody's presence, and every time he shuffles from one foot to the other, I have a surge of both hope and panic that he'll touch me.

But for once, I'm not completely focused on Cody. I can't help noticing that when Mum and Frank do their grandparent bit, they are both looking equally freaked-out.

Something is very wrong.

Ethan gives a loud howl when his head is dipped in water but settles after he's back in Kate's arms. She rocks him, moving from one foot to the other, gently shushing him.

Mum looks like she wants to join him in his howling. Crazily, Frank looks exactly the same.

Judy finishes up with a prayer.

"Heavenly Father, we thank you that by the water and the holy spirit, you have bestowed upon Ethan forgiveness of sins and have raised him to a new life of grace. Sustain him, oh Lord, with your holy spirit, give him a discerning heart and the courage to will and persevere, the spirit to know and to love you, and the joy, the gift of joy and wonder, for all your works. Amen."

"Amen," everyone chants.

Because Ethan's christening is the last one, it signals the end of the service, and there's an outbreak of babble amongst the rest of the congregation.

Our group walks back down the aisle to where Dad and Heather are both waiting on opposite sides of the pews. Kate gathers up all the baby stuff she brought.

"I need to talk to you." Mum grabs Kate's arm.

Kate has a resigned look on her face as she juggles Ethan in her arms. "I'm coming," she tells Mum. She leans down and snaps Ethan into his infant carrier, then turns to Chris. "Can you handle your parents?"

Chris nods, concern etched on his face, but he moves to intercept his parents.

Kate picks up Ethan in his infant carrier and looks at Mum expectantly.

Mum hesitates, then turns to look at Frank. "You should come too," she says. "We'll go into one of those rooms."

Frank doesn't disagree, moving to follow. "I'll be back in a moment," he says to Cody and Heather.

"No." Kate's voice is firm. "Everyone should come."

Surprisingly, Frank doesn't disagree, just nods grimly.

I flick a glance at Cody to see if he knows what the hell is happening, but his face reflects the same confusion I'm feeling.

Dad, Mel, Cody, Heather, and I trail after Mum, Frank, and Kate.

"What's going on?" Mel asks me in a whisper.

"No idea," I say. I'm even more clueless than normal.

Our impromptu family conference takes place in one of the side rooms off the main chapel. I guess they use this room for babysitting kids while church is on because there are crayon drawings of arks and whales pinned up on the walls.

Kate settles Ethan's infant carrier on the floor and starts rocking it with her foot as she turns to face Mum. "What did you want to talk to me about?" Although she's asking it as a question, there's no curiosity in Kate's voice. It's like she already knows the answer.

Continuing the strangeness, Mum's eyes seek Frank's, who's positioned himself by the door next to Cody and Heather, before she replies.

"Why did you choose that middle name?" Her voice is quiet with a slight quaver.

Kate lifts her chin in a defiant tilt. "I wanted to honor my brother."

I shoot a glance at Cody. His eyebrows are drawn together like mine. Cody's middle name is Adrian. And mine is Max after my dad.

"Kate," Frank says. There's some kind of warning in his voice.

"What, Dad?" Kate whirls to face him. "What's wrong? Do you not want your secret to come out? Why the hell would you two keep something like that a secret, anyway?" Anger pulses in her voice.

"What are you talking about?" Mel asks.

"I'm talking about the fact that we had another brother. And he died." Kate's words are like having an iceberg dropped in the room.

Everyone freezes.

"What?" Mel's eyes widen.

"I was sorting through a box of stuff from Mum's attic, looking for photos from when Mum was pregnant with me. And I found his birth and death notice. And some pictures. Joshua Frank Abbot. He was born thirteen months after you. They had his funeral right here, actually."

I blink rapidly. What the hell?

"What?" Mel's voice is even louder this time. Her hand flies to her mouth. She looks between Mum and Frank. "You guys had another child?"

Tears are leaking down Mum's face. She wipes at them distractedly, smearing them across her cheek, turning her makeup into a blurry mess.

"Now is not the time or place for this discussion," Frank says. His face is ashen, and he's got his arms wrapped around himself, like he's trying to hold himself together.

"It's exactly the time and place," Kate snaps. "I'm over all the secrets in this family. All the lies. You can tell all of us the truth. Starting now."

There is a deathly silence. Kate's glare moves from Frank to Mum.

Mum eventually speaks. "Yes, we had a son." Her voice cracks as she says the words.

"Oh my God," Mel says. "What happened? How did he die?"

Mum and Frank look at each other. The grief that is pulsing between them, it's almost like it's a living, breathing thing.

"Meningitis," Mum says finally. There's another deep silence, as if space is needed to absorb the word.

I stare at the walls. The bright pictures now seem mocking.

Mum continues on, her voice shaky. "We thought it was just a viral thing. Your dad had taken you girls out, and I was trying to keep an eye on him, but I'd been up all night and I fell asleep, and when I woke up, he'd gone all quiet. We rushed him to the hospital…"

"But there was nothing they could do," Frank finishes.

"And your father blamed me," Mum says.

Something breaks in Frank's face. He chokes back a sob. "Oh, Julia. I never blamed you. I blamed myself. I knew you were exhausted. I should have listened to you when you wanted to take him to the doctor that morning."

Tears continue to slide down Mum's face.

"It was a terrible, terrible tragedy," Dad says, going over to give Mum's shoulder a squeeze. "No one's to blame."

Oh, my God. My eyelids feel hot, and my throat is

scratchy. I look at Cody. He's watching his dad, his face pale, blinking rapidly.

"I can't believe you kept it a secret from us," Mel says.

"Yes, why didn't you tell us?" Kate demands. "We deserved to know."

Mum's lips tremble. "It was just too hard to talk about. I kept on thinking that one day it would get easier, that he could become something we talked about…" She draws in a breath before continuing. "But it just became harder and harder as the years went by…"

"Is that why you guys split up?" Mel's gaze darts between them.

Frank's shoulders slump, and he rubs at his forehead. "The death of a child is a hard thing for any marriage to bear. And we were young. We had three babies very quickly…"

There's an awkward silence.

Shit, it explains so much. Why they loathe each other. Both of them coping by turning their grief and guilt into anger against each other.

"But you've never dealt with it." Kate straightens her back. "You moved on and didn't talk about it, but how you handled it affected us. He's been a ghost in all of our lives, but we just didn't know it."

I swallow. I don't dare look at Cody right now.

Mum's shoulders hunch up. Frank stares woodenly at the floor.

"Ryan and Cody were right, what they said before," Mel says. "You can't keep going on like this. Turning everything into a battleground between you."

Mum wipes the last of her tears away.

"I know." The words fall from her lips. "I don't want…" She glances down at Ethan who is now asleep in his infant carrier. She takes a deep breath then raises her gaze to Frank. "I don't want things to continue like they are. What the kids said earlier is true. We need to try harder to get along. At least make more of an effort not to argue."

Frank just stares at her.

"Because we both want the best for our kids. That's one thing we've got in common."

Frank continues to stare, unmoving. Finally, finally, he nods. "You're right," he says quietly.

Mum gives him a half-smile. He gives her a weak one in return.

It's like a thousand miracles happening right here. They should update the bible with this.

I want to look at Cody, but I force myself to look at my knuckles instead. I hate that hope is trickling in, despite my best efforts. Will a thawing in our parents change anything between us? Will it mean anything?

"Since we're talking about secrets," Heather says. Her words are slow and laborious. I jerk my head up to look at her. To my surprise, she's staring straight back at me. "Is anyone going to tell me what's going on between Cody and Ryan?"

It's like she's sucked all the oxygen from the room.

"What do you mean?" Frank's voice is strained.

"The way they look at each other…" she trails off. A deep trench opens up in my chest.

"Nothing's going on…" Cody says. His words seem to hover in the air for a minute before he finishes. "Anymore."

The finality in his voice grabs me by the throat, choking me.

Tears sting my eyes.

Damn. I'm going to start blubbering worse than Ethan when he got his head wet. I can feel the storm swirling inside, and there's no way this weather system will die without making contact with land.

I do the only thing I can. I stalk away.

Out the doors, down the steps, and into the manicured gardens surrounding the church. The prickling tears make good on their escape, blurring my vision.

I walk and walk until I find myself at a rose garden at the far edge of the church grounds. The sweet scent of roses choking my nostrils is so at odds with the feeling inside me right now.

There's a wall at the back of the rose garden. It's only when I get closer that I realize it's a memorial wall displaying plaques in the memory of people who have died.

My footsteps slow.

Kate said Mum and Frank had Joshua's funeral here. I walk slowly along the wall, scanning the names, wiping my eyes impatiently. Until I find the name I want.

Joshua Frank Abbot. His date of birth followed by a date of death a mere four months later. Proof that he existed, even if it was only for a short time.

I stand there, staring at the name for a long time. What would have happened if he hadn't died? Would Mum and Frank's relationship have survived? Would Cody and I even exist?

A rustling sound behind me finally makes me turn.

Cody's standing a few feet away, his hands in his pockets.

My heart leaps into my throat.

He moves forward past me, crouching down and reaching out to gently touch the plaque. He runs his hands over the name.

"I can't believe we had a half-brother," he says, his blue eyes staring up at me intently.

I scrub my hand over my face. "Yeah, I know." My voice sounds rough. I clear my throat.

Cody's gaze doesn't waver. "What would he have been like, do you think?"

I take a few seconds to compose myself enough to answer. "A male version of Mel and Kate. It's a scary thing to contemplate."

"Yeah." He stands up, dusting off his hands. "I'm beginning to see what you mean about them. I just got yelled at."

"What?"

"After you left, they took me into the chapel and tore me into shreds."

I raise an eyebrow. "Really?"

There are a few beats of silence between us with nothing other than the noise of birds chirping and the sound of a lawnmower somewhere in the distance.

"Are they right?" Cody asks finally.

"What about?"

"About me breaking your heart?"

I suck in a deep breath. I could joke this moment away, try to hide my feelings. Try to protect myself from getting hurt further.

But screw that.

I hold his gaze. "Yeah, you kind of did."

He smiles a wry smile. "I guess I deserved the yelling then."

I swallow, looking away. "It's about time you got your share of the sisterly telling off."

"They're scary when they gang up."

"Yeah, they are."

"Initially, you acted like you didn't care. I thought…"

I turn my eyes on him. "You thought what?

"I thought I was only breaking my own heart," he says quietly.

"You told me not to wait for you." Even as I say the words, they slice at me again.

He rubs at his forehead. "I'm so sorry." His voice is shaky. "I couldn't handle the… temptation of knowing you were there. I wanted you to move on so I would know there was no going back."

My stomach flutters.

"Well, I haven't moved on," I say.

His blue eyes blaze. "Neither have I."

A fragile thread of hope hangs between us. But hope has betrayed me too much recently. I glance away, my gaze falling on Joshua's plaque.

"I guess this is why we shouldn't be together, right?" I say, staring at the wall. "It will always be complicated, and we'll have our sisters interfering with everything."

He moves a step closer. "Actually, I was kind of thinking it's why we should never be apart. Give them no ammunition against us."

My muscles tense, and the air in my lungs makes a quick exit.

I raise my gaze to his. "You want to be with me so Mel and Kate don't pick on you?"

He bites his lip. "There are other reasons too."

"Oh yeah? Like what?"

"Like the fact you're my shot of tequila too."

My breath rushes out of me.

"And I can't imagine being with anyone but you," he continues, giving me his intense Cody stare.

"I guess that's a decent enough reason," I choke out. "What about your mum and dad?"

He shrugs. "They'll learn to cope. They'll have to." He looks back at Joshua's name. "This kind of puts everything into perspective, doesn't it? He didn't get to live his life. We need to honor his memory by making sure we live our lives the best way we can."

My breath catches in my chest. "What does that mean? Living your life in the best way?"

He raises his gaze to mine. "It means I can't spend my entire life doing stuff just to please my parents or worrying about what people will say. Ultimately, I've got to do what makes me happy. And you make me happy."

"So, you're saying you're going to do me?" I ask.

The smile that lights up Cody's face is brighter than a million sunrises. "Damn, I've missed you so much."

"I've missed you too." My voice sounds like it's been dragged over gravel.

His eyes don't leave my face. "So, like, do you want this to be a thing?" He's trying to keep his voice light, but I can sense the tension underneath.

Those same words he used after we first kissed bring an automatic smile to my face.

We grin at each other for a few heartbeats before I reply. "Yeah. Yeah, I definitely do."

He steps forward, closing the gap between us, and kisses me.

It's a kiss that is happiness and hope and longing and grief all mingled together.

Eventually I pull back, resting my head on his forehead while I regain my breath. But it's not long before his lips are on mine again.

This time, he kisses me like he's making me a promise.

And I kiss him back the same way.

Epilogue
TWO YEARS LATER

"Ethan, come here. No, don't go to Uncle Cody. I'm the one with the yummy raisins." I hold the raisins out as a lure, shaking the packet, but Ethan ignores them and toddles for the ukulele Cody's holding out instead.

"Music trumps food." Cody sends me a triumphant look.

"Obviously takes after your side of the family in the common sense stakes," I say.

"Hey, I've got loads of common sense," Heather interjects from where she's sitting on the couch nearby. "It's those temperamental musicians you've got to watch out for."

"Don't I know it." I give Heather a grin, which she returns.

Yep, I get on fine with my boyfriend's mum. Despite Cody's concerns, Heather adjusted fairly quickly to the idea of Cody and me together. In fact, I overheard Kate moaning to Mum the other day that out of me, Chris, and Mel's new boyfriend Andre, I'm so obviously Heather's favorite.

I still take my wins where I can get them.

Ethan settles himself on Cody's lap, and Cody patiently shows him how to strum one string. Cody's curls fall over his forehead as he leans down, Ethan watching Cody's fingers in utter fascination.

It's almost too much cuteness in one place. It's surprising the laws of the universe allow it.

I get up and wander into the kitchen where Dad and Frank are both cleaning up after the birthday lunch and having a conversation about how the New Zealand rugby team will do this season.

"Need any help?" I ask.

"No, we're fine," Frank says. He gives me a small smile and turns his attention back to Dad.

Frank and I will never be BFFs, but he's accepted that I'm part of Cody's life. At Cody's first concert for the philharmonic orchestra last month, we exchanged proud smiles when Cody completed his solo. And Heather and Frank wrote me a stilted yet sincere congratulations card when I was awarded my Diploma in Paramedic Science last year.

I wander into the dining room, where Mum and Kate are having an intense debate about the positioning of the candles on Ethan's Stegosaurus cake.

"It'll look weird on the head."

"But it has to be on the cake somewhere."

"Why don't you put one on either side of the spines on its back?" I ask.

Kate raises an eyebrow. "That's actually not a bad idea."

"My genius is often underappreciated," I agree.

Kate carefully inserts one candle on the highest point of the back, then another one on the other side.

"We're almost ready. Can you round everyone up?" she asks.

"Sure."

"Cake time," I announce as I head back through the kitchen.

Dad and Frank follow me into the lounge just as Mum emerges from the dining room. Frank and Mum give each other polite smiles.

Things are better between them now. Nothing's perfect, of course. They actually did a parenting through divorce course together a few months after Ethan was born. About twenty years too late for Mel and Kate, but anyway.

Heather and Mum both grab their phones to record while Chris herds Ethan over to wait at the coffee table.

Cody slips next to me. I put my arm around him, and he leans into me slightly. We don't really do the PDA thing in front of our families, mainly because providing our sisters more opportunity for mockery is never a good thing.

"Why don't you spare those of us who are musically inclined and just mouth the words," he whispers to me with a grin.

When Kate brings in the cake with two candles blazing brightly on the top, Ethan's eyes light up, although whether it's for a dinosaur or the fact he's seeing the potential for chaos that fire on cake provides, I'm not sure.

Everyone breaks out singing *Happy Birthday*. Ethan looks around, his face a picture of wonder at everyone singing together.

I glance at Cody, who's watching Ethan with the largest smile.

I can't help the feeling swelling inside me, and all that happiness has to go somewhere.

So I sing the words extra loudly.

A NOTE FROM JAX...

THANK you so much for reading! I really hope you enjoyed reading this story.

As a new author, reviews mean so much to me. I'd really appreciate you leaving a review for this story. You can review this book on Amazon, Goodreads and BookBub.

Also by Jax Calder

Coming out at the Ball Game: a sweet YA LGBTQ+ short story

For Elijah, a trip to the ball game with his dad and his ex-friend Jaxon is a special kind of torture. He's always been a disappointment to his dad, and there's been an awful awkwardness between him and Jaxon since Elijah came out. Elijah hates that he still cares about what Jaxon thinks of him.

But it turns out one afternoon can change everything...

Adult Books 18+

Playing Offside: An enemies to lovers sports romance

Falling for the guy after your starting spot? Never a good idea.

Aiden Jones, aka the Ice King, is one of the best rugby players in the world. And he's not about to surrender his starting spot to Tyler Bannings, the cocky loudmouth who just joined the New Zealand training squad. But when they end up rooming together at training camp, the heat between them threatens to melt even the Ice King. Now Aiden's falling for the same guy who's plotting to take his spot.

But all is fair in love and sport, right?

Playing at Home: A manny romance

Falling for your kids' manny? Never a good idea.

Jacob Browne has never lived up to being the heroic idol his father was on the rugby field. And now he's failed off the field as well with the breakdown of his marriage. When his ex-wife hires a manny, it feels like the ultimate kick in the guts that another guy gets to spend more time with his kids than he does.

But when he actually meets Austin, the connection that grows between them upends everything Jacob thought he knew about himself and forces him to reconsider what it truly means to be a hero.

Playing for Keeps: A friends-to-lovers romance

Falling for your former best friend? Never a good idea.

Luke Hunter's returned to New Zealand, determined to make the national team. So what if one of his new teammates is the person who shredded his heart? Luke's moved past that, and he's happy now. There's no way he's falling back under Ethan's spell.

But it turns out no matter how good you are at evading the opposition, there's one thing you can never escape—and that's the love of your life.

The Inappropriate Date: a heart-warming short novella

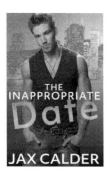

Hunter has always been a good son. Unfortunately, his mother struggles to handle the fact he's bisexual. When she warns him not to bring someone inappropriate to his sister's wedding, Hunter decides to find the most inappropriate date possible.

Blue Hair. Tattoos. Most definitely male. There's more chance his mother will learn to moonwalk than approve of Adam as his date. But appearances can be deceiving. And Hunter is about to learn this lesson along with the rest of his family…

About the Author

Jax's stories are all about light-hearted conversations and deeply-felt connections. She lives in New Zealand with her family and a wide assortment of animals. She's a rabid sports fan, a hiking enthusiast and has a slightly unhealthy addiction to nature documentaries. She is also a massive fan of M/M romance and enjoys both reading and writing it.

Jax is an extrovert living a writers' introverted life where she spends WAY too much time in her own head, so she'd love to hear from you in whatever way you want to connect with her:

You can hang out on Facebook in her authors group Jax's Crew…

https://www.facebook.com/groups/jaxcaldercrew/

Or follow her on Facebook, Instagram or BookBub

And don't forget to sign up to her newsletter via BookFunnel or her website www.jaxcalder.com/newsletter-sign-up

Also, feel free to email her at any time, she'll always respond: jax@jaxcalder.com

Printed in Great Britain
by Amazon

76213442R00177